"Come on, r

The child smeared ~~the tears on her face and~~ hiccuped. Cole was still talking to her, his voice so low and quiet it was like a purr. He stroked her hair and then the little girl put her head on his shoulder and the crying stopped.

This was how Julie found the two of them when she came from the bathroom. When she opened the door and found the kitchen empty her immediate thought was that Cole had left and gone home. But seeing her bedroom door open she understood what had happened.

There was something wonderfully dear, poignantly tender about the way Cole held and whispered to the child, calming her night-time fears. Julie didn't interrupt. She merely watched silently from the doorway, because he was doing just fine. But seeing him with the child sparked a longing in her that caused unexpected tears to well in her eyes. And the sight instantly endeared Cole to her.

ACKNOWLEDGMENTS

Sandra Kitt would like to acknowledge and thank the following officers of the New York City Police Department for their assistance and insights:

Police Officer William Gamble,
20th Prct., Manhattan

Police Officer Ronald Singer,
70th Prct., Brooklyn

Police Officer Samuel D. Sherrid,
retired Director of Special Studies, Planning Bureau

Other novels by Sandra Kitt

Silhouette Sensation

An Innocent Man
The Way Home

SANDRA KITT

Someone's Baby

Silhouette Sensation

First published in Great Britain in 1992 by Silhouette Books, Eton House, 18-24 Paradise Road, Richmond, Surrey TW9 1SR

© Sandra Kitt 1991

Silhouette, Silhouette Sensation and Colophon are Trade Marks of Harlequin Enterprises B.V.

ISBN 0 373 58391 5

18-9204

Made and printed in Great Britain

Prologue

The child knew right away that this place was different. It was nice inside. And it was warm. She didn't like the cold very much. It made her fingers and toes hurt. The other day in another place someone had given her this coat, which was thick and puffy and protected her from the cold air. There were also thick shoes, which were fuzzy inside and allowed her toes to snuggle. Now her feet felt much better, but her hands still got tingly and stiff.

The little girl held tightly to the hand of the young woman next to her. The child didn't want to be left alone again, but she knew better than to say so. There was no choice. And she'd been promised that this was the last time.

In this new place there were rooms, and people going back and forth between them. And there were children. There were strange voices she couldn't understand, like at the other place. Yet the people had always been nice to her. It was bright here, with pretty pictures on the walls and carpets on the floor and even music coming from somewhere. There was so much to see as she was hastily pulled along by the hand.

The young woman was whispering urgent instructions to her, and the fear returned. The little girl looked up into the tired face and saw that that funny light in the woman's eyes had returned just like the last time. The child looked at the

dirty paper clutched in the woman's hand and saw that the
hand was shaking. It was chapped and red. Her cheeks were
pale and her lips dry and cracked. Just like the last time...

Over the woman's shoulder was a blue canvas bag with
clothing. There wasn't very much in it. They'd left everything behind. Until the night before there had also been
some crackers and hard cheese, but she knew it was all gone
now. She had been feeling hungry all day, wondering when
they would eat again.

They walked quietly along the hallway. Past one open
doorway, an elderly man merely nodded as he slowly
mopped the vinyl floor. No one stopped them, although
someone passed by smiling and spoke, pointing down the
hall before walking on. She felt the woman squeeze her hand
and they hurried along. They stopped together in another
doorway and peered into a room where nearly a dozen
young children played. It had been a long time since she had
seen anything like this, and her dark eyes widened at the
laughter and happiness. There was a woman kneeling on the
floor near a window restacking colorful toys and books, and
a whole basket filled with dolls.

The child felt herself pulled away from the open door and
looked at the woman. The fear filled her throat. It was going
to happen again. She knew what was expected of her. She'd
learned quickly over the past few months. She was to be
quiet and good. She was to do as she was told. She was not
to cry. She'd been told that no one would hurt her and indeed so far no one had. Not at all like when they were home.

The woman removed the bag from her shoulder and sat
it on the floor. The little girl reached for the handles that
were passed to her, even though the bag was too big for her
to carry. The woman squatted down in front of her and
looked with longing and regret into her face. The woman
began to whisper, and her words were loving and soothing
and reassuring. She touched the child's hair and kissed her

cheek with cool lips. The child saw tears in the woman's eyes... but she didn't cry.

The woman gently pushed her inside the room and quickly turned to leave. She seemed to have trouble standing again and her breathing was suddenly labored. She held on to the wall as she made her way back to the door, still clutching the paper tightly. At the entrance she glanced over her shoulder at the small bewildered figure standing in the hallway. She waved briefly and quickly left.

The little girl watched the woman leave and was tempted to run after her. She felt her heart pound hard in her chest. The panic rose to her throat, squeezing as she fought against tears. And then it subsided. She stood and watched the door close behind the woman.

The voice above her made her jump, and the canvas bag fell to the floor. The lady standing there was the one from the room with all the children. She had short, curly hair and pretty eyes. And her voice was sweet and coaxing. The child couldn't say a word. But then the lady smiled and reached for her hand, talking to her all the while. Slowly the little girl gave the lady her hand and felt instantly and completely safe.

Chapter One

There was a hard "thump" on the edge of the desk, but the young woman seated behind it never looked up as her fingers flew over the buttons of a calculator.

"Here's your bird," the tall woman said as she then began buttoning her coat. The young woman bent over the desk murmured an absent thank-you but continued to work. The tall woman wound a red-and-black scarf around her neck and dug into the pockets of her coat for red wool gloves. "Julie, it's time to go home. It's seven-thirty almost and it's not going to matter if you get that financial statement done tonight. The board meeting isn't for another week yet."

Julie didn't answer at once. She dramatically pushed the total button and the machine whirred and buzzed and then went silent. Julie began to smile at the answer and looked up triumphantly at the other woman. "Done!" she said brightly. "And all the figures tally."

"I'm sure at the end of the year the bank will be very happy to know that. Right now, it's not very important."

Julie finally noticed the brown paper package that had been placed on her desk. She tried knocking on the surface. It was frozen solid.

"Don't worry. It'll thaw by tomorrow." The woman took a knit hat out of her shoulder bag and pulled it over her short black springy hairdo, a curly fringe sticking out across her forehead softening her sepia features. "Or you could keep it in the freezer for Christmas and have dinner with us. The kids wanted to know if you were coming or not."

Julie got up from the desk and began stacking papers away. "No thanks, Lois. I think I'll just stay home. Tell the kids I'll see them another time."

Lois gathered her shoulder bag and other packages. "Lord knows there will be enough food."

"Yes, but not enough room," Julie replied. Her slightly longer-than-shoulder-length dark blond hair was combed back and wound into a loose French braid. There were loose, soft tendrils around her forehead and ears. Julie's alert gray eyes glanced at her friend and co-worker. "Your apartment is barely larger than mine and you have two kids. I don't know how you do it."

Lois shot a wry glance back at Julie, her eyes speaking volumes. "You do what you gotta do. And sometimes you do it even when you have nothing to do it with."

Julie nodded and laughed. "Isn't *that* the truth."

It had certainly been true of a lot of women they'd both met in the past five years, including themselves. And yet Julie also realized that she and Lois had fared better than most. When she and Lois smiled at each other, it was with warm understanding and empathy for what they'd each overcome.

Lois's dark face was unlined and very youthful, but still often shadowed with a determination and urgency she'd worn ever since the two women had met. At the time she had been recovering from the loss of her husband, who'd been killed in a work-related accident. She had a ten-month-old baby and was pregnant with a second child. She had distant and not well known relatives in Kentucky, but Lois had decided she would try and manage on her own and not give up her apartment to move to a strange city. Like dozens of women in similar circumstances she'd found her way to the center, which had helped her to keep her family together and helped her to remain independent.

"Are we the last ones here?" Julie asked, stuffing her hands into the pockets of her calf-length skirt.

"No," Lois said, turning to the office door. "I think Pat is still here. The light was on in her office and the playroom when I came by a moment ago. But it's unusual for her to be here late."

"Well, I'll be leaving soon," Julie felt compelled to promise. "I just have one more letter to write."

"I have to go get my kids from my neighbor, feed them and put them to bed. Then I'll be in the kitchen till midnight, preparing for tomorrow." Lois gave Julie a skeptical stare. "Are you going to actually cook that bird this year, instead of giving it away again to one of your neighbors?"

"Probably not," Julie readily admitted with a slight shrug of her shoulders. There was still a hint of sadness that Lois noticed, had noticed before, but did not comment on. "If I cook it for myself, I'll be eating turkey until spring—or until I grow feathers myself. Besides, what's wrong with giving it to someone who could use it more than me?"

"Nothing." Lois shook her head. "But if I don't keep an eye on you, you'd give some poor soul the dress off your back."

Julie grinned, but did not dispute her friend's claim. The other workers at the center found them an odd couple. Lois, tall and commanding, efficient and not above using sass and intimidation to make the city bureaucracy work on the center's behalf or in the cause of the women who came to them for help. Julie who was shorter, less imposing, used a more peaceful, unhurried calm to get things done. They were from vastly different worlds, but what bound them together and forged a friendship went way beyond their different backgrounds. It had to do with a need for fairness, the right to respect. The desire to be their own persons and make their own way. They both just wanted a reasonable chance at a productive life.

They had shared many sorrows together, but also many moments of surprise and joy. There had been a time when Julie had stayed with Lois, dependent on her strength and drive, because she had nowhere else to go. That had been back at the beginning, when Julie had just arrived in New York without a dime to her name. Mutual tragedies, and the center, had brought them together.

"I'm not fooled, you know," Lois continued sagely. "You probably won't bother fixing a thing for yourself, and on top of that you'll end up in that neighborhood soup kitchen feeding other folks."

"Stop worrying. I promise I'll spend Thanksgiving in the proper manner, being thankful."

"Umph!" Lois said, turning away to leave. "I'll save you a doggy bag, anyway..." Her voice faded as she walked down the hallway.

"Forget dinner. Just bring dessert!" Julie added, only to be answered with a deep laugh as the outside door closed.

Julie stood for a long moment in the silence, and her smile slowly faded as she began to reminisce about the past. It was unavoidable. And perhaps a necessary reminder now and then of how things had changed, what had been taken away, what she'd lost. The memories returned more frequently than she would have wished for, because along with the good feelings came the bad. Also, there was the natural connection of Thanksgiving to family, to the gathering of loved ones around a feast of plenty. Except that she no longer had a family to gather with, a circumstance that had been of her choosing and the only decision possible in order to save herself. Julie sometimes felt both anger and frustration and a sense of having been betrayed and cheated out of a home. But at least now she was free. It was either freedom or a relationship that would have destroyed her.

Julie looked over at the wrapped frozen turkey. It was a gift from a neighborhood market. The owner each year donated a dozen to the center workers. It was much too big for one person, Julie knew, inadvertently giving truth to Lois's accusation that she wouldn't use it for herself. But for a wistful moment Julie wished there really was a reason to celebrate.

She returned to her desk and sat down. She drew a blank piece of paper from the stationery tray and began to write a letter. The last one had been written in September. Except for a holiday card around Christmas, this was the last one to be mailed until the start of the new year.

"JULIE? I'M SORRY to bother you, but..."

Julie's head came up sharply and she stared at the plump woman in her doorway. "I thought you'd already left, Pat." She looked at her watch. "I didn't realize it was so late. It's close to nine o'clock."

"I know. I'd thought to be out of here an hour ago."

Julie frowned. "Is something wrong?"

"Well, we do have a small problem." Pat stepped aside to show Julie a thin little girl standing round-eyed and silent next to her. "No one's come back for her. She's been here all day."

"Who brought her in?" Julie asked, watching the child, who stared back at her with dark eyes that held curiosity and a silent, almost hopeful appeal.

"I don't think anyone knows. Phyllis found her outside the playroom around eleven this morning. She was simply standing there with this tote. The bag has clothing in it, but most of it is too light for this time of year."

Julie listened, but she was still looking closely at the child. She seemed to be four, maybe five years old. She was wearing jeans and a cotton shirt with Mickey Mouse across the front, boots which seemed a little big for her and a child's winter parka. Her face was heart-shaped and pretty, her features delicate. The eyes, which seemed black, were almost too large for her face, making her appear particularly waif-like and helpless. She stood quietly and obediently, and there was no hint of distress for having been left on her own—just a kind of acceptance that made her seem more mature and older than she was. Julie had an instant momentary identification with the child, recognizing in her some of herself at this age. There was an old look of understanding of what was going on, but without the slightest power to change things.

Julie smiled at the child. "Hello. I'm Julie. What's your name?"

Pat was shaking her head. "It's no use. She won't tell you her name. As a matter of fact, she hasn't said a single word all day."

"Not anything?"

"Nope. She's very well-behaved and was no trouble. She played well with the other children, but it took a while."

As Pat went on to describe the afternoon Julie again turned her attention to the youngster, who continued to stand still and passive.

"At first she just sat in a chair watching everything. She wouldn't even take off her coat, almost as if expecting that someone would return for her shortly. It was more than two hours before she got down on the floor with the other kids, although she mostly just watched what they were doing. She seemed very hesitant to be involved, but the doll basket fascinated her. She still didn't take her coat off, and I didn't want to force her." Pat looked down at the child with some degree of frustration. "She was like a little mouse."

Julie finally got up and came from behind her desk to sit in a chair next to it. She held out her hand to the child. "Come here," she coaxed gently.

The little girl didn't move right away. She seemed to be assessing Julie, looking at her openly before slowly coming forward. When she stood right in front of Julie, Julie could see that her eyes were indeed coal black. Her hair, dark and slightly curly, was long and pulled back into an untidy ponytail and held by a rubber band. She was small for a five-year-old, yet she displayed a lot of strength and durability. Although her very silence suggested that she'd been through a lot, there was also a wonderful sweetness about her—because she was so very young and small, and so self-possessed.

"You're very pretty," Julie said honestly, but the child only looked at her with her brilliant dark eyes. She glanced over the child's head to Pat. "Do you think that something might be wrong?"

"It's hard to say. Her hearing's fine. She pays attention when you speak to her, she just won't talk."

"And there was no identification of any kind?"

Pat chuckled. "There weren't even brand-name labels inside her clothing."

Julie sighed. "Well, I'm sure there's no need for concern. We've had people drop off kids before and never say anything to the staff."

Pat gnawed on her bottom lip. "That's true, but I feel a little uneasy about this. There's just no information to go on. I mean, who do we contact in another hour when it's ten o'clock?"

Julie shook her head. "You go on home, Pat. I'll stay with her awhile longer. I'm sure someone will come for her soon...." Julie reached to ease the coat off the girl's shoulder, but there was an instant resistance and Julie pulled back her hands.

"What if no one comes? What are you going to do then?" Pat asked. But Julie didn't answer, because she hadn't even considered that as a possibility. "I think maybe we'd better take her to the police. Maybe someone reported her missing and we don't even know about it."

Julie got up to get a hanger from behind her office door. She turned and held it out to the child. The little girl just stared at it, and then back up to Julie. Julie sat once again. This time instead of trying to remove the coat she merely pointed to it. All at once the child began to struggle out of the coat. Holding it by the sleeve she handed it to Julie, who put the coat on the hanger and hung it from the office doorknob.

"How did you do that?" Pat asked impressed.

Julie shrugged. "I think she just needed to feel it wasn't going to be taken from her for good. If I leave it where she can see it, she'll know she can get to it anytime she wants." She looked at Pat. "This child isn't lost. Someone left her here. That means they'll probably be back."

"The magic question is, however, when?"

"I'll only worry about that if I have to," Julie said calmly.

Pat straightened and looked at her watch. "Well, in any case, I really have to go."

"Thanks for staying so late, Pat. I hope this didn't ruin your holiday getaway plans."

"Not really. I'm just going to my sister's in Rhode Island. I'll probably start out early tomorrow morning."

Julie tilted her head. "Can I ask a favor? I have a letter I want to mail, but I'd appreciate it if you could mail it once you get to your sister's."

"Sure, no problem," Pat said easily. She saw nothing unique in the request. She'd worked at the center herself long enough to know that the details of people's lives were often complicated, painful and private. Her job at the center was to offer guidance and assistance, a helping hand, not

judgments and criticisms. If Julie wanted the origin of the
letter kept secret, Pat didn't doubt that she had her reasons.

Julie bent over her desk to quickly address the envelope
and to seal the letter inside. There was no return address, of
course, and that wasn't questioned either.

Pat took the letter and began backing toward the hallway. "Are you going to be all right here alone? This place
can get a little spooky late at night when everything's quiet."

Julie laughed lightly and folded her arms across her chest.
"I'm not superstitious and I'm not afraid of silence." She
grinned at the little girl, who seemed to be relaxing somewhat in her presence. "And I certainly won't be alone."

Pat hesitated and frowned. "Do you think Marion Hayes
will show up again?"

Julie's eyes grew sympathetic and she shrugged. "I don't
think so. I know she was having a very hard time adjusting
to her loss, but she wasn't irrational."

Pat rubbed her arms as if to rid herself of a premonition.
"It sure seemed that way to me. I was here when she said all
those wild things, remember? She really believed we were
hiding her daughter from her."

Julie shook her head. "She was just upset. I'm sure that
when the court locates her ex-husband and she can see her
daughter she'll be fine."

"Well..." Pat sighed deeply. "I have to go. I'll get my
things." She waved briefly and turned away down the corridor.

"Umm..." Julie acknowledged absently, her attention
turned once more to the very silent child. She would have
been foolish not to be concerned, but actually she had no
idea what she would do if no one came or contacted the
center about the girl. It had never happened before and there
were no guidelines. Julie began to have a sinking feeling that
she was going to have to play this one step-by-step, but she

hoped, nonetheless, that this wasn't going to be the occasion when a new example was set.

The child rubbed her eyes and yawned.

"Yes, I bet you're very tired. Little souls like you should have been in bed some time ago," Julie commented, but there was no reaction. No response. She continued the one-sided conversation, hoping that something she said or something in her tone would prompt the girl to speak. "And you're being really brave. If I'd been left for a long time with strangers, I'd be scared. Everything is so big and frightening when you're little."

The little girl kept her gaze on Julie, and pulled nervously on the hem of her shirt, distorting the Mickey Mouse image. Quiet like a mouse....

"Well, never mind. We'll just wait and keep each other company."

"I'm leaving now," Pat said several minutes later from the office door. She glanced at the child who now sat on the edge of the chair next to Julie's desk. "I hope everything's going to be all right."

Julie looked quickly at her watch. Nine twenty-five. "It will," she said with more confidence than she felt.

"It's unnatural, her not saying anything."

Julie thought about it. "Maybe not. Don't you remember, when you were very small, how easy it was to be frightened into silence?"

Pat chuckled. "I remember that if I was frightened I'd scream my head off so someone would be *sure* to notice."

"This child was taught otherwise," Julie observed quietly. *And so was I,* the thought went through her head.

Pat shrugged. "Anyway, I hope you're not here much longer. Have a good weekend. I'll see you sometime next week."

"Good night, Pat," Julie responded, as the other woman walked quickly to the exit. In another moment the lock clicked into place on the door and a heavy silence filled the office. The child looked patiently at Julie, as if expecting her to say something, waiting for her to make the next move. "I bet you're hungry. Why don't we go see what's in the kitchen. Hot cocoa would be nice, don't you think?"

As she spoke, Julie held out her hand to the girl. The child looked at Julie with her great dark eyes and finally wiggled from the chair and stood up. After another moment of hesitation she put her hand in Julie's. Together they left the office, Julie continuing to talk slowly and quietly, somehow knowing that reassurance was needed. She wanted the little girl to trust her. She talked of nothing in particular, she just wanted the tone of her voice to be comforting.

"Here we are," Julie said, opening a door.

They entered the kitchen and Julie turned on the light, releasing the child's hand to search through the cabinets over the sink. Inside was a haphazard collection that included tea bags, instant coffee and creamer, an opened box of saltines and a new box of Fig Newtons. Julie moved things aside and found the tin of cocoa.

"So far, so good," she said, showing the tin to the child. After a second thought, she also added the box of Fig Newtons to their bounty.

Next Julie looked into the refrigerator, but as she suspected, there wasn't much inside. An orange, a few cans of diet soda and a container of yogurt.

"Well, so much for dinner. I guess it will have to be cookies and cocoa. How does that sound?"

She didn't expect an answer, and actually when she turned around it was only to find she'd been talking to herself. Julie started to call out, but in frustration remembered that she had no name to use. Instead she hurried from the kitchen, quietly calling "Where are you?" down the hallways. She didn't have to go far. Julie was about to rush back to her office, thinking the child might have gotten her coat with the idea of leaving on her own. But she noticed the light on in the playroom and looked inside to see the child kneeling on the floor in front of the basket that held all the dolls.

Julie silently watched in curiosity as the little girl began looking through the collection of dolls, obviously searching for something in particular. After a moment she pulled out an object that was red-and-white on one end and green-and-white on the other. She straightened it out, and Julie could see it was a doll, but one that had two heads. On one end the doll had a pink face with blue painted eyes and yellow yarn for her blond hair. Her calico dress was red-and-white and she wore a white apron over it. But if you turned the doll upside down, the dress turned inside out to reveal a doll with a dark brown face and black eyes, and black yarn for her hair. The dress on this end was green-and-white and it, too, had a white apron like the other side.

Julie watched as the child turned the doll back and forth, back and forth in silent fascination. Then she sat back on her heels holding the doll, smoothing the dress carefully and neatly. She was so intent that Julie wondered if she had ever had a doll before of her own. But it was obvious she knew what to do with it. The little girl held it briefly before settling the doll in the crook of her small, thin arm.

Julie watched the actions of the little girl for a while, deep in thought, but shortly returned to the kitchen to make the cocoa. It was clear to Julie that despite the child's stalwart spirit, she was very much just a child with a child's simple needs. What she needed, of course, was her mother or some other family member. Short of that, Julie reasoned, there was herself and the doll.

The responsibility of being a mother had always fascinated Julie. For one thing, at the center she had seen her share of women who had children they didn't want, who seemed impatient and unprepared for the responsibility. Resentful of the time and energy needed. She had also seen many whose lives were wrapped up totally in their children. She had seen women who had suffered the loss of children. Lois's second birth was to have been twins, but she lost one to respiratory failure. Nevertheless, she saw her children as a gift from her first marriage.

Julie's own mother had never seemed easy in the role of mother. But then she'd married too young, a boy who joined the navy and who'd died in someone else's country and war. She'd had a baby too young. Not that she was indifferent, but Julie had a memory from the age of three or so, of her mother in a constant state of worry, of always moving and resettling. Nothing ever seemed sure, and even as a toddler she lived with a fear that her mother might forget her one day, forget that she had a child who needed her love. That she'd be moving so fast that she would just leave her behind somewhere.

Instead, her mother had found someone else who wanted to marry her and love her, and who gave her everything. Martin Gardner was almost fifteen years older than Cynthia Conway and found in her not only youth and beauty but adoration. And he had not been unkind to the child Cynthia had brought to their marriage, but Julie had grown to realize she was a constant reminder that his wife had loved someone else first, and Julie didn't belong to him. Martin had fed and clothed her, sent her to the best, most expensive schools. He'd denied her nothing of a material nature, but she'd never really been made to feel like part of the new family. Just a visitor, more or less, to her mother's more rewarding life with Martin. Julie had never overcome the sense that she might be forgotten and lost, and in some ways that was exactly what had happened.

Good, bad or indifferent, a mother was still the most important person in a child's life. When mother wasn't there, something or someone else was needed to fill the void. The little girl had found the doll. How simple her answer had been, Julie thought, as she put the plate of cookies and the cups of hot cocoa on a small serving tray. How much harder are the solutions when one becomes an adult.

Julie made her way back to the playroom. The child was still on the floor, now with several other toys around her, although she still held the doll across her lap. She looked up when Julie came into the room, and although she didn't smile, her bright eyes were a little less cautious than they had been just an hour ago. Julie carefully put the tray on the floor and took a seat next to the girl, curling her legs to the side.

"This is not exactly a well-balanced meal," Julie said dryly as she handed a cup to the girl. "But it's still better than nothing."

The little girl used both hands to hold the cup. She looked into the contents for a long moment. She even went so far as to use a finger to do a taste test before sipping from it, which made Julie laugh. The child watched as Julie ate a fig bar, but wouldn't take one herself. Julie could see clearly that the child was hungry and she offered her the next cookie. The youngster took it carefully and nibbled at the cookie politely until it was all gone. Julie gave her a second. And a third.

"I think we were fortunate the cookies were in the closet. I don't know about you, but yogurt is not one of my favorite foods." She made a face and grinned, but the child only watched her silently. Julie coaxed the child into eating as many of the cookies as she wanted and was amused and charmed when the child judiciously left the last two on the plate for her.

"Thank you, but it's okay for you to have them." Julie pushed the plate forward and the last two cookies quickly disappeared.

But after the snack the thought of what was to be done if no one came for the little girl became a growing concern for

Julie. She tried once more to get some sort of response, some information from the child.

"Won't you tell me your name? Do you know where you live?" Julie asked slowly and patiently. But the child merely blinked at her.

"Do you have sisters and brothers? Don't you want to see them again?"

The girl looked at the doll in her lap, patting it gently. Julie sighed in frustration. Then she took the doll from the girl and held up the part wearing the red-and-white dress.

"Her name is Fannie..." Julie flipped the doll over to the other side "...and her name is Annie." She put the doll back in the child's lap. Julie pointed to herself. "My name is Julie. Julie Conway." She pointed to the child. "What's your name?"

The girl yawned and rubbed her eyes again, and Julie merely smiled ruefully.

"I agree. I'm tired, too." She glanced around the room, as if expecting to see something, anything, that would tell her what to do next, but there was nothing. The choices were very simple. They could continue to wait, straight through the night if necessary, or she could follow Pat's suggestion to go to the police.

When Julie again looked at her watch it was ten-thirty. The building was beginning to get cold because the superintendent had already turned off the heat for the long weekend, when it would be unoccupied. Staying the night would actually be very uncomfortable.

"Well," Julie began, tilting her head at the child. "If we stay here we'll freeze. I think we might have to go to Plan *B*, after all. We have to do something."

She got up with the tray and returned it to the kitchen, rinsing out the things they'd used. When she returned to the playroom the little girl was standing, waiting. Quickly Julie returned all the toys into their various storage places. She looked at the doll under the child's arm and then at the child.

"Why don't we take the doll with us," she said, turning off the light and beckoning the girl from the room before closing the door.

Julie was still inclined to believe that someone would be back for the little girl, but she also had come to fear in the past hour that it might not happen tonight, just as Pat had suggested. That didn't leave many alternatives.

She got the child dressed in the coat, and was concerned when there was no hat or scarf or gloves for all her small exposed parts. Julie got her own things together and, buttoning her coat, realized that she was leaving with considerably more than she'd arrived with this morning when she came to work. There was her bag, the canvas tote, the turkey . . . and the child.

Using a black marker, Julie quickly wrote out a sign that said, "IN CASE OF EMERGENCY CALL . . ." and she put her home telephone number on the bottom. She would leave it stuck on the door. Then, trying to balance her load, she and the girl walked to the door. But as Julie was about to close and lock it behind them, the little girl held back. For the first time there was a clear look of apprehension and confusion in her face. She didn't want to leave. She looked with wide eyes into the dark night and then behind her back into the center. Julie held out a hand.

"Come on now. If someone comes for you they'll find us. I promise . . ."

She realized that the child had felt safe and protected at the center. Perhaps she'd been left there for just that reason. Perhaps the child thought that, if they left, then her mother or guardian, or whoever, would never find her again. But she did finally step out of the door, even though her eyes remained saucer-shaped, and she suddenly reached out to grab hold of Julie's coat. There were few options left to her, and she clearly chose being with Julie as the best one at the moment.

Julie spoke softly to her. "Don't worry. Everything is going to work out just fine." They started toward the corner, and even though she had a tight hold on Julie, the child continued to look back toward the center building until it couldn't be seen any longer.

The nearest precinct was only seven blocks away. Julie had learned from her experience in New York that you could often get somewhere fastest by walking. She simply had to slow her steps to accommodate the child's small, weary ones. Even though it was very late Columbus Avenue was bright and alive with traffic and people, and they were just two more going about their business in a city that never closed down.

New York still held enormous excitement and possibilities for Julie. She realized that she was one of the lucky ones who'd managed to get the most out of one of the most vibrant but controversial cities in the world. She'd never been able to figure out, however, why she'd come to New York, of all places, when she'd found herself without resources or family support. And there had been other choices at the time. She could have submitted to the will of others and lived her life as ordered. It would have been a very comfortable and responsibility-free life, but it wouldn't have been her own.

Instead Julie had opted for leaving her past, to live her own life. It was true that at first New York had been a tougher taskmaster than she'd bargained for and she'd lived in near poverty for almost a year. She'd given up a lot to achieve autonomy, but Julie knew she'd gained even more in self-respect. One couldn't put a price on self-respect and one's life.

Julie looked down at the small dark head of the child walking beside her. The little girl had the doll under her arm, and the short, sometimes tripping steps told her that the child was exhausted. "Just two more blocks," she whispered, but she, too, was beginning to feel the weariness of the day, which had been filled with unexpected turns.

It continued to amaze Julie how resilient both the human mind and body could be when it was needed. That's what she liked most about the people of New York, most certainly the women who came to the center. They were all determined to survive.

At the end of the next block Julie turned into a narrow one-way street of brownstones, small apartment buildings and the precinct. It was her turn to hesitate. She stopped walking and watched two uniformed officers exit the precinct and climb into their blue-and-white car. For a fleeting, unexpected second a brief fear and memory shot through her and quickly disappeared. The officers paid no attention to her, probably weren't even aware of her.

The little girl must have sensed the fleeting change in Julie, for she looked up at her, her head tilted to the side in question. Julie smiled and took a resolute step toward the entrance. She couldn't turn back now.

"We're here," she said with much more calm than she felt.

The inside foyer was very small. There was an information counter to the left with a glass partition and a middle-aged woman seated behind it, on the phone. There was a bench along the wall where a sullen young man in dirty clothes sat slumped. There was an officer standing in front of him asking questions and not getting many answers.

There was an office directly in front of Julie and she began to walk in that direction. It had a Community Affairs sign on the door. Under that was another that said Youth Squad. But then Julie felt a sudden resistance in the child, who was trying to pull her hand free. At that moment there was an awful scream from a distant corridor and the child's body stiffened. Julie quickly squatted down next to her, letting the bags and packages fall where they might.

"It's okay. There's nothing to be afraid of..." Julie tried stroking the girl's cheek and hand, but the child's eyes were filled with fear.

The scream came again, followed by an authoritative male voice shouting firmly, "Sit down and be quiet." The child jumped. Through the door behind them Julie felt a swishing of cold air. Yet another officer came in escorting a man whose hands were handcuffed behind him.

"I almost ran right over you," the officer said to Julie with some indifference. "Could you move away from the door?" He pointed to the right wall where there was another bench. Taking the arm of his prisoner, he headed down the hall in the direction of the noises and other voices.

Julie did as she was told, still trying to calm the little girl, and struggling with all the bags. "Shh. I know it's very strange..."

A phone rang. Someone shouted from a doorway for someone else. She had stepped into a crazy jack-in-the-box atmosphere of activity. It was a world unto itself. It was just another night of men in dark blue and sad people in trouble. The place had a certain sterility to it, the hallways bare and everything so flat. It was not the night before Thanksgiving here. No warmth, no hint of holiday spirit, no sense of family. It was *not* the place to leave a small child. Julie looked around and realized that the child's instincts had been better than her own.

She looked at the little girl. "All right. We won't stay. It isn't very nice here, is it?" She stood up quickly, making another decision. She wasn't sure it was absolutely the right thing to do, but there weren't any other choices tonight. The child would come home with her. Tomorrow she'd think of something else, if she had to.

Julie touched the little girl's hair with a gentle, reassuring stroke. She made sure the coat was closed tightly around the child's throat. She herself had not worn a scarf or hat, or she would have given them to the little girl, but they would both have to manage with what they had. Then Julie shouldered her bag and the canvas tote once again. She wondered if she could get a cab on the corner, but quickly remembered that she didn't have enough money on her for the fare. It was less than two miles to her apartment, but there was no question that they could not walk that distance. It would have to be a bus.

"Is someone helping you?"

Julie was startled by the male voice and her head snapped around as she faced its owner.

The man was not in uniform. But he belonged here. His blue eyes were appraising, holding her overly bright gaze and forming an opinion. There was no particular expression on his face other than polite inquiry. Yet Julie forced herself into a calm, almost blank state, giving nothing away.

But she couldn't just ignore him, either. For one thing, his physical presence alone commanded attention. He wasn't standing particularly close to her and the child, but there seemed to be so much of him. Julie felt a sudden tightening in her throat because she had an instant awareness of his strength and power, yet also recognizing that this assessment was not based on his physical presence. He was tall and broad. Very sturdy, like an athlete with a well honed and muscled body. His hair was the same dark blond as her own, but was also dusted generously with gray, giving it a sort of wood ash color. There was something youthful and alert about the way he stood with both hands in his trouser pockets, and she sensed that he could spring very quickly into action if he had to. The thought made Julie feel nervous, and she resented it. She resented that he seemed so imposing and resented even more that it might be deliberate.

His white shirt was rolled up at the sleeves, exposing thick wrists and strong forearms. His tie, an unexpected outrageous splash of clashing colors, which oddly suited him, was askew at the throat, the collar of the shirt unbuttoned and displaying the equally strong column of his neck. Julie's gaze then saw the small bulge near his arm where it rested on his waistband. She couldn't see the gun, but she knew he had one. She began to shake her head.

"No. No, I . . ."

"Do you *need* help?" he interrupted Julie's stammering.

She looked back at the little girl who was watching the exchange from behind the protection of Julie's coat. The fear was still there. Julie turned back to the man. "No," she said with more conviction.

He raised his brows, although his expression didn't change, and it was clear to Julie he was skeptical of her reply.

She stood tall and lifted her chin. "No," she repeated. "I just had a question to ask, but . . ."

"Did you change your mind?" he asked astutely, "or did you get an answer?"

Julie's smile was swift and guilty. She averted her gaze, busying herself with balancing the bags once again. "I found an answer," she nodded, although she wouldn't look at him.

"I'm Detective Bennett. If there's anything I can do . . ."

"No, nothing," Julie said too quickly, although she detected more than professional concern in the offer. But she wasn't going to let him be Father Confessor and coax more information from her. The last time she'd done that, her trust had been used against her. The child had known better. It was a mistake to come here.

Detective Bennett looked at the wall clock over the precinct entrance. "It's midnight. It must have been a pretty important question to bring you here," he probed, not willing to take her at her word.

Julie felt her heartbeat jump. He could certainly not be accused of indifference. She shrugged. "You were on the way."

"To where?" he asked pointedly, looking her over thoroughly, seeing the small child standing behind her.

"Home," Julie answered, taking a step away from him and toward the door. She reached blindly for the little girl's hand, and felt the tiny fingers grab hold trustingly. "Thank you for your concern, Detective Bennett, but everything is fine."

The detective's eyes narrowed imperceptibly, but he only inclined his head. It would do no good to push her. But he slowly began to follow her and the child to the door, still curious and alert. At this point, he ordinarily would not have cared anymore. He knew that people were often fickle and indecisive. Easily influenced. But this woman seemed surprisingly different.

"I'm here most afternoons if you change your mind," he offered suddenly. He wanted to make it easy for her.

Julie was compelled to stop. She frowned at him. "If I change my mind about what?"

He looked at her carefully, taking a moment to examine her features, her shiny hair in its intricate, almost old-fashioned style, her gray eyes with the warm center. He glanced at the little girl with her dark ponytail and darker eyes. Detective Bennett winked at the child before returning his gaze to the woman.

"About needing help," he said smoothly.

Julie felt herself blushing, but she only nodded and turned to the exit, the child on one hand, everything else on the other. It was awkward getting through the door, knowing the officer stood silently behind them, watching.

He was inclined to just let it go. He'd seen his share of confused, lost people over the years. She was cautious, but she wasn't in trouble. At least, he didn't believe so. Still, something had been off. Something had brought her here to the precinct. Precincts were *not* just on the way to anywhere. They were in the middle of neighborhoods as a control, a buffer against crime and trouble. People came to the precinct, not out of choice, but because it offered the only solution most often, to problems that went beyond normal everyday existence. The precinct was a depository of the down side of life.

Detective Bennett wasn't sure what had brought someone like her into the precinct at midnight with a child in tow. But whatever answer she'd found here, he was sure it wasn't the one she'd been seeking.

Chapter Two

Outside the precinct once more, Julie found herself taking a deep lungful of the cold November air. Beneath her layered clothing she'd begun to feel overly warm and confined. The heat was slowly fading now that she was in the open again, but the reaction had come as a complete surprise.

It was only the second time in her life that Julie had ever been in a police station. The first time had been seven years ago at the age of twenty-three. And it had been the night before she was to have gotten married. At the time, panic, embarrassment and utter defeat had made her flee to the precinct. Not as quickly as tonight, but then as now she knew there'd be no help for her there.

Many years ago the officer Julie had spoken to had been young, cocky, assured of his manhood by virtue of being in a uniform, and absolutely in charge. He'd also been inexperienced and insensitive, making light of her fear and humiliation, sweeping aside her accusations and even the proof that would bear her out. It had been devastating to feel so powerless and alone.

Julie took a quick look over her shoulder and caught a glimpse of Detective Bennett as he now engaged in conversation with a black man in shirtsleeves who was probably also an officer. For a moment she indulged her curiosity about him. He was not at all like the other young police officer she'd spoken with all those years ago. Detective Bennett was definitely more seasoned. There had been incredible alertness in his blue eyes, a sort of all-knowing look that said he was not easily impressed and certainly not easily fooled. He did have a tall, broad masculinity, which was overwhelming, but in that moment of watching him unguarded, Julie changed her earlier impression. She was sure he wouldn't necessarily use that edge to get his own way…unless he had to. And she had to admit, now that she had a moment of time and space in which to consider, he hadn't been the least threatening to her. Her caution with him had been for other reasons.

In New York people were very conscious of themselves, of their power, looks and abilities. Detective Bennett didn't strike Julie as being that pretentious. He had a square forehead and jawline, a wide, generous mouth that Julie had noticed first of all before focusing her attention on something else. His voice had a quiet low timbre to it. She didn't imagine he'd have to raise it often. Detective Bennett had not shrugged off her denial of needing assistance. He had silently, in his own way, pursued it all the way to the door as she'd left the precinct with the little girl. It had only served to make Julie realize that her excuses had probably not been very convincing to him.

And now she felt disoriented because the blue of his eyes said he recognized that she might indeed need help. The next move had been hers, to accept the offer or not. Julie wished that she could trust the detective.

Julie remembered the little girl and looked down at her. The child's large dark eyes seemed to see and understand everything, including the sudden confusion that Julie herself was now feeling. What, in heaven's name, had this child been through to make her so old? Julie smiled at her.

"That was Plan *B*," she joked quietly. "It was probably a bad idea, so now we launch into Plan *C*. Tonight it's me and you." But the little girl only blinked, her small face soft with exhaustion, the eyes drooping more and more.

Together they made their way back up the block to the corner where Julie saw they'd just missed the bus.

HE FELT A LIGHT SLAP on his shoulder and turned his head.

"Any particular reason why you're staring at the door, Cole?" asked the man standing there. He didn't wait for an answer but turned to walk back to the office marked Community Affairs.

Cole Bennett slowly followed, but he stopped at the door entrance and just leaned against the frame, hands still in his pockets.

"I was watching someone leave," he responded absently as he watched the other man toss some papers into a dog-eared manila folder and then drop the folder on top of a precariously balanced pile in a metal tray.

The other man, Ben Bradshaw, smiled knowingly from his dark face, his mustache twitching in amusement over his full mouth. "Was she pretty?" he asked, reaching for his jacket, which was draped over the back of his chair. He and Cole were of equal size, although Cole was firmer in muscle and sinew than his colleague. But also like Cole, Ben had an economy of movement typical of men who'd been trained to respond quickly. Ben gulped down the last of a very cold cup of coffee and began turning out lights in the office. He grabbed a leather trench coat from a peg behind the door and walked out past Cole, closing the door behind him.

Cole was still considering the object of Ben's idle question. "Yes," he finally murmured.

Ben chuckled. "Are you sure? It sure took you long enough to say yes." He was headed toward the information counter. He moved quickly, and it could fairly be said that he was a man intent on leaving. Cole was behind him.

"I was thinking about why she was here."

"Why was she here?" Ben asked, tapping on the glass partition of the information counter.

"You're asking questions I don't have the answers to, Ben."

Ben looked skeptical. "What kind of detective are you? You had a woman here who, by your own admission, was pretty, and you didn't get her life story... or a date?"

A corner of Cole's mouth lifted in humor at the teasing.

"'Night, Pete. Betty," Ben said through the glass to the two workers. "Have a nice Thanksgiving." He turned back to Cole, looking carefully at him. "She wasn't that kind of woman, eh?"

Cole didn't have to think about that. "No, she wasn't. She didn't seem the kind who'd ever have a need for a place like this."

"But she was here. There must have been something," Ben observed.

Cole was once again thoughtful. She had beautiful smooth skin, and her eyes were clear and her hair was almost a honey color. "Oh yeah. There was something."

"Now don't go off on me, Cole. I know how you get when your intuition starts working. Those little gears..." he pointed to Cole's head "... start doing somersaults."

Cole finally straightened and pushed the thought of the woman with the soft gray eyes aside. "No mystery. She was in and out of here so fast there was no time for one to form. What are you doing here so late? Is this a new dedication to the force?"

Ben laughed, and ambled over to the exit. "I could ask you the same thing." He stopped and shrugged. "It was the usual stuff. Shop owner on Eighty-ninth complaining about the kids from the local junior high. They come into his store in groups after school and he gets ripped off. Then a senior citizens' group filed a charge that they don't feel safe on their street and want to know why there aren't more foot patrolmen in the neighborhood.

"While I was trying to soothe those ruffled feathers, a woman collapses in front of a produce store near Amsterdam and goes right into a coma. And if that wasn't enough, the substance-abuse treatment center had local people demonstrating outside the facility all day, tying up traffic." Ben smiled sarcastically. "How was your day?"

"Not as bad as yours, apparently," Cole said.

"Not even a homicide?"

"Not even."

"So it's my turn. What are you doing here so late?"

Cole shrugged, becoming evasive. "Still investigating the homicide from last night."

Ben looked at his watch. "If you didn't crack it by six o'clock this afternoon, it ain't gonna happen. Tomorrow is Thanksgiving. Lighten up. Go home and stuff a turkey. Or you can still come with me. One more mouth to feed won't matter. My mom is cooking for an army."

Cole shook his head. "Thanks for the offer, but I've got to get some reading done for next week."

"How are the classes going?"

"They're long. And a lot of work. I had a class until nine this evening, then I put in a couple of hours at the library. I came back here to go over the case. It's not going to be a long one."

"Then it can hold for the weekend unless the suspect has a sudden attack of conscience and comes in to confess. I'll see you Monday..."

Cole watched as Ben waved briefly, and then was gone. Moving slowly, almost aimlessly, he turned down the corridor and up one flight of stairs to the second floor and his office. It was eerily quiet of people and voices. The precinct was not in a particularly high-crime area and on nights like this, before a holiday, nearly half the staff got to go home to live normal lives. The ones that didn't have much family, well...they never talked about where they went.

Cole strolled into his office and over to his desk. It was one of three in a space best suited to a single piece of furniture. It was not an attractive office, not homey with personal objects such as photos and mementos. It was stark and functional because it suited the work that was done there. The men and women who worked for the department found other ways to break the monotony and stress. They joked among themselves with words and gestures. Otherwise, it wasn't exactly a fun environment.

There were three thick books opened on Cole's cluttered desk, plus a notebook and various notes scribbled on loose sheets of paper. He, too, had a half-finished cup of cold coffee, but Cole knew better than to drink it. He closed the heavy volumes and stacked them, then reached for his suit jacket and put it on.

Ben had been right. The homicide he'd been working on with Joe and Mario would wait the weekend. The evidence gathered so far was pretty conclusive, and he and his partners were reasonably confident of an arrest. They had a suspect. They were even sure of the motive. It had been a crime of jealousy and revenge. But it was too late at night to be thinking of other people's affairs. Yet Cole also stayed because it was an atmosphere conducive to his study, and because it was a lot easier than going home.

The work Cole Bennett had chosen for his life he was very good at. He'd come to it as a twenty year old, believed in it and had worked hard at it. He had not had the role model of a father or uncle to mold himself after. Actually he'd never known his father at all, a man who'd one morning just walked out on his sickly wife and son and had never returned. Instead Cole had allowed himself to be influenced by a truant officer who had found him at thirteen on the streets of Queens, where he'd grown up, playing hooky when he should have been in school.

Cole had never really understood what it was about Walter Haas that made him want to do the right thing. Maybe it was simply that Walter had been there and had cared a great deal. Walter had made him realize, thankfully early enough, that although he'd had to live in foster care for ten years he had options and could make his life what he wanted it to be. With Walter's encouragement and belief in him Cole had gone from breaking the law, in adolescent mischief, to enforcing it as an adult.

Walter had died, along with Cole's constantly ailing mother, before he'd graduated from the academy. But the legacy Walter had left him Cole knew he could never repay. The gift of his pride and self-esteem.

He'd become, at twenty-seven, one of the department's youngest detectives because he was smart. He'd never been satisfied with just solving a case, or piecing together the elements of a crime. He'd never been content with just walking away when it was over and going on to the next. Cole also wanted to know the why. Nothing was ever just black-and-white, and it was the gray areas, the subtle and complex details of people's lives that brought them to crimes of passion, acts of hate and senseless pain, that fascinated him. Once an act was done, it was already too late for both victim and criminal. What brought people to violence? And what happened to them afterward? Walter had taught him to care about that.

Cole lifted the heavy books and papers and, hoisting them under one arm, left the office. Here at the precinct his life was predictable, his purpose clear. He tried to help people in need. But once he left the building Cole more often than not felt lost. He would go home now and probably not even bother with dinner because it was so late. Tomorrow, he thought with vague dissatisfaction and sadness, would take care of itself.

He had no family, and no casual friends. There was mostly only the precinct and his fellow officers. The people he was closest to were all from there, because being a cop made him different from everyone else.

For one thing, nothing was ever simple. Cole looked at everything through the eyes of someone who saw a little bit more, in each person or circumstance he came across, than met the eye. It meant his trust was not easily placed, because he knew how easy it was to be misused. Cole had developed a certain cynicism over the years and it made it hard for him to relax, to accept things at face value, not to be suspicious. It came with the territory; everyone had a story.

Even the woman who'd come and left so quickly with a frightened little child holding tightly onto her.

As Cole started back down the stairs to leave he went over again the split-second meeting and even quicker impression he'd gotten. The woman had certainly been pretty, and in a way that his instincts told him she wasn't from New York. It went beyond the obvious lack of an East Coast accent. Cole had also noticed it in everything from the way she smiled to her hairstyle. But also she didn't seem as though she really was expecting anything at the precinct, which made her presence there even more strange.

She'd had a reason for coming into the station, but had quickly changed her mind. Cole wondered why. He was certain that she wasn't in any trouble or danger, but his few words to her had set her on edge and made her withdraw. Well, Cole thought dispassionately, if she needed help she would probably be back.

He followed the same ritual that Ben Bradshaw had as he'd left twenty minutes earlier. He said good-night and wished everyone a nice holiday. He, too, received good wishes, even though it hit a hollow chord in him because, like most holidays, he knew he'd be spending this one alone.

"Hey, Cole! Wait up a minute..."

At the door Cole turned reluctantly at the urgent voice. He saw a middle-aged officer in blue, hurrying toward him waving a sheet of paper. The desk sergeant came to a puffing halt in front of Cole and looked up into the bigger man's face. The clerk hitched himself up to his full height and tried to look every bit as commanding as Cole did.

But Cole automatically began shaking his head. This was a familiar scenario. He gave the clerk a pointed look of refusal. "I'm not here, Bert. I clocked out five hours ago, and you haven't seen me."

Bert waved the paper under Cole's nose. "It's a message from the Captain."

"The answer is no." Cole pulled open the door and a gust of cold air rattled the page in the desk sergeant's hand.

"Ah, come on. Give me a break, Cole," Bert whined, looking harassed. "He only wants you for a couple of hours. He asked for you especially." Bert added the flattery.

"Ask someone else," Cole suggested in annoyance. It bothered him that he'd get asked to pull extra duty merely because he was one of only a few men who didn't have family obligations and it was assumed he'd have nothing else to do. He was doubly annoyed because they were right.

"Look," Bert said, putting up his hands in a pleading gesture. "The Captain told me to give you anything you want...within reason."

"What's so important?"

Bert shrugged. "You know that homicide you guys got the other night? The family of the victim wants to see some action on the case. They want results and they want them now."

Cole sighed. "There's nothing more to be done right now. Forensic hasn't sent its report up yet, and we're still running fingerprints downtown. We may have a witness but she's disappeared, probably for the weekend," he hinted, but Bert only lifted his shoulders helplessly. "So who's calling in sick?" Cole questioned dryly.

Bert looked around the hallway to see who was in earshot. "Marino and Savage. Marino's folks are flying in from Miami, and Savage's wife is overdue by a week. He thinks it'll happen this weekend."

Cole looked off into the distance, into the peculiar void of his life, and although his annoyance didn't completely vanish, part of it dissolved into understanding. He turned back to Bert and arched a brow. "You owe me."

Bert looked relieved. "You got it. Just say when."

"I'll let you know. And another thing. I'm off the books for Christmas, right?"

Bert again looked harassed. "You know I can't promise you that."

"How important is it to you to make the Captain happy on the night before a major holiday when he suddenly finds himself in a jam?"

"All right, all right..." Bert gave in, muttering as he walked away.

When Cole stopped outside it was cold and it was late, but he felt at once the pulsating rush of the city. It had a vitality that caught you up quickly, bringing you into the center of its energy. And for those who couldn't keep pace, the city could just as quickly leave them defeated and wasted. It was a place he managed very well in, but the life was nevertheless hard and lonely.

Cole headed for his car, an inexpensive compact that got him around. Out of habit he glanced around the dark street and up toward the corner as he opened the car and put the books on the back seat. There was an elderly man walking his dog, another young man in his shirtsleeves putting out garbage. Up on the busy corner of Columbus Avenue stood a woman and a small child.

Cole got into his car, once more alert. He'd had a basic curiosity about the woman, which had no place to go given the haste with which she'd left the station. But seeing her so unexpectedly sparked his interest all over again. He started the car, pulled out from the curb and headed for the corner. Cole nosed the car back toward the curb in a space left vacant by the presence of a fire hydrant. He pressed the horn...

Julie didn't hear the horn at first. Her eyes, squinting up the avenue, could at last see a bus approaching. Her hands were almost numb with cold, and the late night wind crept through every fiber of her coat. But if she was beginning to feel miserable and frozen, she couldn't imagine what the silent child beside her was going through.

The little girl was completely still and obedient, and if she was cold, there was no sound or motion or indication that she was. Julie tried to shift the strap handles of her various bundles across her bent fingers, which were starting to hurt, along with the rest of her body, from exposure. The horn sounded again.

Julie looked over her shoulder and saw the small powder blue compact car, its headlights on and motor running. She turned to the little girl. "Here comes the bus." She squeezed the child's hand. Julie began moving to the curb, at about the spot she thought the bus would stop.

She heard a car door slam, watched the bus coming, still a full block away, felt her heart begin to pound in alarm as she detected a man walking toward her from the corner of her eye.

"You didn't get very far."

Julie heard the voice, recognized it and looked in surprise over her shoulder. The bus crossed the corner and slowed to the stop. A weight suddenly gave way on Julie's left arm and it felt instantly lighter. Something thudded to the ground and began to roll.

Julie's attention was diverted from the bus as she realized the turkey had fallen through the brown bag and had awkwardly rolled some distance away to the feet, actually, of the man. She looked up into the amused eyes of Detective Bennett. For a stunned moment Julie just stared and listened to the hydraulic swish of the bus door closing and the bus pulling away.

Cole bent to retrieve the still-hard poultry, ignoring the curious glance of a couple passing by. He held the bird easily in his hand and looked at Julie.

"I believe you dropped something," he said smoothly.

"I..." she began, but didn't know what else to say, or even what to do. She was beginning to feel both silly and unaccountably irritated.

Cole watched the bus lumber away. "Have you been waiting all this time for a bus?" he asked, watching the little girl hide herself behind the woman again.

"Yes." Julie sighed. "And I just missed it again, thanks to you. I'll take that," she said trying to reach for the turkey and finding she didn't have enough hands.

Cole witnessed her awkward but determined attempt to control herself and her belongings. "Don't I even get a thank-you for saving your Thanksgiving dinner?"

Julie felt her cheeks grow warm with embarrassment. He was making fun of her. "Thank you," she replied stiffly, still waiting to be handed the turkey.

Cole made no move to give it to her. "Where do you live?" he asked, noticing that she was cold enough for her hand to shake.

She didn't respond.

"You realize you can easily stand here another half hour for the next bus. Can I offer you a lift home? It's the least I can do for making you miss the bus."

Julie could detect not so much amusement as sarcasm this time. She was about to decline firmly when she felt the child lean her head against the back of her legs and her resolve weakened. She glanced back at the detective. He had a large, comfortable presence that, if anything, should make her feel perfectly safe. But in a fit of unreasonableness Julie wanted to prove she could take care of herself. She quickly took the turkey from his hand, but it was heavier than she remembered and she held it awkwardly.

"I don't mind waiting," she said.

Cole smiled slightly. She was very independent. And stubborn. But after midnight in New York with the temperature somewhere around thirty degrees was not the best time to show it. "I believe you, but think of the little girl. She's just about had it." He took the turkey back.

Julie knew he was right, but still she felt uneasy and on guard. She wished she'd never gone into the precinct, but unfortunately he was right. The child would not last another half hour of waiting for a bus.

She considered the offer for a long moment, and Cole felt some impatience that she thought there were alternatives preferable to accepting a ride home with him. But he stood and waited, his hands getting cold and wet from the damp wrapping of the turkey.

Julie looked at him examining his face. His motives.

"You'll be perfectly safe," he assured Julie dryly, but he could see that the irony was lost on her. She was being very careful.

"All right," she sighed reluctantly. Then her eyes looked into his with a sudden earnest appeal. "We're not taking you out of your way, are we?"

Cole's brows rose at the sudden question and concern. She certainly didn't know him well enough to care, but he believed that she did. "It's not out of my way. As long as you weren't taking the bus to New Jersey." Cole was rewarded with a brief smile and a short shake of her head. "Then my car's right over there."

He turned away to the car, leaving Julie to follow with the little girl. She put her arms around the child's shoulder and urged her to the small car. Cole discarded the ruined bag that had held the turkey and put the bird in the back with his books. He held the door as Julie settled into the passenger side, putting her packages between her feet. She held out her hands to the girl.

"Come on. You'll sit on my lap."

The child didn't respond right away and Cole simply bent and lifted her under her legs, and put her on Julie's lap. Once he was behind the wheel and pulling away from the curb Julie was once again aware of how tall he was, yet he seemed to have the easy fluid grace of an athlete. There was nothing awkward about his movements. It was just that the car didn't really seem to be big enough for him.

The child leaned back against her chest, her dark hair just under Julie's chin. It was a strange new sensation to feel the weight of a child against her in this way, helpless and trusting. Julie felt suddenly very protective, wanting her to be warm and safe. Wanting her to know that everything was going to be all right and that she was not going to let anything happen to her. Julie, of course, had no idea how she was going to accomplish this, but she continued to believe that there was someone somewhere who loved this child and had trusted that she would be watched after. Until there was another answer, Julie knew she would continue to do that. She closed her arms around the small body and smiled somewhat sadly. Had she not come to New York seven years ago, it was entirely possible that she might have her own child of about this same age.…

Cole was aware of the gentleness with which she touched and held the little girl. He knew that she was not the child's mother, yet there was a kind of curiosity and fascination in the way she regarded the child, and he wondered what their relationship was.

"The car will be warm in a moment," Cole said solicitously, making adjustments to the heating system. "Where do you live?"

"West End Avenue near Seventy-first Street," she answered, settling back more comfortably in her seat. For several blocks there was silence in the car. Julie felt the child's body slowly relax against her and go slack.

Cole took a quick glance at the woman and child. He had not forgotten that they'd come into the precinct less than an hour earlier. But Cole also knew that if she was unwilling to talk before, nothing had changed since then.

"Mind if I ask your name?" he began conversationally.

Julie glanced at him with a very tired smile. "I'm sorry. You must think I'm rude."

He shook his head slowly. "Exhausted and a little put-out would have been my guess."

Julie chuckled lightly. "That's a pretty good guess. I'm Julie Conway."

"And the little one?"

Julie froze. Her arm tightened convulsively around the child for just a second causing her to jump. Julie felt her heartbeat increase, because she hadn't the vaguest idea what to say. "Ah…" she began. "Well…" she began again. *Mouse. Quiet as a mouse*… "M…Mickey. She's called Mickey. It's a nickname." The lie settled uncomfortably like an albatross around her neck. Julie realized that she probably should have told him the truth; now would have been the ideal opportunity. But somehow it still felt like she would have been betraying a trust, and the responsibility she had accepted this evening of taking care of the child until she was returned to her family. And, after all, she wasn't doing anything more than keeping the child overnight. Tomorrow everything would work out.

Cole picked up immediately on the hesitancy, but again let it slide. He couldn't quite put his finger on what was unusual, but knew that it all came back to the quick appearance this Julie Conway had made at the station house. *Julie*...Cole liked the name, and mentally ran it through his mind and formed it with his tongue. It had a very light, almost ethereal sound to it.

"Well, Julie Conway, don't you think it's a little late, cold and unsafe to be wandering around with a small child and a frozen turkey?"

"I think you enjoy making fun of me," Julie said, but without any rancor. "I wasn't just wandering around. I was trying to get home."

"From where?" Cole asked quickly.

Julie turned to him with another smile. "You're interrogating me, Detective."

Cole came to a stop at a red light and looked at her with his own smile. "I guess I was. Force of habit. I'm just trying to make sure everything is okay. You did come into the precinct," he felt compelled to remind her.

Julie's smile wavered and she looked down at the small dark head against her chest, moving with the gentle force of her own breathing. The child had fallen to sleep. "Everything is fine. I was on my way home from work."

The two adults caught each other's gaze for a moment and Julie was uncomfortable with the way Detective Bennett waited for her to go on, as if she wasn't giving enough information . . . or he wasn't satisfied.

"I work at Helping Hands. It's a counseling center and sort of halfway house for women needing assistance. We help in finding jobs, housing, schooling or child care."

"What? No help for men?" Cole realized almost as soon as the words were out of his mouth that his question was inappropriate. He also knew that Julie Conway wasn't going to like it, and he was right.

It was a moment before Julie could respond, and when she did it was with a complicated mixture of anger, sadness and futility. "It's been my experience that men don't need halfway houses. When families are in trouble the men seem to manage very well on their own."

Her voice was not angry, but Cole was properly chastened. For one thing he knew she was right, and second because he had been entirely too flippant. "What do you do at the center?"

"I manage the business end of it. I make sure the bills get paid, the staff is hired, the supplies get ordered and that we stay within the state guidelines as a not-for-profit. I stayed to finish some financial reports. I stayed much later tonight than I intended to."

"And . . . Mickey?" Cole paused most deliberately at the name. "You're either hiring awfully young, or someone got left behind."

Julie's stomach curled in alarm as he came painfully close to the truth. It was already apparent that he knew Mickey wasn't her own child. "I'm baby-sitting. She's just staying with me until her mother returns," Julie said very simply and calmly. No lie there.

Cole thought about what she'd just said and saw some holes in the explanation. For example, it still didn't explain the in-and-out visit to the precinct. But his attention was diverted to trying to read the street numbers as he turned onto West End Avenue. In another few minutes he was pulling up in front of a limestone three-story row house.

Julie began to whisper to the little girl to wake her up, but Cole touched her arm as he opened the door on his side. "Leave her. I'll come around..."

He got out and came to the passenger side. Cole opened the door and reached in to slowly lift the limp child from Julie's lap. He leaned the child against his chest, his left arm supporting her under her buttocks, and her head dropped onto his shoulder. The doll the little girl had been clutching all evening fell to the sidewalk.

"I'll get it," Julie said, gathering her own bags and the doll, and remembering the turkey in the back seat before closing the door with a slam. Rather unbalanced, with everything in her arms threatening to drop, Julie hurried up the entrance steps behind Cole. With his free hand he took the turkey from her while she fished for keys from her coat pocket. For a moment Julie had an odd sensation of familiarity. They seemed a family. A rather odd one, since they were all strangers to each other. Yet Julie liked the fleeting sense of appeal and comfort she got from the thought, glancing at Cole as he held the little girl so naturally in his strong arms.

The outer doors opened into a very small vestibule. Cole was pleased to see that there was an intercom system that allowed visitors to be announced. It was a safety measure that was more a necessity than a luxury in New York. An inner door then opened into the hallway. Julie began climbing the stairs with Cole right behind her. The gentle creaking of the wooden staircase had never seemed so loud as it was now, as Julie hoped the noise would not awaken the tired child. She looked over her shoulder and whispered.

"I'm on the second floor."

There were two apartments on the floor, one to the rear and one to the front. Julie turned toward the front. Her keys clinked and clicked and the door to the apartment opened. She turned to Cole, her arms out.

"I'll take her now."

Cole lifted a brow at her. "You could barely manage when she was walking on her own. She's small but still too heavy for you to carry." He moved past Julie into the apartment and Julie had no choice but to follow.

"I've already inconvenienced you enough..." she said, closing the door.

"Where do you want me to put her?" Cole interrupted.

Julie flicked on a switch for the ceiling light and pointed to a dark doorway behind him. Then she hurried forward to turn on a light in the minuscule space she called the bedroom. Already Cole was carefully laying the sleeping child on the bright yellow comforter on the bed.

Julie had dropped the bags on the floor by the bed and was shrugging out of her coat. Cole stood back and watched as she pulled off the small boots and slowly maneuvered the short limbs out of the winter jacket. The little girl never moved, having succumbed completely to the need for rest. Cole stood patiently aside as Julie bent over the child to undress her. His attention was distracted briefly by the details of the room. There was the platform-style bed, a bureau with many drawers against the opposite wall, with a TV on top. There was a wicker stool being used as a nightstand, which held a lamp and clock radio. There was a fluffy shag rug on the floor. The space was tight and small, but felt more cozy than cluttered.

He heard Julie murmur something low and soothing to the child who, of course, was still sound asleep. But the quiet reassurance of her voice, the gentle attention to the child, held Cole's interest. He recalled nothing of this kind of loving treatment from his mother, and certainly not from the two foster homes he'd lived in. He had been well taken care of. He'd never lacked for the basics. But it was the *other* necessities, the tender loving care, the safety and stability that Cole had missed out on. Julie said she was only baby-sitting, but he had lived and worked enough years seeing childhood neglect and indifference to recognize genuine kindness. It made him look more closely at Julie Conway, made him more curious about her.

Julie, realizing that Cole was still standing just behind her, turned to him. She felt odd, knowing that he seemed to be watching her so intently, his gaze questioning and personal. The turkey was in his hands, forgotten.

"The kitchen is out there across the floor..." she instructed quietly and gave her attention back to the child.

Cole left the room and found a kitchenette partitioned off from the living-and-dining room by a tall four-paneled screen. It was black-lacquered with an oriental mountain-and-forest motif painted in gold leaf across the panels. Cole found that there was no way the turkey was going to fit on the narrow shelves of the refrigerator and he set it, to thaw, in the sink. Then he took the opportunity to look around the rest of the apartment.

Many of the brownstones and row houses in New York had been subdivided into small apartments with as few as two per floor, like Julie's, but frequently more. It meant that you had two windows, at most, either overlooking the street and a constant line of cars and traffic, or the backyard with weeds and a possible tree or two. Because the apartments were so small, it was easy for the space to take on an unhealthy cramped feeling with not enough light. They say if you live in one place long enough your dwelling will tell your whole life's story. But if that was truly the case, then Cole could tell nothing about Julie Conway, other than she had an eclectic, whimsical style and was apparently sentimental. She kept things.

The space was simply furnished with an odd assortment of furniture styles. It wasn't modern or regional, nor did the rooms have a traditional look. It was just an assembly of functional pieces that, when put together, was attractive and peaceful. Yet all the space, almost every available inch was occupied with something. There were plants and even trees in floor pots and they were all healthy and leafy. There were lots of books, neatly stacked, some piles even leveled and used as a base for an end table with a lamp. One wall was filled with framed artwork, letters and photographs, although they were all of children of various ethnic backgrounds. There was a huge open basket in one corner that held children's books and toys. If Julie Conway baby-sat, then she did so often.

But for all the visual evidence, Cole would also guess that she was a private person. She did not let people into her life easily. Her surroundings were lively, almost festive, but none of it told him much about the woman except that she liked being around children.

"I'm sorry I took so long. I didn't think you'd still be here."

Cole turned around at her quiet voice and looked at Julie for a moment. Her eyes were soft and tired, and her hair, braided the way it was, was beginning to crawl loose. Her whole appearance was calmer, less harried and confused than when he'd first seen her. And she looked a lot prettier. She wore no jewelry other than a pair of small pearl ear bobs. And there was nothing distinctive about her way of dress, yet she had a presence that did not fade into the background. It was the way she held herself: tall and straightforward, as well as the way she so obviously kept neutral ground between herself and others. Julie Conway was prepared to be a friendly person. But only on her terms.

Cole smiled in appreciation for the side of Julie Conway he was seeing now, because what he saw he was beginning to like. Julie merely blushed as if embarrassed and fingered her hair nervously, misunderstanding his smile.

"You were right. I must have looked a complete lunatic with a child on one hand and a turkey in the other. I'm really sorry if I was a nuisance."

"I wasn't, you didn't...and don't be sorry," Cole said lightly. He saw her relax at his banter. Her gray eyes, although warm and bright, still held him at a distance. Cole began walking slowly across the floor to stand right in front of her. She held her ground.

"Well, thank you, anyway."

"No problem."

There was a small silence as they looked at one another. Gone was the setting that had made them strangers. Suddenly having Cole Bennett stand in the middle of her apartment, tall, broad and male, brought clearly to mind for Julie that she'd never before had a man here. It didn't seem exactly threatening—after all, he was a police officer—but it did seem odd. Actually what Julie saw at the moment was a very attractive man, and she felt a growing sense of inadequacy. They were no longer on neutral territory, in the street or at the precinct. They stood in her home.

And it also felt odd because her apartment, while more than comfortable, had now taken on a hint of intimacy with him commanding so much room. They weren't very close together, but it was the closest Julie had allowed herself to a man in a long time.

Cole was now looking at her with a great deal of interest, and it was a moment before Julie realized it was purely and simply a man's interest.

Cole could see the softened, less controlled Julie disappear into the cautious woman he'd first met. She was putting them each back into their proper place, but it was too late at night to start speculating on what made Julie run. He turned toward the door.

"I put your turkey in the sink. It will thaw completely by morning."

She shrugged. "Then I guess I'll have to cook it," she said lightly, not thinking of how Cole would take her comment.

"Tomorrow's Thanksgiving. You're suppose to cook it," he reminded her with a smile. He only saw unease in her expression.

"Yes, of course." She didn't seem to know what to say. "Are you planning a big family celebration?" Julie asked politely, and was surprised when Cole's eyes flickered with a moment of uncertainty.

He put his hands into his pants pockets. His jacket gaped open and Julie caught a glimpse of the gun again. Cole pursed his mouth and averted his gaze before bringing it to rest on her once again.

"No. No, I'm not" was all he said, and his tone indicated very clearly that there was probably to be no celebration at all. "Besides, I'm working."

Julie nodded. Then she suddenly reached out her hand to Cole, stiff-armed and awkward. "Well, I can't keep you standing here all night. Thank you for the lift home. I appreciate it, Detective Bennett."

Cole raised a brow at how formal she'd become again. He liked her better the other way. But he took the offered hand. It was warm and felt very small in his own. Soft. Inadvertently he rubbed his thumb across the back. Julie pulled her hand free.

"Cole. My name is Cole. I'm only a detective when I'm on duty."

He turned around and walked to the door. He felt reluctant to leave, and he didn't understand why. He opened the door and stepped halfway through before looking back at Julie.

"The offer is a standing one."

She frowned. "What offer?"

Cole didn't know how to phrase it so it wouldn't sound empty and meaningless. He shrugged. "If you ever need me. 'Night..."

Julie was late in waving to him and the door closed. His choice of words stunned her. They were odd, inappropriate, and right on target. Even though she'd never thought to need anyone again...

As he left her apartment, Cole felt the sudden chill of the empty hallway and the late hour. The cold of November, and his life. It was going to be a long ride home to Huntington. For those quick moments in Julie Conway's apartment, he'd forgotten all about that.

Chapter Three

Her body felt cramped and stiff. Her shoulder was bent in an uncomfortable position and a foot dangled in the air off the edge of the cushion. Julie groaned softly and, when she opened her eyes, found herself looking at a framed print, now at a cockeyed angle on the living-room wall. From her prone position on the love seat, tangled in a cotton spread and nightgown, Julie wondered what she was doing on the sofa.

She bolted up abruptly, her hair in disarray, and blinked the sleep from her eyes. She stood, letting the cover fall to the floor, and stepping over it walked to her bedroom. She'd left the door partially open the night before and slowly pushing it open all the way, Julie saw the small figure curled up in the middle of her bed, still fast asleep. Julie smiled at the total abandon of the little girl. She lay diagonally across the bed, half under the covers and half out. One pillow was on the floor and the doll was wedged in a space between the mattress and headboard. This was how Lois's kids slept when they stayed over. All over the place.

The child's sleep was normal again, unlike the middle of the night whimpering that had awakened Julie and brought her quickly to the room where she'd left the girl. The sound had at first been soft and mewling, just part of her vague dreaming until Julie had realized that she wasn't dreaming and she was listening to the sound of a child in distress.

The little girl was sitting up in bed, her eyes closed as tears rolled down her forlorn, sad little face. The doll was under her arm. Julie had tried to be careful in touching the little girl the night before. She'd tried to respect that the child was a person with rights, something that Julie herself had never been taught as a child, and she didn't want to take too many liberties. She'd simply held the little girl's hand for safety, and that was it. But now, without a moment's hesitation, Julie sat on the bed and gently pulled the child across her lap. Somehow she knew just how to hold her, and just how to rock her, just how to pat her cheek and cuddle her against her chest. The child wanted her mother, it was that plain and clear.

The girl was not resistant to Julie holding her, but her tiny body was stiff in her arms. But the tears had stopped and the whimpering turned to sleepy sighs. Julie had hummed under her breath trying to recall any nursery song, any childhood tune that would be familiar and therefore comforting. But it wasn't long before the little girl was sound asleep again. For a long time Julie continued to hold her, continued to slowly rock back and forth, finding her own peace and need in the motion. She'd missed this as a child. She missed not having children of her own to love. Julie had learned very early not to cry in distress, not to ask for comfort, because it had never been there for her...gentle hands and soothing voice...but Julie knew instinctively that this was how it was done.

Now Julie walked to the bed and carefully pulled the bed linens free of narrow legs and arms and over the child. At the rustling of the sheet the little girl turned over fully on her back, her dark hair fanned out around her. Julie quickly grabbed clothing, jeans and a sweater, and left the room again.

It was just seven-thirty, and they'd slept through the night without the telephone ringing as Julie had anticipated, so there was no way to know if anyone had returned to the center for the girl and seen the note. But that didn't necessarily mean that someone was *not* looking for the girl.

While taking a quick shower and getting dressed, Julie frantically tried to consider her options. They were the same ones she'd had the night before; the police or herself. She was still convinced that the police would do something necessary and logical like temporary foster care, but Julie also recognized that she was not able to keep the child indefinitely, and she was not prepared to break the law, whatever that was in this kind of case.

She did not doubt that her decision to keep the child with her had been the right decision, but her encounter with Cole Bennett had also shown her he was an exception to Julie's experience with police and he might very well have understood her circumstances. As a matter of fact, it was hard to think of him as a policeman at all. His whole demeanor, even to his teasing her, had been far too cerebral and also very human. In retrospect, he hadn't seemed to mind at all the spectacle she'd made of herself leaving the precinct or her evasiveness in answering even the simplest question. But he was not a fool. He must have realized that she did have a small problem . . . she just wasn't prepared to let him know what.

When she'd combed her hair into a French braid, Julie headed for the kitchen to make coffee. She remembered, suddenly, Pat's comment the night before that the child might be reported missing. Julie turned on the radio on the counter and searched for the local all-news station. For twenty minutes she listened to all the politics, sports, weather, traffic, crimes, even a listing of Thanksgiving events and goings-on about the city. But there was no report of a missing child.

Julie was just finishing her second cup of coffee when the phone rang. She turned off the radio and ran to answer before the sound woke up her small guest. She was almost breathless when she reached the phone. Was this the call?

"Hello?"

"Happy Thanksgiving."

Julie smiled. "Lois, it's only eight o'clock. What are you doing up so early on a holiday?"

"Someday, when you have two or more kids under the age of seven, you'll know," Lois said airily. "They're better than an alarm clock but a *lot* noisier."

And indeed Julie could hear the voices of the children in the background.

"And if it's so early why are you up?"

Julie sighed and sat with her legs up on the sofa as she answered. She carelessly pushed aside the discarded pillows and bedspread that she'd used during the night.

"Oh . . . I slept on the sofa last night and a cramp in my shoulder woke me up."

"Okay. I won't ask why you slept on the sofa . . ."

"You won't have to. I'll explain everything in a minute. Actually I'm glad you called, Lois. I need your advice."

"Well, that's only fair, since I'm about to ask a really big favor. Are you sitting down?"

"More or less."

"Good. Look, I have an opportunity to do some Christmas shopping on Saturday and I'd like to take advantage of it. My church has put together an all-day bus outing to one of the suburban malls, and I'd like to go. Are you free to take the kids?"

"That's the favor?" Julie asked. "Of course I'll mind the kids. A few more won't matter."

"Now don't be so quick to say yes. I haven't finished yet."

"Oh, oh," Julie murmured wryly, but she wasn't really concerned. Lois was one of the most straightforward, honest people Julie knew, and one of the strengths of their friendship was that they could call on each other when help was needed.

"The bus leaves at seven-thirty Saturday morning and isn't due back to the city until nine o'clock in the evening..."

"And you'd like me to take the kids Friday and hold them until Sunday. Sure, I'll be happy to."

"Oh, Julie, thanks. I can't begin to tell you how much that would help. I really want to try and avoid the crowded department stores next month."

"That's a sensible thought, but you know it never works out that way. You'll have to take the kids to see Santa at Macy's, and you'll have to get a tree, and of course at the very last minute you'll find you don't have enough wrapping paper."

Lois groaned. "We won't even talk about making cookies and getting something for...wait a minute. What did you say? What do you mean, two more won't matter?"

"That's what I wanted to talk to you about."

"What's going on?"

Julie took a deep breath. She really didn't know how to begin. "Someone left a child at the center yesterday and never came back for her."

There was a lengthy silence on the line and Julie could imagine Lois's mouth dropping open in disbelief. In fact, her next words bore this out.

"You're serious, aren't you?"

"Very."

Julie then told Lois about Pat coming to her the previous evening with the child and the fact that she had been at the center all day.

"I remember Phyllis mentioning that she had a little girl there who'd been dropped off and no one at the center remembered the mother. About five years old?"

"That's her."

"So..." Lois began slowly, speculation in her tone of voice, "you're telling me that no one came for the girl...and she's with you?"

"That's it. And I don't know what to do. I left a note on the center door with my phone number and I thought someone would call me during the night. No one has.

"Pat wanted me to take her to the police, but I just couldn't. I couldn't bring myself to leave this little girl in such an awful place. Not on Thanksgiving."

"Well..." Lois said, with a very deep sigh.

"Exactly," Julie responded. "It was hard trying to convince Detective Bennett that everything was okay when it wasn't, and then he insisted on driving me and Mickey home..."

"Hold it, hold it," Lois interrupted. "You're losing me again. Who's Detective Bennett? And who's Mickey?"

"Detective Bennett is from the precinct, of course. And the child is like a mouse because she's so quiet. Anyway, he wanted to know her name, so I said Mickey. But that's not her real name. I had to call her something and she was wearing this Disney T-shirt."

Suddenly Lois started laughing. "Your explanation isn't helping me, Julie. How did it get so complicated? All right, start from the beginning and tell me everything."

Julie couldn't figure out what was so funny, but Lois kept bursting out into laughter, particularly when Julie told her about the frozen turkey falling through the bag onto the street at Cole Bennett's feet.

"Goodness, Julie. I hope you at least invited the poor man to share the turkey with you, after almost crippling him with it."

Julie sighed. Lois had taken a personal interest in her lack of a love life, but she knew better than anyone that Julie had good reason to be skittish. She had loved a man once, and it had almost destroyed her. It had stripped her of her dreams and hopes, of her trust. It had stripped her of her dignity. Julie once thought that more than anything in the world she just wanted to be loved. But in her world, love had exacted too high a price. She wasn't sure she was willing to risk so much again.

"I'm glad you find this so funny, Lois. But I still don't have a clue as to what I should do now."

Lois sobered. "I don't know what to say. I think I agree that you don't want to give her to the police. They'll only turn her over to the Bureau of Child Welfare and she could get lost in the system forever. On the other hand, you have a child that someone may be looking for."

"I thought of calling Marjorie Kennedy. As the director of the center she might want to know what's going on. Also, there could be all kinds of legal ramifications."

"Mmm... No, I wouldn't do that yet. That's hitting the panic button. Besides, Marjorie, like everyone else in creation, is away for the weekend."

"I feel like I'm right back where I started late last night," Julie said in defeat.

Again there was a long silence on the other end.

"You are taking a chance, but I don't think it will matter very much for the weekend. I mean, maybe whoever left the child just wanted her taken care of for the weekend. Maybe on Monday they'll show up with a crazy explanation and no one will be the worse for it."

Julie could sense the hesitation in Lois. "But you don't really believe that, do you?"

"Honestly, Julie, I don't know what to believe. Have you considered the possibility that the child might have been abandoned?"

"Yes," Julie said in a small voice, her stomach tensing because the responsibility was growing into monster proportions. "But I'm just not willing to believe that, yet."

"Then you have until Monday morning to find out. In the meantime..."

"In the meantime I guess I'll be cooking my turkey after all."

"There's something else you and the little girl can do to help pass the time together."

"What?"

"Go watch the Thanksgiving Day parade."

COLE HAD FORGOTTEN all about the parade. In truth there was no particular reason he should have remembered. He was not all that familiar with the holiday assignments from the station. As a rookie, he'd never been assigned to the route of the parade. As a regularly assigned officer, his duties had always been more serious. And without children of his own, it was not something he gave much thought to.

When he left the precinct, the sunny streets were busy with movement and a level of festive excitement that suggested something was about to happen. For a change Cole realized that the "something" was going to be pleasant and not the scene of some riot. For a moment, as he stood on the corner, he felt strangely isolated and out of place. He seemed to be, he noticed, the only one alone, unattached. The only one who wasn't anticipating the event to come.

Even as a youngster Cole could not recall ever having seen any parade, let alone the most famous one of the year in New York City. He therefore couldn't appreciate what all the excitement was about. Nonetheless, with a restlessness that was born of an unsatisfying morning, and a casual curiosity, he found himself slowly headed toward Central Park West. His eyes roamed over the crowd slowly with some interest. When he allowed himself, he still became fascinated with the concept that people met and came together with someone special, someone with whom to build a life, to share, to form a family. There were hundreds of people who had lives that weren't dangerous or on the edge. There were people who didn't live and work toe-to-toe with the seedy underbelly of the city.

Police married, of course, and had families all the time. And then they lived with the ever-present chilling fear that their sworn duty to uphold the law and to protect citizens' lives wouldn't lead to the loss or maiming of their own. It had been nearly twenty years, but Cole still wondered what his life would have become if he'd married Sharon Marie Sutton. Would they be living now in the small cape house he'd bought when they'd become engaged, his first year on the force? Would they have had together the three children they'd talked about, going so far as to select names? Would Sharon have succeeded in talking him off the force and into a safer line of work? Or would they have been divorced now, the casualties, like so many others, of a life that was too stressful and uncertain to maintain?

"Hey. What are you doing here, Bennett?"

Cole came out of his reverie and looked at the older officer in uniform offering to shake his hand.

"I wanted to see who was giving away money on Central Park West," Cole joked smoothly, releasing the officer's hand.

"I wish!" Officer Tim Brady chuckled. "I'm standing here to make it safe for Snoopy and Big Bird to float downtown."

Cole grinned. "It's the easiest job you'll have this year."

"Probably. But wouldn't it be easier and save a lot of wear and tear, not to mention taxpayers' money, to stage the whole thing and just let everybody watch on TV?"

Cole caught sight of a toddler, no more than three, being lifted in his father's arms so he could see the lining up of a colorful float that had ice skaters atop. The child's face was awestruck. Cole shook his head. "I don't think so," he murmured.

"What's happening with that homicide?" Officer Brady asked.

Cole felt his annoyance level rise. Just on a hunch this morning, after reviewing the case, he'd gone back to the crime scene. There were a few questions he wanted to try to find the answers to, like why the victim had been in an apartment that had been locked from the inside. And why the neighbor who'd claimed to have heard constant arguing days before had heard nothing the day of the crime.

When Cole had reached the site, it was to find that someone had managed to get into the apartment past the police barricades. Further indications were that he hadn't missed the subject by much. He might have made an arrest—chancy when you're alone and frowned upon in the department. But Cole suspected the perpetrator was young, scared, with no place to go . . . so he was still in the neighborhood. The other thing Cole had discovered was that Helping Hands was back-to-back with the building where the homicide had occurred.

"The holiday is slowing things down" was all he'd say to Officer Brady.

"Well, this is certainly better than a homicide. Hang around for a bit. It might be fun." He nodded to Cole and turned to several of his waiting colleagues.

It might be, Cole thought with unexpected wistfulness, but it might also make him too thoughtful, and the day might seem endless. He looked around the mass of people and decided that it might be best to leave. But then his eyes caught sight of a dark blond head with a very distinctive hairstyle, and a woman with a beguiling look of confusion. And he changed his mind.

The sidewalks on either side of the street were already packed with people positioning themselves for the best possible view of the parade. Julie and the child had found themselves swept up in the flow and movement, and Julie had to admit to feeling almost giddy herself. There were policemen and police cars and barricades all over the street. It was very apparent that she and the little girl were too late for finding a good spot to stand or sit, and her hold on the child's hand tightened so they wouldn't be separated.

There was pushing and shoving, people unavoidably getting too close and touching. Julie had not anticipated this and for a quick moment she felt panic rising in her throat. It was instantaneously there, and then it was gone causing a quick jump in her pulse, which eventually settled down. She held her breath a moment longer in surprise. It was almost exactly the same feeling that had come over her in the precinct the night before. As if she couldn't catch her breath.

Then she felt fine again. She looked at the child who was busy turning her head about, taking in all that was going on around her. Julie was glad that the child had not noticed her disorientation, but it bothered her that a visit to the precinct the night before had apparently sparked the embers of an event long ago that she would just as soon not remember and which she thought she'd gotten over.

Someone inadvertently pushed her aside and Julie found that they were in an even worse viewing position than they had been merely moments ago.

''Do you need some help?''

For a moment Julie was stunned and thought she was imagining things. She looked to the left and right quickly, but only saw men, women and children who were all strangers. Finally she looked over her shoulder and there stood Cole Bennett. She felt a funny tension in her stomach. Part of it was due to recognition, but it also spoke of an attraction. It was so quick and so natural that Julie's eyes widened in surprise. Then she began to smile rather shyly and in confusion. She wasn't sure if she was glad to see him or not.

Julie found also that she had to reaccess Cole Bennett because the man who stood before her now was somehow different from the man last night. In his dark suit he had looked official, authoritative in a no-nonsense way. The night had cloaked him in a way that wouldn't allow him to be taken lightly. Now he looked far less imposing.

He was wearing jeans, with a pale yellow shirt under a bulky navy blue pullover sweater. He also wore a light-weight unzipped ski parka and sneakers. In his left hand his fingers were stretched to hold a thick text and a gray notebook. His hair was much lighter in daylight than she recalled, and his eyes much bluer, aided by the darkness of his sweater. If it was at all possible, he looked even more masculine than he had the night before. The thought brought a sudden rush of heat to Julie's face.

"What are you doing here?" she asked in a thin voice.

"Following you, actually," Cole said easily, his eyes running over Julie quickly, liking her casual attire, the soft features of her face. He'd known women who were far more attractive, some quite beautiful, some rather sexy... but none who had Julie's feminine appeal. She blushed, and Cole wondered what had caused it. He grinned at the little girl who, instead of hiding this time, merely showed a childlike shyness toward him. She had a knit cap pulled down over her hair for warmth and a scarf wound thickly around her neck. She also wore a pair of mittens, which were way too big for her, leading him to believe that Julie had supplemented the girl's wardrobe from her own. "Hello, Mickey," he said, and turned back to Julie. "I saw you from across the street."

"Why aren't you in uniform?" Julie asked. "I thought you were supposed to work today."

"I'm finished for the day. And I don't usually have to wear my blues."

Julie nodded, unnecessarily smoothing back the stray wisps of hair from her cheek.

"You didn't answer my question."

Julie laughed lightly. "You're really determined to help me, whether I need it or not."

Cole shrugged, watching her carefully and liking the light sound of her laugh. "An overdeveloped chivalrous streak. Are you here to see the parade?" Cole directed to the little girl.

Julie sighed, looking around her and answering for both of them. "Well, we'd hoped to. I've never seen one before. But I can't seem to find any place to stand that won't be blocked by people a lot taller than we are, and where we won't get stepped on."

Cole shook his head with a smile. He knew for certain now that she wasn't from New York. "You have to be aggressive, otherwise you won't see a thing."

"Then I'm in trouble. I'm afraid I'm not aggressive at all."

Cole's smile broadened, showing grooves at the sides of his mouth. "Good," he responded. But he could tell that Julie was confused by the response.

The fact was that Cole had also never known any but aggressive women. They came to him strong, independent and wanting to be in control . . . too much on guard. Julie Conway was on guard, too, but it was not because she held people generally suspect. Cole liked that, but he was aware that she had a certain naïveté, which in New York could be dangerous.

He looked away over the street, squinting against the bright sunlight. "Follow me . . ." he said to Julie, not waiting for a reply, but moving in the direction of the corner to the south.

Julie noticed how easily he maneuvered his way through
the deep throng of people, leaving a narrow path in his wake
that made it easy for her and the child to follow. They
reached the corner, and Cole stepped off the curb to move
the police barrier there about two feet to the front. Catching the eye of a uniformed officer standing in the street, he
pulled out a folder from his jacket pocket, showing a photo
ID and badge. The other officer merely nodded his permission. Then Cole beckoned Julie and the girl forward so they
were first against the new space created by moving the barricade.

She looked up at Cole and smiled brightly. "I'm impressed. It obviously pays to know people in high places."

Cole arched a brow. "Sometimes. But I suspect you're
very easy to please."

Julie grimaced. "Sometimes."

There was a sudden thunderous pounding of snare drums
signaling the start of the parade. There was a surge forward
in the crowd and in the mounting excitement the child, so
much shorter, was nearly swallowed up. Julie placed the little girl in front of her, but then the barrier was in the way.
She looked at Cole.

"We'll be fine. I don't want you to feel you have to look
out for us. And I don't want to keep you from whatever you
had planned to do today..."

Cole watched her struggling to hold her position and
manage the child, heard her trying to talk over the start-up
of the lead band. He looked around the crowd again, at the
small individual units of families. He had nothing to do but
go home and perhaps study. Maybe call Walter Haas's
widow, who now lived in Florida. If he left now, he'd think
about Julie Conway the rest of the day—and about the fact
that they kept meeting in the strangest ways. Cole, in that
moment, chose to take it as a sign that their meeting and
being together had some meaning. He was normally not a

frivolous person and not given to flights of fancy. He certainly didn't believe in fate. His line of work precluded that. On the other hand, it was foolish to tempt fate unnecessarily. He wanted to stay with her.

"You're not keeping me from anything. Besides, I've never seen the parade before, either." Cole didn't add his own observation that both Julie and the child could still get swamped by the exuberance of the viewers.

The first marching band started out and the crowd set up a roar of applause and shouting. The noise all around them rose deafeningly and the procession began. Julie kept looking down at the little girl to see if she was enjoying it, but she only seemed silently bewildered. Cole, seeing the additional problem, took action once again.

"Hold these for me," he directed Julie, then thrust the two books into her hands. Reaching down, Cole lifted the girl up from the street. "Come on, Mickey. Up you go..." Holding her under her arms Cole hoisted her higher, placing her in a sitting position around his neck, her legs hanging over his shoulders.

A quick glance showed Julie that she held a notebook and a thick law textbook. It came as a surprise to her that this was the kind of reading material Cole Bennett carried around with him, but she had no time to reflect on it. Julie was suddenly concerned how the girl was going to respond to being touched, whether she was going to protest, even a little, as she'd done with each new thing she tried. Julie's face must have reflected her doubt, because Cole smiled at her.

"Relax. She's fine. She's got a better view than either of us."

Indeed, the little girl seemed to be taking her position in stride, holding onto the collar of Cole's jacket for additional support. But with the ability to see unobstructed and feeling safe from the crush of people, her attention focused now on the unfolding events.

Cole held the girl securely by one foot and with his free hand pulled Julie so that she was standing right in front of him. So protected, the three of them could enjoy what was going on. The parade was bright and cheerful and occasionally very noisy. The floats were colorful and elaborate, and all around her Julie saw pure pleasure on the faces of the viewers. Julie found herself brushing against Cole's chest and thighs in their closeness. The contact was wholly innocent, but nonetheless made Julie more than aware of his virile presence. It also stirred within her for a moment, that hint of intimacy again.

Twice he reached across her shoulder to point out an attraction or a celebrity sitting on a float. Once he leaned forward to ask her if she was warm enough, and Julie was startled by the gentle whisper of his breath against her ear. When some adolescent boys tried to push their way past Julie to get under the barricade, she went off balance, her shoulder pressed into Cole's chest. She murmured an embarrassed "sorry," but his hand found the waist of her coat to steady her, holding on to her for a long moment. She liked the reassuring feel of his presence, but nonetheless tried to avoid further contact.

An hour and a half later, it was all over. The time seemed to go very quickly and when the last of the floats went by with Santa in his sleigh, the excitement and energy slowly died down and people began to happily drift away.

Julie turned around to look at Cole and she sighed. Their gaze met and held for a long moment in which each could see reflected surprise, delight, a kind of mellowness that came from a purely enjoyable experience. Julie's cheeks were rosy from the cold, her nose very pink. The natural effect of the elements on her features was charming. They began to smile slowly at each other, and they were both thinking the same thing. The parade had been a lot of fun.

"Well, that's that," Cole said. Julie nodded silently, hugging his books to her chest. Cole lifted the girl back to the ground.

"Thank you. I hope having her on your shoulders like that wasn't too uncomfortable."

Cole rotated his shoulders easily. He didn't seem the least uncomfortable. "I'll let you know tomorrow if I can't get out of bed," he teased with a slow smile. But he noticed that neither of them made a move to say goodbye. "Where are you off to now?"

"Back home," Julie answered. "As a matter of fact I'd better get back quickly." She looked anxiously at her watch. "I left a turkey roasting in the oven."

"Is that the infamous turkey of last night?"

Julie laughed. "The one and only turkey of last night."

"It probably wasn't a good idea to leave the house with your oven on," Cole cautioned smoothly, slowing taking his books back. But Julie sensed more concern than criticism.

"I'm sure you're right," she answered. They were back to the silence again, and Julie realized that she was searching for some further conversation, as if she was reluctant to say goodbye and not aware of the reasons why. "I...I didn't know it was necessary for policemen to study after they were policemen," she said, feeling foolish.

Cole was puzzled. "Pardon?"

She pointed to his books. "Are you studying law?"

He shrugged. "I'm *trying* to study law."

Julie blinked at him. "Why?"

Cole sighed. How did you explain how complicated the system was? How did you explain a simple curiosity to know how it worked, and why it often didn't. "Some law study is required at the academy for all candidates..."

"But you're not a candidate," Julie observed.

"No, but ... I wanted to know more."

Julie let her eyes examine him for a moment. This was, indeed, quite a different Cole Bennett than the man she'd met the night before. *Above and beyond the call of duty* ... came to mind, and Julie realized that he had much more depth, was much more concerned and curious than she had first given him credit for.

"How much more?"

Cole shifted from one foot to the other. "I'll finish the degree next May. The bar exam is in September."

"You don't like talking about it, do you? This is not because you're a policeman, but just for yourself," Julie observed astutely. "Are you a crusader, Detective Bennett?"

Cole arched a brow and slowly smiled. "I warned you I had an overdeveloped chivalrous streak."

"I think it's wonderful," Julie said.

He tilted his head. "What? That I'm studying law?"

She shook her head. "That you care enough about what you do to study law."

And Cole liked the sense of encouragement that was suddenly inherent in her smile. Ben was the only other person who understood immediately that he wasn't trying to impress anyone. He was just trying to be more effective at what he did.

Someone brushed past Julie's shoulder, reminding her that they were standing in the middle of the street. It reminded her she had to get home to see about a roasting turkey ... much too big for just two people. She also recalled that twice Cole Bennett said he had no plans for the afternoon or any to celebrate Thanksgiving. Without knowing anything about him, even Lois had suggested he be invited to dinner. Before she could think any more why she shouldn't, Julie blurted out, somewhat awkwardly, her invitation.

"You're more than welcome to have dinner with us..."
she said, putting her hand on the little girl's shoulder. "I
mean, it's not going to be fancy..."

"Yes..."

"And I probably don't even have all the trimmings,
but..."

"Yes. I'd like that."

He'd said yes. And he was letting his eyes roam her face
with an intent, speculative look. Julie suddenly felt uncomfortable. What if he thought she was being forward, or
suggesting more than just dinner? She began to regret her
impromptu invitation. But before she could change her
mind, and indeed Cole could see swiftly changing emotions
racing through her, he spoke again.

"Does this mean you forgive me?" he asked simply.

"For what?" she asked confused.

"For making fun of you last night, as you said."

"Are you admitting you were making fun of me?"

Cole's smile was slow and mischievous. "Of course not.
I am saying yes, I would really like to have dinner with you
and Mickey..."

For a foolish minute Julie didn't know who he meant by
Mickey. And then she looked down at the little girl whose
head was craning back and forth between the two adults as
they talked.

"Do you have cranberry sauce, at least?"

Julie looked blank. "I don't know."

"You have to have cranberry sauce. That's what
Thanksgiving is all about."

Julie thought for a moment, and then she smiled slowly.
"Then I better make sure I have some."

Cole nodded. "I'll bring the dessert."

COLE STOOD AT THE SINK, his hands in hot soapy water. He
was concentrating on washing the food remains from a plate

that had a delicate pattern of blue-and-white flowers stenciled over the surface, just the sort of service ware for someone like Julie Conway. Cole was feeling an odd sensation of peace doing the task, a much more satisfying experience than when he did his own dishes alone and it was just something that had to be done. He was also listening to the low, lilting cadence of Julie's voice from the bathroom. It floated, disembodied and soothing, through the air, even though he couldn't see her. In any case Julie wasn't talking to him, but to the little girl who was getting an evening bath.

The tone was the perfect kind a mother should use with a child. At least as he perceived it. Cole himself had never heard the kind of sweet murmurings that Julie was using with the child. His own mother, more often than not, had been too ill and out of sorts to concentrate on his needs or on things he wanted to hear. He remembered her tone as one of complaint, pain and sadness. There had never been tenderness.

What Cole had liked about Sharon Marie was her softness and tenderness. But it was precisely those things, contrasted against his everyday world of mayhem, that had caused Sharon to withdraw from him and the life they'd planned. Cole had never blamed her for the choice she made in not marrying him. But he had felt defeated and fatalistic, and it had left him not wanting to try again.

It was ironic, Cole had always thought, that people expected men like him to be available—on call, so to speak—when needed. His job made day-to-day life in New York possible. He did the dirty work. But he, too, would have liked to have had the sense of safety that others took for granted.

Cole rinsed the plate, putting it on the drain board, and reached into the depths of the sink for the next item. He thought with some amusement that he had never expected Julie to take him up on his offer of help although it had been a sincere gesture. Cole was used to the experience of being sent off to the living room, the guest oasis, while the host or hostess or both busied themselves with entertaining preparations that more often than not made him feel like he was on display. Not only that but that he was expected to behave in a certain social way.

Cole could recall the women he'd dated or been involved with who never relaxed enough to treat him as ordinary. He became exotic, dangerous, too special, with a life that held a macabre fascination. There had never been a sense for Cole of the possibility of a real relationship or a chance for sharing, because he'd been relegated to the status of a curiosity. With Julie from the start . . . so far . . . it was different.

He was a cop, but she was neither impressed nor threatened. She'd accepted his offer willingly, and whether or not Julie realized the consequence, instead of feeling like a temporary visitor Cole had been made to feel he had the run of the house, her home was his. And he liked the feeling. He was enjoying the homey clutter of Julie's apartment with its comfortable lived-in atmosphere. He had been overwhelmed with the sense of it after they'd arrived from the parade, walking through the door and being assailed with the rich, buttery aroma of a roasting turkey.

Spending the day in the company of Julie and the child had made him feel normal, typical. It was an illusion that would disappear the moment he went back to work, but for the afternoon Cole felt grounded. Even watching the parade with the three of them a huddled little unit against the enthusiastic crowd had served to point out to him the sacrifices he'd made, the ones that had been thrust upon him as a young man, in order to do the work he did now. On days such as today, and there certainly were not many, Cole wondered if it had all been worth it.

He was starting to look at Julie in the considering way a man looks at a woman that he could see having a relation-

ship with. And yet Cole knew he had to be careful to keep a
proper perspective on the day.

They'd stopped for the all-important cranberry sauce and
had found a bakery and bought several apple turnovers for
dessert. Once at the apartment, in the flurry of getting off
coats and hanging them up, Cole had made his first offer.
The child had wandered off to the toy basket in the corner
near the window.

"Is there anything I can do to help?"

Julie had looked at him with an expression of vague dis-
traction, as if she herself wasn't sure what to do. And then
with some hesitation Julie pointed to the handle of the gun,
just visible at the hem of the blue sweater where it was
pushed into the waistband of his jeans.

"Do you think you could not wear that?" she'd asked.

"Of course. I'm sorry..." Cole said. He pulled the gun
free. "Where would you like me to put it?"

Julie looked around and finally opened a cabinet over the
sink. She took the gun gingerly from Cole, surprised at how
heavy it was, and quickly put it away. She turned back to
face him.

"You can also help out by keeping Mickey company while
I start on the rest of dinner."

Cole looked blank. "What do you mean, keep her company?"

Julie smiled at him. Watching small children was obviously not what Cole Bennett was used to. "I mean, talk to
her and play a game or something. You know. Keep her
company."

"I'm sure you've noticed that she doesn't say much,"
Cole pointed out evenly. Of course he had noticed that the
child was silent, for whatever reason. But she was bright and
alert. She wasn't mischievous and she didn't explore or run
or climb or touch or pull at things around her. She didn't do

anything that would make her noticeable. She wasn't fidgety like other five-year-olds who demanded attention.

"I know. But think how terrific you'll feel if she does." Julie smiled coaxingly. "It's not hard. You only need to be patient and interested. She'll do the rest."

"Okay. Then I'll try," Cole said good-naturedly.

"One more thing..." Julie said to him as he stepped toward the living room. Cole looked over his shoulder. "Promise to tell me if it's really awful."

Cole was surprised. She seemed so earnest about it, so anxious as to whether dinner was going to be pleasing. "That's not going to be necessary. Besides, I never bite the hand that feeds me. You might not invite me back," Cole teased before continuing on to the living room.

Julie watched him in silence. She'd given no thought to inviting him back. Not that she might not want to, but just that it might not be a possibility. What would they be to each other? Friends? Or more? More might be difficult.

When the two adults and one child sat down to the pinewood table, the Thanksgiving dinner was simple, no fanfare, no candles or lace tablecloth...and perfect. For a few moments the child sat staring at her plate of food and it had never occurred to Julie that she might not like turkey.

"Go on and eat, sweetheart, before the food gets cold..." Julie coaxed.

Cole was alert to the exchange. "Here, let me try..." He took the fork and knife and cut the turkey slices into smaller pieces, and then he speared some and offered it to the little girl. She looked at it, then at Cole before finally opening her mouth to accept the food. After that she ate on her own, although it was quickly apparent that she liked the sweet cranberry sauce best.

Cole grinned at Julie. "I told you you have to have cranberry sauce..."

Cole was drying his hands on a towel, the dishes done, when Julie appeared from the bathroom. They just looked at one another and, like another moment that had been purely spontaneous, they smiled as they both realized how easily they managed together. It was a surprise to both of them, but for very different reasons.

He noticed a kind of tired contentment about Julie. Perhaps it was because of time spent with the little girl doing a nurturing task, but Cole wanted it to be because the afternoon and evening with the three of them together had been so good. Quiet. Peaceful. Real. Julie's hair had softened and loosened over the course of the day and Cole also liked that she didn't fuss with it. It had a tendency toward gentle disarray, which he found appealing. Maybe because it meant Julie was not concentrating on herself but on those around her, making him and the child comfortable and welcome.

Julie didn't exactly feel shy standing across the room from Cole, but she did feel a wonderment at how willingly he fit in, how agreeable he'd been to making the day easy and fun. For the first time as she looked at him, Julie let herself fully appreciate that Cole was not in the least like other men she'd ever met. He had nothing to prove, no masculine ego to protect, no need to control, which would have caused her to feel inadequate. If anything, Cole had unwittingly made them equals.

His sweater and shirtsleeves were rolled up to his elbows. He was wiping his large hands on a towel and for a second Julie was fascinated with the strong, sinewy shape of them. He still had another towel, which she had insisted on tucking in around his waist to help keep his clothes dry while he washed the dishes. But the fact that Cole *had* been willing to do dishes bolstered him in her esteem about one hundred percent. She had begun to relax with Cole around her, to accept him. She had been particularly taken with his ease with the little girl. Cole had shown not only patience but an attentiveness and curiosity and playfulness that had at one point drawn an excited giggle from the girl.

The sound of simple childhood delight had surprised her, and Julie had turned to the living room to see what was going on. Cole was stretched out on his side full-length on the floor, his upper-body weight supported on a bent arm. With the other hand he was working a hand puppet, and he had created a voice for the character the likes of which Julie had never heard before and which sounded so whimsical and funny that she went into peals of genuine laughter. It was that memory, that feeling of absolute pleasure that made her smile at him now.

Cole's smile, however, turned to one of amusement, and Julie turned to find his attention now focused on the girl who stood in the bathroom door. She was dressed in a T-shirt, which was being used as a nightgown and which was obviously much too big for her. The shirt had the slogan printed in red and green, Ray's Famous Pizza.

"I don't remember children's sleepwear being so creative," he said.

"It probably isn't." Julie shrugged. "But I had to improvise."

"Did you get behind the ears?" Cole asked, standing with his hands on his hips.

Julie had the oddest sensation then, a feeling of the possibility of Cole as a father himself. It was also his display of both strength and gentleness that she liked a lot. Julie stroked the little girl's hair. "Inside and out."

"Then I guess it's time for bed," he said smoothly, and watched as Julie suddenly began to blush.

"Yes..." she answered, averting her gaze from his.

Her reaction surprised him, but it also pleased him that Julie was so easy to read. He squatted down to balance himself on the balls of his feet. Then he silently beckoned the little girl toward him, and she came without hesitation.

Cole tugged at her ponytail, and playfully tickled her, again getting a giggle from her. Then he stood and reached for the Annie-Fannie doll, which had been left on a chair during her bath, and gave it to her.

"Good night, Mickey," he said to the girl, winking at her as Julie led her to the bedroom.

Cole watched them leave. He stood, putting his hands into the pockets of his jeans. They were warm and wrinkled and he realized with some wry humor that he suffered from dishpan hands. He wandered aimlessly into the living room. Behind him there was only the hushed voice of Julie as she said good-night to the child and tucked her into bed. Everything else was quiet. He suddenly experienced a churning in the pit of his stomach, because now with the day over, he knew he would have to go home, back to his own life . . . back to the other life.

He didn't belong here with Julie and Mickey, and in fact, the day had held an aura of both the possible and impossible and he had tried to reconcile them. He had managed to fit in for the course of the day. It had been wonderful. For the space of a few hours, and with the company of a pretty woman and the sound of a child's laughter, he had belonged to the real world. Julie Conway had provided him with much more than just Thanksgiving dinner. Cole sensed that she was behind him and turned around.

"She likes you," Julie said very softly. "You have a way with women."

Cole just looked at her. "Some women," he qualified. "The little ones are easy. I'm not always so successful with the bigger ones."

Julie shook her head. Somehow she couldn't imagine that. In fact, after their afternoon together she found it incredible that Cole Bennett didn't have somewhere else to be today . . . with someone else. "Well, you really only have to be successful with one."

He grinned. "I'm still trying..."

Julie tilted her head. "Then, you've never been...married?" she asked cautiously, aware that she was being personal.

Cole shrugged. "Close, but no cigar."

Julie was puzzled, and it must have shown in her expression. Cole began to walk toward her, and his movement was so slow, so predatory, that Julie stared at him in fascination. He was stalking her, and she began to feel a little trapped. She could feel her pulse rate rise, and she concentrated on breathing evenly. The interest in his eyes changed and became much more focused and directed on her.

"I was almost married once. It was my rookie year."

"What happened?"

"I got shot...and she changed her mind. It hadn't occurred to her that I could be killed doing my job. She decided she couldn't handle the possibility."

Julie had not considered that herself. She, of course, realized that police died all the time in the line of duty, but she had not yet considered that meant Cole was vulnerable, too. At least, not until this moment, after coming to the conclusion that she liked him. He kept coming forward until he was within two feet of her.

"Was...was it serious?" she asked in a small voice, looking up into his face and seeing a man who had lived an unusual life, a dangerous one taken for granted by people. Until this afternoon she had only seen Cole in the context of his position, and had responded with a kind of remoteness that kept them separate. She was suddenly seeing him as just a man.

"Not really. It was a flesh wound on my side. It hurt more having my fiancée walk out," he said lightly, as though he had completely forgotten the episode and put it behind him. But his eyes told a different story. The mixing of gray hair with blond, and the lines around his eyes and mouth, spoke of a life that had still not been easy but for which he'd been suited. He didn't have many regrets, except for the moments when he was with someone such as Julie Conway who, in an abstract way, reminded him of Sharon Marie.

Julie looked down at her hands, too unsettled by what she saw in his gaze. "You can still get married. You don't have to give up."

Cole let his eyes roam over her hair, her smooth skin and the expressive shape of her mouth. "I haven't..." he whispered. He reached out his hand to push back an errant wisp of her hair when Julie suddenly turned away from him.

"We...we forgot all about dessert. Would you like some coffee and one of the turnovers?"

Cole frowned, rather surprised at her sudden evasiveness. But he let his hand drop and thought wryly that, after all, it had only been dinner. She hadn't granted him license for anything else. But he was still confused and disappointed.

"I don't think so," he said easily as he watched her move some distance from him. "I may have overdone it with the turkey. I had three helpings, remember?"

She twisted her hands nervously, but managed to smile at him. "You do have an amazing appetite. I hope it wasn't just to be polite."

"Julie, it was a great dinner. I mean it. I consider myself very lucky to have been invited," he said honestly.

Julie nodded, and the silence fell between them. It wasn't awkward but it did hold an expectancy, one that she was afraid to think about.

Again Cole found himself walking toward Julie. He didn't like the distance between them, didn't want it. Meeting Julie Conway had been totally unexpected, and the circumstances of their involvement, of getting acquainted, had been buffered by the presence of the little girl. With the child asleep he thought there was a chance to be less on guard, less formal.

Julie would have liked that, too. And there was a time when it might have been possible. But that was long before she'd committed herself to someone who'd then betrayed her trust. She kept the distance in place because she was not yet ready to deal with anything else between them.

"If you like, I can put together a doggie bag of leftovers. I'll never be able to eat it all."

Cole reached out and took hold of her hands. They were slender, cool...so small in his own. She suddenly seemed very fragile and not at all like the independent, able woman he'd been with all afternoon. "I would much prefer to be invited back. I understand there are one hundred and one things you can do with leftover turkey..."

He meant to make her smile, but she couldn't. Julie was acutely aware of how close Cole was to her. She had a strong, overwhelming sense of his masculinity.

Cole waited for an answer, but when Julie didn't give one his disappointment grew. "On the other hand, perhaps I've overstayed my welcome."

She looked up at those words, into blue eyes that were clear and earnest and surprisingly hopeful. "No, you haven't," she said softly, wondering how to make him understand.

But Cole believed her. He slowly smiled at her, unaware of her ambivalence. He liked the way her lips were suddenly parted slightly, and her eyes were very bright in anticipation. He slowly pulled Julie toward him, feeling the natural resistance she made. He found even that attractive in her.

"Then let me say thank you..." he murmured. Cole released Julie's hands, taking hold instead of her upper arms to bring her closer. A small shiver coursed through her, but he ignored it. He bent his head and let his lips press against her own. Julie wasn't exactly responsive. She seemed to be waiting, holding her breath, but again Cole saw this as merely a bridge that had to be crossed as they slowly came to know one another.

He liked the feel of her mouth, the shape of it against his. Hers was soft and pliant. He pressed closer and gently tried to manipulate her lips open. He was not looking for passion and wasn't giving it. He was merely using this kiss to let Julie Conway know how much he'd enjoyed the afternoon with her. Cole heard her breathing deepen, felt her sway a little to him and was encouraged when her lips parted beneath his a fraction. Cole let his tongue explore against the soft surface of her lip. Julie's hands braced against his chest in a nervous little movement and he let his mouth rub gently over hers.

Cole felt the brief touch of her tongue against his, heard a faint sound of some kind…a moan, and he went with the subtle stimulation of their softly kissing mouths. But then Julie pushed against his chest. She pushed again, harder and with more purpose and Cole felt a complete stiffening of her body. Before he could react, Julie tore her lips from his and uttered a strangled sound.

Chapter Four

"No..." The sound came out in a whispered rush.

Julie turned within the half circle of Cole's arms as her hands came up defensively. She was not out-of-control but she was very obviously frightened.

"Julie..." he said easily, automatically in a voice of understanding. Cole kept the surprise out of his voice because it was clear he had to keep things calm. He wrapped his arms about her, capturing hers against her chest. But Cole could feel her readying for a struggle, her body rigid and straight. "Nothing's going to hurt you," Cole said and softly repeated it until, in a matter of seconds, her body began to relax.

Julie bit her lip trying to breathe evenly. Part of her wanted to break free, to run to safety. But part of her fully realized that she wasn't being held against her will. She was being comforted. Cole's arms were not closed tightly and there was no force at all. He was simply holding her.

Julie let her eyes close, concentrated on where she was...and with whom. She didn't struggle because this time she didn't have to. She was being held by Cole Bennett in a familiar way, and her sense of one danger slowly dissipated to be replaced by another. Julie was actually cradled against him, but found that it was not a threatening position. Even though Cole was in control of the situation, she let him be.

She felt incredible warmth from his natural body heat. She felt the firm strength of his chest against her back, could detect the steady, even beat of his heart. That calmed her even more. His voice was a deep caressing whisper of reassurance, and Julie listened to his words, believing him. She wasn't in any danger. She began to feel safe again.

When Cole sensed that it was time, he let Julie go and stepped back. For a second Julie stood still, her back turned to him.

"I'm sorry," Cole began. "I didn't mean to..."

Julie was already shaking her head vigorously. She turned around to lean against the wall. "I...just couldn't breathe," she tried to explain, her voice sounding thin.

"Are you all right?" he asked, watching her very carefully, trying to gauge her emotions at that instant.

Julie nodded, the wispy tendrils of hair he'd thought to touch before, now feathered about her face, giving her a softly tousled look, a helplessness that had been very real a moment ago.

She didn't meet his gaze and Cole could see a flush come over her features. He realized that along with her momentary outburst of panic, Julie was also feeling embarrassment. But he couldn't just tell her she needn't be. To do so would be to admit he recognized the cause. To put it into words would only embarrass her more. Instead, Cole dared to try and turn the drama of the moment and its implications into easy humor, making himself the target.

"I'll have to say that that is the first time I've ever taken a woman's breath away," he said and gave her a totally self-deprecating grin. The words were light, but his eyes were serious as he continued to watch her.

A moment of sadness and relief flashed across Julie's face, but still she wouldn't look at Cole. She was not yet ready to risk the questions she thought she'd see in his eyes, because she knew she couldn't give him answers.

"Sit down," Cole ordered gently. Julie looked at him then, her eyes wide. She slowly sighed and it was the last effort that she needed to be herself again. In fact, she rather proudly raised her chin at Cole.

"I'm not going to faint," Julie stated, almost as if willing herself not to.

Cole pulled out a chair from the dining table. "Humor me. Sit down, anyway," he said.

Julie pushed away from the wall and carefully made her way the four feet or so to the chair. Still, she was annoyed to find that her knees were wobbly and she sat down none too gracefully.

"Can I get you something?" Cole asked, and although he kept his voice and tone even, not emphasizing at all that they'd both been through a minor emotional trauma, he continued to keep a close eye on her.

The flush on her face deepened. "Nothing, thank you. There's nothing you can do."

Cole automatically put out a hand to touch her, but caught himself and rested the hand instead on the chair back. "Are you sure?"

Julie's eyes were suddenly filled with a confusion and pain that was heartbreaking. She tried to smile, but failed. She clasped her hands together, squeezing them tightly until the blood drained from her knuckles. Cole's jaw tightened in anger as he saw her struggle. Someone had hurt her badly.

"I'm sorry, Cole. It wasn't you . . . it's me. This wasn't your fault."

Cole let his gaze soften, let his eyes fill with concern that was genuine. He slowly squatted down next to her chair, and he saw her eyes register brief apprehension and then surprise because he was so close. But Cole knew that to back away from her, to keep a distance, would have given the wrong signal, as well.

"Don't be sorry," he said, an earnestness in his face that had Julie staring at him. "And it's not your fault, either." Cole gave her a slight smile. "Your kiss told me that."

Julie blinked at him and began to gnaw at her bottom lip with her teeth. Her hands twisted together. "You're probably wondering..." she began, her voice cracking with emotion.

"Julie..." Cole interrupted quietly, leaning a fraction closer. "You don't have to explain anything," he said. Cole recalled Ben Bradshaw's flippant remark to him the night before about getting her life's story. Cole would guess that the details were complicated. "You seem caring and sincere. You have a sense of humor and you're generous. I like you. I found all that out this afternoon, and it's all I need to know."

Julie looked closely at him, seeing a tenderness in his blue eyes that belied his hard edge and the very nature of his life. "No questions?"

Cole's gaze roamed over her face. Her coloring was better, but her mouth was still tight. He had a few questions, but knew that now was not the time to be outraged or to play cop.

"Just one," he said, holding up an index finger, and watched a guarded look cloud her gray eyes. "Can I change my mind about dessert?"

Julie just stared. It was a moment that again changed everything between them. She had been stripped before him of her pride and self-control, in a way, of even her womanhood. It really had not been his fault, but Julie would have understood his leaving her now because the evening had somehow been ruined. Yet Cole didn't seem inclined to leave.

Julie remembered as if it was yesterday going to her mother and stepfather with her horrible story, with physical evidence to prove her claim. She had never known the loneliness possible as when people who were supposed to love you and care for you, didn't believe you. More than that, Julie had had an astonishing realization that their disbelief and rejection had nothing to do with her. It had to do with her parents wanting to distance themselves from the truth before the taint spread. Her mother, whom she might have counted on in other circumstances, had aligned herself with her husband and his opinion, and Julie had stood alone.

Julie didn't have to say a word to Cole because the knowledge was in his eyes. Perhaps it was training and because he was a cop. Yet he was hardly behaving toward her like a civil servant. Julie knew that his concern was sincere. He had respect for her feelings and for her need to contain any further damage to her already bruised ego.

Cole was aware of the skeptical, considering way in which Julie seemed to be regarding his question. It would not have surprised him if she had asked him outright to leave, but when she didn't Cole realized they had crossed some sort of bridge of understanding, and empathy lay between them.

Slowly Julie began to smile, raising her brows. "You're not very subtle, Detective," she said softly.

Cole lifted a corner of his mouth. "It's not one of my strong points, I admit," and then the smile slowly faded, and his blue eyes were once again serious. "I just wasn't sure if I'd be given another opportunity."

"After what happened, I wouldn't think you'd want one," she replied dryly, looking at her joined hands.

Cole looked down at her hands, too, for a second. Then he reached out and gently pulled them apart. He took one of her hands, now cold, and held it for a while, looking down into her eyes. Julie didn't pull away. Holding her hand, Cole stood up finally and drew Julie to her feet beside him.

"You were wrong," he said smoothly. "Why don't you put some water on for coffee."

Julie thought she should make some sort of protest. She didn't want him feeling sorry for her. But Cole was already walking away, so she found herself heading for the kitchen counter and the coffee maker. She felt unnatural in what she was doing until she realized that Cole was not standing behind her watching her every move. He made himself at home and helped out as he'd pretty much done all afternoon.

Knowing that Julie didn't need to feel any more awkward than she already did, Cole made himself useful. While she prepared the coffee, he found two dessert plates in the cabinet, and opened drawers until he found fresh silverware. He set everything out on the dining table with paper napkins, all the while talking and asking questions. Julie at last came to realize that he was once again treating her as he had earlier in the day.

He talked about the dinner again, and said the only other thing he would have liked to have had was stuffing. Julie admitted she didn't know how to make stuffing, to which Cole responded he would show her sometime. That offhand remark was a surprise, but she hid her pleasure at the idea by expressing doubt that he could cook. Cole, however, got cocky enjoyment out of telling her he could do anything around a house that she could. Julie grinned. She'd never met a single man in her life who knew how to cook and would admit it. But then, she was already discovering that Cole Bennett was not exactly your ordinary garden-variety kind of man. And she laughed lightly as he recited his domestic qualities.

"It sounds to me like you'd make a wonderful wife," Julie teased in a quiet, amused voice.

Cole shrugged and raised a sardonic brow. "I think I'd make a better husband."

They stood staring at each other for a long second, the implications of their banter bringing forth past memories for both of them. It was an awkward little moment that they then shied away from.

Cole said how much he liked her apartment, that it was weird and sort of fun. That made Julie smile. He was particularly fascinated with a felt-covered bulletin board in the living room that was purely visual, a revolving display of changeable items. It was not intended to hold pinned phone messages and office snapshots. There were dried orange and yellow leaves from fall, a button that said, "just do it...." There was a Calvin and Hobbes cartoon and a handkerchief printed with a street map of London. There was a used and colorful popcorn bag and the curled and yellowed newspaper clipping that was the complete text of Dr. Martin Luther King, Jr.'s "I Have a Dream..." speech.

Cole spent some time in front of the board, gaining additional insight into Julie Conway. He was discovering a woman who was, in some ways, simple and genuine, and in others, complex and mysterious.

When the coffee was ready and two turnovers had been heated in the oven, Julie softly called for Cole's attention. He approached the pine table slowly, thoughtfully, with his hands stuffed in his jean pockets. He watched her as she poured the coffee and cut the turnovers in half. Cole sat down.

"You're a romantic, Ms. Conway," Cole said.

Julie sat opposite him. "Why? Because I keep cute restaurant napkins and save fortune-cookie proverbs? My friend Lois says I'm strange." Julie laughed gently at herself.

Cole lifted his mug, watching her with sparkling eyes. "I'm sure your friend was teasing. No, I think because even the little things seem to give you pleasure..." Cole took a sip of coffee and raised his brows. "And you make a good cup of coffee."

"It was a fluke," Julie said wryly.

Cole drank his coffee in silence for a moment. Then he shook his head. "You don't give yourself nearly enough credit."

Julie didn't respond, and they turned their attention to dessert. Julie, however, kept taking furtive glances at Cole, wondering what was going through his mind. What was he really thinking about that instant when he'd kissed her and she'd very nearly panicked? Could he tell, for instance, that she wanted to enjoy the kiss?

Julie had overcome a lot in seven years. She would, of course, never be able to forget that the man she would have married, whom she would have lived her life with intimately, in trust and promise, had violated her. It was no longer the hurt it had been. She didn't dwell on it. It had taken a long time to come to terms with, but she had managed that, as well. Most importantly she no longer blamed herself. For a long time afterward, particularly after the debacle with her parents and the police, Julie even doubted that she had been violated. Was it rape when your fiancée, fresh from overindulging at a bachelor party and very drunk, forced you to have sex, leaving bruises on your body, disappointment and heartache in your soul? They would have been doing the same thing just twenty-four hours later. But he would have been sober and hopefully more gentle ... and she would have lovingly given her consent.

"Julie..."

She jumped and felt Cole's large hand close over her own, preventing her from further mutilating her turnover with her fingers. Julie looked at Cole and saw anger, understanding and helplessness. Then it all settled into determination. His jaw muscles twitched and his blue eyes probed the troubled look in her own.

"Don't think about it," he commanded quietly.

For a moment Julie spontaneously squeezed his hand before he released hers and picked up his mug again.

Julie took a deep breath. "Where do you live?" she asked, trying to get off the subject of herself. She wasn't a victim anymore. Anyway, her life was hardly exciting, and not so unusual as she'd come to learn since working at the center.

"Long Island. The North Shore."

Julie only nodded. She knew nothing about Long Island. "Is that where you're from? Is that where your family is?"

Cole pursed his mouth. He used his finger to absently dab crumbs from the table, flicking them onto his empty plate.

Julie watched his hands. He had very strong, large but gentle hands. She remembered with surprise how they'd felt holding her. Securely, but with care.

"No, I'm not from Long Island. I grew up in Queens. And no I don't have family there. I don't have family anywhere."

"Oh..."

He made a vague gesture of dismissal with a hand, and then leaned forward onto the table with his folded arms. It brought his face closer and allowed Julie to see clearly that he was a handsome man. There was enormous maturity about him, even though Julie judged he could only be in his late thirties. She wondered, finally, if the gray hair, which blended so attractively with the dark blond, was due to heredity...or his job.

"I bought a house there when I was a rookie. I saved for a year to make the down payment. It was going to be the house in which I married and raised a family. When that didn't work out I kept it anyway."

"Why? Wasn't it a constant reminder of how things had fallen apart?"

Cole shrugged. "Not really. It was only a house. I still had to have some place to live, and I liked that part of the island."

It was only a house... Julie repeated to herself silently. Cole watched as some sort of memory, some sort of recognition made Julie lift her head alertly.

"A family, people around you that you love, those are the things that make a real home. It's a great house and I like it," he said without any hint of complaint. Then Cole looked over his shoulder into Julie's colorful and crowded living room. "This is homey. Why is your place different?"

She smiled wistfully, brushing absently at a tendril of hair, shifting in her chair. "Maybe it isn't. But I felt it might well be the only home I ever have. I wanted it to be comfortable and as complete as I could make it."

"Is it?" Cole asked quietly.

Julie hesitated, thinking about his question and thinking about her loneliness and the sometimes emotional ache of emptiness she experienced thinking of the children she might have had. "Mostly..."

"I know one thing that does make a difference," he said but he was looking at her significantly, almost personally, and Julie blushed under his sudden intent regard.

"What?"

"House plants."

She blinked at him, not sure she'd heard correctly. And then she began to laugh.

"How did we get onto the subject of house plants?"

"It wasn't easy." Cole grinned, pleased to hear her laugh, and gratified that her attention had been diverted from her pain.

For a time there was a warm companionship in their mutual gazes, and then it became particular, more special, and for the first time Julie did not look away as Cole's eyes roamed from her hair to her face and mouth and back to her gray eyes.

"Would you like some more coffee?" Julie asked as the silence stretched on.

He pushed his mug toward her. "Just enough to keep me awake on the drive home," he said, inadvertently reminding them both that it was getting late.

Julie got up to get the pot from the counter and Cole silently watched her, letting his eyes follow her movement, again feeling that surprising sense of comfort in her company, feeling that he could relax here, realizing that even after a potentially disastrous moment—worse for her than it had been for him—he *wanted* to be here. His eyes stayed on her as she leaned in front of him to pour the coffee.

Julie tried not to notice that he was scrutinizing her, but she pulled the coffeepot away too quickly and ended up with hot coffee dripping on the table and then down the leg of her jeans.

"Wonderful..." she said in exasperation, looking down as the dark stains spread.

"Did you burn yourself?" Cole asked, quickly standing.

"I don't think so, but I'd better go and inspect the damage," she said, putting the pot down and hurrying off to the bathroom.

Seeing that the accident was not at all serious, Cole settled back in his chair. He used his napkin to wipe up the spilled coffee, and began sipping at his refill, reflecting on the extraordinary events of the day, which brought him to the present moment. In the silence, Cole thought he heard a low whine, a whimper actually. It was another second before he realized it was coming from Julie's room. Quickly the cup was put down and he was out of his chair headed for the room.

When Cole opened the door he could distinguish at once that the little girl was crying. She was lying on her back, the covers kicked aside, the Annie-Fannie doll pressed tightly to her chest.

For a moment Cole was perplexed. He had no idea what he should do. He gave a quick thought to calling Julie, but in the end found himself whispering in a low voice to the child. Cole walked over to the bed and looked down at the small body shaking with tears.

"Hey. What's the matter?" he asked in a voice he didn't recall ever having used before. But it seemed pretty natural, nonetheless. He reached slowly and lifted the little girl from the bed, holding her in his arms against his chest. "Did you have a bad dream?" he crooned, getting into the comforting mode and wondering if he sounded foolish.

The child leaned back from his chest, and Cole found the head and arm of the doll pressed against his mouth and chin. But there was little time to appreciate the comedy in it. The child's eyes were closed tightly and her little chest heaved with emotions as she used the back of her hand to wipe the tears away. Cole patted her back gently, and began to pace the small confines of the room.

"Come on, now. Don't cry."

The child smeared the tears on her face and hiccuped. Cole was still talking to her, his voice so low and quiet it was like a purr. He stroked her hair and then the little girl put her head on his shoulder and the crying stopped.

This was how Julie found the two of them when she came from the bathroom. When she opened the door and found the kitchen empty her immediate thought was that Cole had left and gone home. But seeing her bedroom door open she understood what had happened.

There was something wonderfully dear, poignantly tender about the way Cole held and whispered to the child, calming her nighttime fears. Julie didn't interrupt. She merely watched silently from the doorway, because he was doing just fine. But seeing him with the child sparked a longing in her that caused unexpected tears to well in her eyes. And the sight instantly endeared Cole to her.

It was not long before the girl was once again fully asleep, and Cole was putting her limp body carefully back to bed with the covers secure around her. He had no awareness that Julie stood watching until he walked from the room and closed the door behind him.

Whatever emotions she was experiencing, for a fleeting moment, Julie was sure she saw reflected in Cole's eyes. They regarded each other silently, but it was not an uncomfortable silence. Cole shrugged.

"I heard her crying."

Julie nodded. "It happened last night, too."

"She seemed okay this afternoon."

"She *is* okay," Julie assured him. "It's just that late at night children get a little scared in the dark."

He merely nodded. He had no experience with that.

"Thank you for seeing to her. I think she just needed a little cuddle." And she recalled, however, that that was exactly what she herself had gotten from Cole only an hour or so ago.

Cole glanced briefly at the door to the bedroom. "Well, at least when you go to bed she'll have someone beside her."

"I've been sleeping on the sofa."

He frowned. "That love seat is a lot shorter than a sofa. It can't make for very comfortable sleeping," he commented.

"It's not so bad. But it's a good thing I'm not very tall."

Cole chuckled silently at her humor.

"I think the coffee is cold. Should I heat it?"

Cole thought about it, but sooner or later he knew he'd have to go. He shook his head. "Don't bother. One cup will have to do the trick."

Julie nodded. She was already beginning to feel the quiet solitude of her small apartment close in around her. For a while today it had seemed much bigger, much livelier. Cole looked at her, wanting to say something, but he wasn't sure what. And he wasn't sure why. Instead, he walked past Julie and headed for the closet and his parka. He wondered if it was really easier going home now, having had so good an afternoon, much better than he would have hoped for with Julie, or if it was worse because of it.

Julie took the cups and plates and coffeepot to the counter and, reaching into the overhead cabinet took out a blue-and-white cereal bowl. She turned to Cole and offered him his handgun, which was sitting in the center of the bowl like a piece of strange exotic fruit.

They looked at each other and smiled at the presentation before Cole took the gun and put it back into the waistband of his jeans. And then they walked to the door.

They did not make any promises, did not make plans for another time. There were no awkward thank-you's. Somehow they'd come too far for that, gotten past being merely polite. The next step was, nevertheless, uncertain. Cole put his hands into the pockets of his jacket. It was a very deliberate movement as he stood in front of Julie looking down into her face. Again his eyes made a careful, thorough assessment of her. Just their eyes communicated, but they were both considering the same thing.

"Shall we try again?" Cole asked, his voice low and a bit gravelly. The texture of it sent a nervous flutter up Julie's spine.

She looked at him, unafraid of him. He had been strong and understanding. He had been patient. Julie slowly nodded even though her heartbeat was starting a little tap dance in her chest.

Cole kept his eyes on hers as he slowly bent toward her. But soon he transferred his gaze to her soft mouth, seeing the slight movement of uncertainty. He let his lips part before they settled on her mouth, because that was the way he wanted this kiss to be. He wanted to be gentle with her, but he wanted no misunderstanding as to what he thought she could give. And Cole wanted it to be a man-and-woman kiss, not a kiss between friends.

Her eyes closed, and so did his. He tilted his head and slowly moved his mouth over hers, and there was a tentative response, a puckering of her lips against his. It was just what he wanted. Cole slowly broke the kiss and raised his head.

"Okay?" he asked softly.

Julie was standing a little stiffly, almost in anticipation. When she opened her eyes there was a startled brightness to them, and the start of warmth...and pleasure. She stopped holding her breath.

"Okay," Julie confirmed with a sigh.

Cole smiled at her and opened the door. "The equipment works perfectly," he told her gently. "It just needs practice and time."

Her features colored over. "Who has that much time?" she responded wryly.

Cole stepped out into the hall.

"I do..." he whispered, closing it shut.

THERE WAS A YELP of childish excitement followed by a chorus of giggles, and the three little bodies streaked through the living room, rounded the corner and disappeared into Julie's bedroom. Shortly there was the sound of the mattress thumping against the support board of the platform bed as the three children used it for a trampoline and the banshee screams expressed their joy.

Lois covered her ears and shook her head at the noise. "I don't understand how you can take all that racket."

Julie grinned. "On Sunday two of them will be going home with you. That will reduce the racket considerably."

"I'm surprised you haven't been evicted. Every time the kids come over to your place they know you'll let them get away with anything short of murder."

Julie smiled peacefully, not the least disturbed by the commotion but rather liking that the children were having such a good time among themselves. She glanced at the cheerful destruction of her living room and shrugged.

"I'm not worried about being evicted. I'm worried about my mattress. In another week I might have to replace it."

"I'll chip in. After all my kids use it almost as much as you do."

"I don't mind. Although I was concerned that it might be a problem with three of them in the bed."

"How are you going to work out the sleeping arrangements?" Lois asked as she finished the last of a cup of tea.

"Well, I'll just get them all ready for bed, and then everyone can have milk and the last of the turnovers, and I'll send them in to bed. I've decided to let them figure it out on their own, who is going to sleep where."

Lois laughed and shook her head at the purely democratic way in which Julie had solved the problem.

"They'll manage fine."

"Yeah, somehow kids do," Lois sighed thoughtfully. "Don't you wish sometimes that your own life was as easy to deal with? Instead you have to decide what to do about a child you call Mickey, and a cop named Cole Bennett."

Julie used her fork carefully to slice off a chunk of Lois's homemade sweet potato pie. She didn't respond at first because the mention of Cole had a tendency to kindle a lot of confused emotions in her. She'd told Lois everything about her meeting with Cole, and pretty much everything that had happened on Thanksgiving Day. She had not told Lois, however, about the fact that Cole had kissed her, or how she'd reacted.

She had not mentioned, for instance, that while she had been initially frightened that things would get out of hand between her and Cole, she had also been rather surprised by the excitement she felt from kissing him before she'd finally lost her nerve. It had been the first time in a long time that Julie had actually wanted a man to kiss her, although she hadn't realized it until after Cole had done so.

Julie had been hurt and humiliated by her experience with her fiancée, but she'd finally been able to reason that not all men lost control so senselessly in the way that he had. Julie still believed that love and affection between a man and a woman was possible, that respect and caring helped in treasuring a relationship and in treating each other well. She had not actively sought to find such a relationship for herself again—but that didn't mean she didn't want one. She just hadn't a clue as to how to start all over again. And she was still not sure if she could.

Lois had said go out and date. That was easier said than done. For one thing you had to be asked, and Julie realized that she had not exactly put herself on the front line as being available. For another thing, although a date sounded fine, maybe a dinner or movie, maybe a small party where there's safety in numbers, sooner or later it was just going to be you and him, and saying good-night. A good-night kiss she might have been able to handle, but if there were other expectations, Julie already knew from terrible experience that saying no was not always enough to put an end to things going too far.

But she had liked Cole's kiss. She had liked it especially because it had been so extraordinarily gentle. He was not aggressive and he didn't assume anything from it. She had liked it because his lips had been firm and warm, and their masculine fullness had sparked an instant awareness of her own femininity that had lain dormant for so long. That awareness, that reminder because of Cole Bennett's kiss, had also alarmed her.

"She still hasn't said anything?" Lois asked.

Julie looked blank. "Who?"

Lois looked tolerant. "Daydreaming again? We were talking about the kids. Has the little girl said anything?"

Julie took a deep breath and shook her head. "Not a word. But she's been giggling and laughing more frequently. She seems to like Tanya and Darren and will probably get along fine with them this weekend."

Lois made a gesture with a tilt of her head. "Yeah, well . . . with my kids it's either beat 'em or join 'em."

There was another ear-splitting scream from the room. A pillow came sailing through the door, hitting the three-paneled screen in the kitchen and rocking it unsteadily back and forth for a second. Darren appeared from the room in his stockinged feet, retrieved the pillow and dashed back into the fray.

Lois rolled her eyes heavenward, but Julie only smiled complacently.

"Oh, and thank you for bringing me those things for Mickey," Julie said, reaching to put a shopping bag on her lap that Lois had given her upon arriving. Julie looked idly through the folded pile of children's clothing.

"I'm glad you asked me about it before I left the house. I probably would have sent most of it to a thrift store."

"She had no pajamas," Julie said, holding up a corduroy jumper and smiling at the pockets, which were embroidered to look like a pair of hands. "She's been sleeping in a T-shirt of mine."

"Well, there should certainly be enough clothing to last until . . ." Lois stopped.

Julie looked at her. "Until her mother or someone comes back for her," she stated smoothly.

"What do you think will happen on Monday?" Lois asked carefully.

Julie glanced at her briefly. "I don't know. Quite honestly I've been trying not to think about it. I was hoping that someone would have contacted the number on the note I posted, but there's been nothing."

"Do you still believe someone will be back for her or are you only hoping?"

"Both," Julie admitted. "I'm hoping someone will come for her, because she should be with her family. And I know that staying with me is not the real answer."

Lois knew Julie was right. The system for foster care in the city was barely adequate and not very efficient. If Julie committed herself to the little girl she could have the child taken from her at anytime, for any reason. Lois understood that Julie did not need that kind of emotional uncertainty and neither did the little girl she called Mickey. Lois patted Julie's hand in reassurance.

"Well, don't drive yourself crazy over it today. Tomorrow is another day," she said airily, sounding nothing like Scarlett O'Hara. Lois sat back in her chair and took a deep breath, regarding Julie. "Now tell me more about this detective."

Julie flushed and looked at her friend with wide-eyed appeal. A memory flashed quickly into her mind and out again, not of the awkwardness of what had happened between her and Cole Bennett, but of that gentle moment in which he held her against himself in solace.

"There isn't any more to tell."

Lois smirked. "Is that why you're turning all shades of pink?" she said teasingly. Julie didn't answer. "You haven't told me if you like him. Do you think you'll see him again?"

"I don't know," Julie replied with a sigh, even though she'd gone over his parting words to her again and again. Had they been thrown out carelessly? Had she interpreted them the wrong way? Did it bother her that it might have been a superficial gesture? Yes... "He was very nice, but it was just one day, one evening."

Lois was shaking her head slowly. "He still gets ten points, as far as I'm concerned. You know when Ray died and I found myself struggling with two very small children, I couldn't even think of loving anybody else or of getting married again. And let's face it, there isn't a whole lot to choose from out there..." Lois wisecracked, making Julie laugh. "I'm still not exactly looking for another husband, but if a good man came along, he'd never know what hit him." Julie laughed again. "What I'm saying is, maybe you're ready, too."

Julie gnawed gently on her lip, because the pain of the truth was so bittersweet. And because the warmth of Cole's kiss had stayed with her... and because he'd made her feel so hopeful once again. "I've managed fine on my own in the past few years. I've been lucky and I'm content."

"Lucky isn't the same as being loved. Content isn't the same as being happy. You're really good at helping other people, Julie. But don't forget about yourself. You have a right to try for the magic ring and you deserve a second chance to fall in love."

Julie looked up at Lois, her eyes soft and filled with dreams. It frightened her that the image of Cole Bennett came to mind as Lois spoke. Perhaps because he was the first man in so long that she'd allowed herself to be attracted to. She didn't want to hope foolishly, but it would be nice if...

"Do your tea leaves say how this is supposed to happen?" she asked quietly.

Lois grinned, nodding her head. "Don't be afraid to say yes."

THE LIGHTS WERE OUT in Cole's living room. If he happened to be home at the right time in the afternoon the lights were turned off so he could enjoy the sunset in progress seen magnificently from the window. It used to be a clear, unobstructed view, but nearly twenty years of trees and bushes growing had altered it somewhat. Not enough, fortunately, to prevent him from watching the sky turn to the black velvet of night.

The view never ceased to fascinate Cole, and there was something soothing and stable in the predictability of the sunset, unlike the occasional chaos of his everyday life. It was a subtle appreciation he'd never been able to share properly with anyone. It would have been nice to be able to stand at this window with someone who could absorb the tranquility and peace as he did. Someone special, whose presence, like sunrise and sunset, added sanity to his life. At the moment, however, the benign view did nothing for his frame of mind.

He was thinking of Julie Conway.

As a matter of fact he'd been thinking of Julie since he'd left her on Thanksgiving night. Much of his consideration had been with contentment and pleasure, with some surprise and amusement. But there had been some anger, as well. Cole realized he had stumbled across the remains of a dark secret about Julie Conway, and the knowledge was having a strange, unexpected effect on him.

As a cop he was not unfamiliar with assault cases that came through the precinct or that were reported with graphic details and morbid relish in the daily tabloids, but they were beyond his jurisdiction and concern unless the victim was also killed. Cole remembered the rudimentary training that had been necessary for all police who might come in contact with assault victims. It had all been technique and form. The content of understanding was something that was harder to teach. Someone who'd possibly been violated might still not get the patience, understanding or the benefit of the doubt that was called for.

A curl of tension went through Cole's gut, and he impatiently ran his hand through his hair as he tried to envision what might have happened to Julie Conway to make her shy away from a man's touch. He was not interested in the details. The point was, someone had forced her into something against her will. Someone had frightened her, possibly even hurt her. Someone had made her a victim.

Whatever had happened, Julie had overcome it for the most part, Cole recognized with some relief. She showed no particular fear of people. And while she had been somewhat evasive with him at first, Cole saw it merely as common-sense caution...not fear. She smiled rather easily, and was easy to tease. Julie might have been made a victim, but she had not remained one.

The other observation Cole had to make was that Julie had not been frightened that he had kissed her, only that it might have gotten out of hand. Cole had been completely taken with her courage and strength, with her straightforward approach to those first painful moments after he'd released her. Julie had shown pride and modesty, and Cole wanted to see that she didn't lose either.

It had all become personal so quickly. It had been one thing to respond intuitively, because he'd immediately recognized the cause of her distress. But it was hard to know if he'd responded because of training, or because she was someone he might care about.

And had he done the right things?

His sudden doubt had led Cole to call a hot-line number at a women's crisis center for guidance. It had never occurred to him to call a precinct, even his own, and talk to any female officer assigned to the sex-crimes unit because his inquiries were not as a cop, but as a man. He didn't want textbook rhetoric. He wanted insight.

Cole had explained briefly what had happened. He didn't try to dress it, analyze it or place any blame. He just wanted to know what he should have done to help Julie. Cole got a deep, rich chuckle from the end of the line.

"Just on the basis of your telling, I'd say it was handled well," the woman from the hot line responded. "I'd say you were pretty alert."

"I'm not looking for Brownie points," Cole said bluntly, "I just want to know if I've made things worse for her."

"Look, sometimes these things are hard to call. You never know what's going to trigger a memory and you certainly had no warning beforehand that there was even anything wrong. Whatever happened probably happened a long time ago. You probably also took her a little by surprise. I don't think it was being kissed that shook her up, but what she thought you might have expected after the kiss. You handled it very well when she gave the signal she wanted to stop."

"But what about her?"

"Well, I'd say she handled it very well by not blaming you for anything or withdrawing. You took her fright seriously and tried to comfort her. And you didn't ask embarrassing questions.

"I think kissing her again might have been a little chancy, but it's sort of like therapy for a person who almost drowned. Getting them back in the water as quickly as possible."

Cole smiled sheepishly to himself. "Actually my motives were probably a little more selfish than that. But I asked first."

"At least you didn't take it for granted."

"Then I haven't been a jerk?" Cole asked wryly.

The woman laughed again. "Look, I'm real impressed that you even bothered to call. Men don't, usually. I think because they take what's happened to their women personally. Just don't make an issue of the past. Don't treat her differently. Your instincts are pretty good. Trust them."

When Cole had gotten off the phone he'd felt not only relieved but hopeful. And he knew a certain level of anxiety that was totally new to him. What if Julie didn't want to see him again? That thought, along with the reaffirmation that he wanted to see her, was enough to give Cole determination. It was different from the resolve to do his job well, or to finish law school. Those were all things he'd committed himself to because that's what his life was all about. This was different because it was more personal and because he sensed that he had a chance to make one part of his life normal.

It was Friday night, and it was now completely dark outside Cole's living-room window. It was the end of a week of unexpected surprises. He had spent much of it thinking of what his life had become and what he still hoped it could be. It had not been unrewarding, but he had come to realize what seemed to be missing. It seemed ironic that he was now most aware of it because of a day spent with a pretty young woman whose presence was quiet and peaceful, and a mysterious, silent little girl whom he could make laugh.

Cole stood thoughtfully in the darkened living room. It created an atmosphere, a screen that allowed him to see Julie in his mind, with her softly combed and braided hair, her gentle smile, the warmth of which generated easily from her and which made him feel so comfortable.

Cole knew he would like the time to really get to know Julie Conway, to gain her trust and regard. He would like time to kiss her again and teach her that it is to be shared...not taken. He wanted time to know what she might feel like if he held her close, not just to comfort her but to love her. And if she let him, he was perfectly willing and able to do just that.

Cole turned from the window, wondering if Julie would like the sunset view. In time he would like to show it to her.

He had all the time in the world.

Chapter Five

The small voices were actually comforting, an added welcome background noise to the usual malaise of Saturday mornings. Now that the children were awake and soon to complain about being hungry, Julie was also glad to have the mechanics of making breakfast for them to keep her occupied. From the refrigerator she removed a plastic container of pancake batter, prepared the night before, and the orange juice. She looked in the meat tray and found a package of bacon.

Every now and then laughter and childish voices flowed from her bedroom. Sometimes the voices raised in excitement or momentary bursts of disagreement and then settled down into a low hum. The children's presence and their antics provided a preferable alternative to being alone and thinking. She was doing quite enough of that in the stillness of the night. And the fact that she wasn't sleeping well had little to do with the space limitations of the love seat in the living room where she was sleeping at night.

It was never far from Julie's thoughts that her life had changed significantly since coming to New York. She had her own home and a job to support herself. She was no longer dependent on anyone for anything. She had a good friend and confidante in Lois, and in that she considered herself lucky. But Julie also believed she was no longer like other women because of what had happened to her. She, therefore, no longer perceived men in the same way as other women. That is, as possible friends, companions, husbands... or lovers.

Since coming to New York Julie had not come even close to meeting a man whom she could see as anything more than as a member of the opposite sex. Not until she met Cole Bennett. Just in the past few days, since knowing him, she'd been feeling a tightening and tension in her stomach and chest that suggested she wasn't indifferent to him. Not that Julie had never known the sensation before, after all she had loved another man once, but it had been so long ago since it had happened to her. And she wasn't really sure she was prepared for the implications of caring.

The response had begun suddenly, when she and the little girl had met Cole at the start of the Thanksgiving Day parade. It had settled inside her like a low bubbling, changing several times during the course of the day and evening. Julie had never felt actually threatened, but the sensation had turned to apprehension when Cole had kissed her—but only because she had not been ready to be treated as a woman that a man was attracted to. Julie had come to believe that somehow that ability had been taken away from her on the eve of her wedding to be replaced by a sort of numbness and desire not to be noticed.

It had not occurred to Julie that she might ever be interested again in a man in any but the most superficial way. But Cole had changed that, too. That's why she couldn't sleep. Her entire being was going through a metamorphosis in which her mind knew that she had been held and kissed by a man again... and her senses were now telling her it had been a pleasant experience. Yet even admitting that made her nervous.

The children's voices again broke into riotous laughter at whatever was entertaining them on TV, and Julie quickly tried to clear her mind of daydreaming, shaking off the lethargy that made her too pensive. She stepped over a toy truck and some wooden blocks in the center of the floor. She busied herself with stacking the many books and puzzles that the children had played with the night before, so that the pine table could be set for breakfast.

''Are you guys getting dressed in there?'' Julie called out absently and received a chorus of ''yes'' that sounded entirely too compliant, making her wonder what the three children were up to. But she didn't have a chance to investigate because a buzzing sound captured her attention.

At first Julie didn't believe the downstairs buzzer had actually been pushed. It never sounded unless she was expecting a delivery or unless Lois was coming with the kids, as she had the night before. And Julie's buzzer was never sounded by mistake. So she waited until it buzzed a second time before approaching the metal box next to her door, pressing the top button and speaking, her voice quizzical.

''Yes? Who is it?''

''Hi. It's Cole Bennett'' came back the now familiar voice.

Again, Julie felt the immediate pulsation of tension in her stomach. All she could think of in that instant as she heard Cole's deep voice was the bewildering episode of their last meeting a few nights ago. At night the memory of both her embarrassing behavior and Cole's tender concern had kept her confused and off balance. And awake.

Julie had assumed that she wouldn't see Cole again because it would be too difficult for both of them to overcome her history, and certainly there was no reason why Cole should want to. Julie had no doubt that he never had to search for willing companionship, and not for a moment was she going to imagine herself one of them, because she couldn't.

She had gotten as far as acknowledging that Cole's kiss had been more than nice. And she could still sometimes evoke the feel of his strong arms about her, creating a sort of haven with her back to his chest, after her panic had subsided. But when the door had closed behind Cole later, Julie had believed that that had been the end of it for both of them.

It was just that with Cole virtually on her doorstep again, Julie found herself filled with surprise, doubt and a flickering of excitement. She had not succeeded in making herself invisible to him.

"Cole..." she repeated blankly. She heard him chuckle.

"Yeah, you remember? Your friendly neighborhood cop. Can I come up?"

Julie came to life. "Oh. Yes..." she answered, pushing the bottom button that would release the lock on the downstairs door. She was trying not to second-guess why he'd returned.

She quickly opened her door, hearing Cole's footsteps on the stairs. Then Julie went back to the kitchen to lower the temperature under a skillet.

"Aunt Julie."

Julie turned her head to find six-year-old Tanya, Lois's daughter. The little girl had most of her clothes on, but no socks, and her long-sleeved knit shirt was inside out. Her dark curly hair, normally parted into two twisted ponytails over each ear was loose and bushy from recent sleep. Right now she was also pouting and her eyes were woeful and pleading.

"What is it, sweetie?" Julie asked, already taking hold of Tanya's sweater and beginning to pull it off. Tanya's head became momentarily lost in the fabric and her little voice was muffled.

"She won't let me hold Annie and Fannie," Tanya whined.

The shirt came off and Julie turned it inside out and pulled it back over Tanya's head. She held it so the little girl could get her arms through the sleeves.

"...and Darren keeps pushing me off the bed."

"There's another doll in the toy basket. And tell Darren he gets no pancakes if he pushes you off the bed again."

Tanya's dark button eyes brightened in her small brown face and she did an about-face heading for Julie's bedroom, calling out in a satisfied voice.

"Darren, Aunt Julie said you better stop..."

Julie returned to the stove to place strips of bacon in the ready skillet, and had no more time to feel awkward and uncertain as Cole came through the door.

Cole could hear the frenzied animated voices and TV music as soon as he entered the apartment. It was coming from Julie's bedroom. There was also the unexpected sound of children's voices, which caused him to raise his brows. To his left from the kitchen was the sizzling crackle and smell of frying bacon. The many sounds were slightly amplified by the fact that the apartment was so small, but Cole nevertheless still experienced an overwhelming sense of cheerful welcoming activity that was so informal and cozy to walk into.

Cole closed the door and glanced at Julie who stood busy at the counter. She gave him only a brief furtive look in return and Cole was astute enough to know he'd caught her off guard, which was exactly what he'd intended. The noise from her room drew his attention and he walked to peek into the door only to find not one but three children piled in the middle of the bed. They were surrounded by a mess of sheets, blankets, pillows and children's clothes. All three were paying rapt attention to the creatures on the TV screen. Cole backed away and turned again to Julie.

Her hair with its blond streaks was combed and braided, as always. She again wore jeans, this time with an oversized white shirt with wide sleeves, that made Julie look very young and lithe. Her feet were bare. There was something about the way she stood, sort of ignoring him but also casual and domestic, that pleased Cole. He had a sudden desire to walk up behind her and slide his arms around her. He was feeling odd and new inside, a sense of intimacy that had less to do with his thoughts about Julie than it did with feeling almost happy just being with her. Cole tried to be dispassionate about it, to remember that Julie so far had not given him any encouragement. But again, that's why he was here. He slowly approached Julie while unzipping his winter parka.

"I didn't realize that children multiplied overnight. Did you sprinkle some magic powder about your room?" he teased. Julie finally turned to face him.

Cole let his eyes roam over her face, again experiencing her calm prettiness, her simple appeal. There was no question that Julie was quite different from what he was used to in a woman, but Cole also realized that his surprise and his reactions to Julie were for exactly the same reasons. Although she seemed unsurprised to see him, Cole could detect the heightened color in Julie's cheeks and the uncertainty in her eyes. Still she met his look in a straightforward manner.

"It doesn't happen quite that way," she responded smoothly. "The other two are my girlfriend Lois's kids. She wanted today free, so I have the children for the weekend."

The cold from outside still clung to Cole, and he seemed so big, to exude so much vitality and energy. His light-colored hair was slightly windblown and he absently used his fingers to comb it into order. Julie found his action so distinctly masculine that she quickly averted her gaze back to the frying pan, suddenly appalled at the image of running her own hands through Cole's hair.

Cole arched a brow. No words of greeting had passed between them but somehow as they stood in silent reappraisal none seemed necessary. They were not strangers anymore. He slipped off his parka and hung it in the closet.

"If you're always baby-sitting, what do you do when you need a day off?" he asked. When he turned around from the closet he found Julie waiting to hand him plates and glasses for the children's breakfast. Cole took the items and went to the pine table to lay them out.

She chuckled quietly to herself, carefully draining the strips of bacon on sheets of paper towels. "What would I do with a day off?"

Again Julie was quickly absorbing him into her home. She didn't make an issue of his being there, and she also didn't make him feel that it mattered. Cole knew it wasn't indifference. Julie was treating his presence almost as a matter of course, and he liked that. He came back to the counter and stood smiling down at her. Cole's eyes were assessing and serious.

"Spend it with me."

It was not a question. But Julie got the feeling it *was* a very clear invitation. She took her time pouring the bacon fat from the skillet, letting the surprise of his comment sink into her mind and her heart. To cover her confusion she suddenly passed him a handful of paper napkins and the container of orange juice. When she looked into Cole's face it was with equal assessment.

"I was going to ask why you were here," Julie voiced quietly.

Cole suddenly had an understanding of her doubt, but nevertheless still felt it was best not to have given Julie warning of his arrival. He let his gaze hold her own, hoping that she would see what he couldn't and wouldn't put into words. That the past, hers or his, need not stand between them.

"I'm not working, I didn't have school, and you're not on the way home or to anywhere else for that matter. I should probably be studying for an upcoming test, but I'm here because I wanted to see you."

Julie blushed and lowered her gaze from the honesty in Cole's blue eyes. She was equally affected by the hoarse sincerity in his voice.

"If... if you'd brought your books I could have helped you study," Julie offered foolishly.

Cole leaned toward her. "That's not what I had in mind, either," he said quietly.

Julie gestured behind her. "As you can see I've got company."

Cole shrugged. "I assumed Mickey would be here. The other two are a surprise, but that's okay. I'll even out the odds. They look like they're going to be a handful. That is, if you want me to stay," Cole prompted, watching her reaction.

It came to Julie then that she wanted him to stay. She couldn't say so, of course, because it would be like a confession. Julie also realized that Cole's presence was not just a friendly little visit. It was the fragile start of a man-woman thing. She had been very careful in the relationships she'd formed over the past several years, surrounding herself with people she felt safe with. By Julie's own choice it had precluded any intimacy. For a long time she had felt raw, sensitive to too much closeness, and hurt and angry that she couldn't allow closeness. She was sure that Cole had guessed that part of her past which now made it difficult for her to consider a relationship. But even Julie now knew it no longer seemed impossible.

As Cole said, she merely needed time and patience. He seemed himself set on changing the boundaries and her rules. But it was still going to be her choice, and Julie knew from the probing intensity in Cole's eyes to the tensing of his jaw muscles that the challenge had been gently issued.

Still she was glad the children were present, and her reply to Cole was cautious and indirect.

"I can promise you it's going to be a noisy, hectic and exhausting day," Julie said with a slow smile.

Cole raised his brows and grinned at her assumption that a day with three children and herself would wear him out. Given the crazy unpredictability of his own days and nights, he thought it best not to enlighten her.

"I think I can handle it," Cole responded with a straight face.

"Aunt Julie," came a thin, small voice.

Cole and Julie turned their heads to see Tanya standing shyly next to them. She held her sneakers, a comb and some colorful plastic hair barrettes. Tanya stared at Cole openly, and moved to lean against Julie in much the same way that Mickey had the first time Cole had seen her. Then the little girl absently put an end of the comb into her mouth to run the prongs against her teeth, creating a clicking sound.

"Who's that?" Tanya finally said, pointing the comb at Cole. At her question, Darren and Mickey also came into the kitchen to see what was going on.

Darren, peering through glasses that rested on the end of his round nose, frowned at Cole.

"Who are you?" he also asked boldly.

"Don't be rude," Julie admonished, taking the comb and barrettes from Tanya and deftly combing and containing the little girl's hair into its customary ponytails. "Say good morning first."

"Good morning," piped up Tanya and Darren obediently.

"But who is he?" Darren persisted.

Cole merely grinned in enjoyment as the two youngsters aligned themselves with Julie and she put her hands on each of their shoulders. She was totally at ease now, and unconscious of herself, exuding a great deal of natural care and affection.

"I want you to meet Cole Bennett," Julie said, looking at Cole.

"Cole!" the two kids repeated, scrinching up their faces as if the name was strange and foreign.

"Yes, Cole," Cole spoke up. "As in Ole King Cole. As in Natalie Cole."

Tanya giggled, shaking her head and causing the two ponytails over her ears to whip back and forth. "No you're not. Natalie Cole is a singer."

"You're right," Cole agreed. "I can't sing."

"He's a cop," Darren observed in a clear, sure voice.

Cole and Julie exchanged surprised glances.

"How do you know?" Tanya asked her brother.

Darren pointed at Cole. "'Cause he's got a gun."

Again Cole and Julie exchanged glances, and while Julie's eyes held no censoring, Cole's was nonetheless apologetic.

Tanya took Julie's hand and gently tugged, looking up at her with troubled eyes. "Aunt Julie, did you do something wrong? Are you going to jail?"

There was so much fright and real concern that Julie quickly hugged the little girl. "No, no sweetie." She looked at Cole, almost for guidance but also with an acceptance in her warm smile to put the children at ease. "Mr. Bennett...Cole, is a friend of mine. He...came by for a visit. And maybe he'll spend the day with us," Julie said haltingly, still with some uncertainty as to what her relationship to Cole really was.

Darren came forward to tilt his head up as he questioned Cole. "Do you have a police car outside?"

"I'm afraid not. Just my own."

"Oh…" Darren murmured, disappointed. Then his eyes brightened behind the glasses. "Can I see your gun?"

"Me, too," Tanya said, skipping closer.

Cole did not look at Julie and he made no attempt to hide the gun from the inquisitive children. But he wanted to be careful how he dealt with their curiosity, which was understandable.

"I'm going to give it to Julie to put away. You'll see it once, but I can't let you touch it. It's not a toy. Understood?" Cole said in a firm voice, but one which also was very smooth and quiet. The children slowly bobbed their heads up and down.

Julie quickly turned to get the blue-and-white bowl from the overhead cabinet, as Cole slowly and carefully took the gun from his waistband. He held it flat across the open palm of his large hand and just close enough for the children to get a good look at it.

Tanya was decidedly unimpressed and quickly lost interest. Mickey never bothered to come forward to look. Only Darren leaned closer.

"That's not real," he challenged with little-boy skepticism.

"I'm afraid it is," Cole said, placing the weapon in the bowl that Julie then put away.

Cole looked down to find the third member of the trio silently standing next to him, waiting to gain his attention. "Hello, Mickey," he said, reaching to pat her cheek.

"Mickey!" came back the identical chorus from Tanya and Darren again.

"Her name isn't Mickey," Darren said, as if anyone should know that.

Again Cole was caught by surprise. "Oh?" He glanced quickly at Julie, only to find her standing just as confused and curious as he was.

"Her name is Domy," Tanya said, pointing to the other little girl who remained silent.

"What do you mean?" Julie asked in a thin voice, frowning at Tanya.

"Her name is Domy," Darren nodded in a confirmation, but it was clear from the blank expression on Cole and Julie's face that that made no sense.

"She's not a dummy, and it's not very nice to say so, Darren. I'm surprised at you," Julie said sternly.

Darren only looked exasperated and rolled his eyes. "Not *dummy. Domy. Do-my!*" he said louder, as though that would help the adults understand. But they didn't.

Tanya began to laugh and even the other little girl giggled.

Cole looked down at Mickey for a long considering moment, and then to Julie who now seemed not only confused but uncomfortable. Cole turned his attention back to Darren.

"I suppose she told you that?"

"She did," Darren replied, shrugging his shoulders.

Cole wasn't sure what to make of this new development, and apparently neither did Julie.

"Does she talk to you?" Cole asked the little boy now.

Already he was getting bored with the topic, having already explained. "No," Darren said, turning to stand in Julie's bedroom to watch what was happening on the TV. "She won't say anything."

"But she told you her name," Cole tried to clarify.

"Umm-hmm," Darren answered, distracted.

"It's a stupid name. I like Mickey better," Tanya said, trying to take the Annie-Fannie doll from the silent little girl's hands. Before a tug of war could take place Julie quickly intervened, taking Tanya by the shoulders and turning her around.

"Tanya, put your shoes on. Darren, turn off the set and come put the truck and wooden blocks away."

Darren sighed, looking aggrieved. "But Aunt Julie, Tanya used the blocks."

"I did not!" defended Tanya from the floor, where she sat pulling on her sneakers.

"Never mind. I'll help," Cole said easily to Darren, squatting down to pick up the blocks.

Darren came to watch Cole with renewed interest. Together they got the toys stored in the basket, and Cole even talked Darren into helping him fold away the linens Julie used at night when she slept on the love seat.

Julie had gone back to making the pancakes, still trying to figure out what Tanya and Darren were trying to say about their silent companion. Had she, indeed, tried to tell the children something? The possibility made Julie a bit uneasy, because the little girl had still not said anything to her. For the first time she was beginning to feel foolish and ill-advised for not having told Cole everything she knew and didn't know about the child. But perhaps it wouldn't matter. Surely on Monday someone would come back for her.

Julie looked over her shoulder to see that everyone was doing something. Even Mickey was down on her hands and knees pulling a forgotten book from under the coffee table, following the example of the other two children putting away their playthings. Julie smiled rather complacently at the hum of activity in the apartment. She also had another wistful thought, although she didn't immediately attach any significance to it, that Cole *would* make an ideal husband. Of course, the very word husband evoked other thoughts for Julie, as well, but not with the same pain or confusion that she used to have.

Darren carelessly tossed a toy into the basket and then sat back on his heels. He used a finger to push his glasses back up his short nose, and thoughtfully regarded the tall man sitting on the floor next to him.

"Are you Aunt Julie's boyfriend?" Darren asked bluntly.

Cole raised his brows, but kept his expression otherwise bland as he continued to dump things into the toy basket. "It depends."

The little boy frowned earnestly at him. "It depends on what?"

"Whether or not you like the idea," Cole improvised, but seeing a serious regard fill the boy's eyes.

Darren thought deeply for a moment. He shrugged, the task of deciding the fate of adults way beyond him. "I guess it's okay. Aunt Julie never had a boyfriend before."

Cole beamed at the youngster's guilelessness. "Well then, the answer is, I'm working on it."

Darren's confusion grew. "What does that mean, 'you're working on it'?"

Cole grinned at the boy. "It means I'm waiting to see if your Aunt Julie likes the idea of me being her boyfriend."

"Okay, breakfast is ready," Julie called out and there was an instant noisy stampede to the table.

Cole had set the table so that each of the children had a side, and he and Julie shared the fourth side. Julie didn't particularly notice until she was seated, after having poured coffee for herself and Cole. Then she noticed that there was no avoiding physical contact. Their thighs touched under the table. Their shoulders sometimes bumped and rubbed together. It was not uncomfortable but, again, Cole's physical nearness continued to reinforce his masculinity and size in Julie's mind. Yet she was beginning to enjoy having him near. It felt normal and easy. It felt . . . seductive.

Cole had decided that the best way not to frighten or upset Julie was to get her used to him in small stages. Harmless moments of contact, such as the way they now sat, innocent touches and long glances that said very clearly his

interest lay in her. It was already evident that Julie wasn't
afraid of him, just uncertain and very careful. And it probably had less to do with the person she was than the *woman*
she was. It was up to Cole to show her that someone could
want her for all the romantic, even sexual reasons.

Breakfast was a sort of family affair. It had all the drama
and exchange and complaints and fussing and laughter of a
family. At least the kind of family that Cole had always
imagined. He was amused by Darren's proprietary attitude
toward Julie. Not that Darren didn't like him. It seemed that
the young boy just wanted to establish that he knew Julie
first. Cole was equally charmed by the gregarious Tanya,
who talked constantly and had wonderfully funny obser-
vations to make and questions to ask. Such as wanting to
know if Cole was going to stay over, too, for the weekend.

Cole glanced at Julie to find out her reaction. She was
embarrassed and nonplussed.

"Tanya, that's not a question to ask..."

Cole shook his head at the inquisitive little girl. "Not this
time," he replied.

"You can sleep in the living room like Aunt Julie does
when Darren and me come, 'cause her bed is too small,"
Tanya suggested sagely.

"I'm glad you warned me," Cole said with a straight face,
but his eyes twinkled wickedly as he caught Julie's helpless
expression.

Mickey remained silent as usual, ever watchful, however,
of what was going on around her. Curious, but not totally
involved. Cole thought again about the conversation with
the two other children, who seemed to be insisting that
Mickey was not the child's name. It was not the right moment to pursue the subject again, but they had stirred Cole's
curiosity, too. He tried to remember what Julie had told him
about the little girl, or about baby-sitting with her. Where

was the child's mother? How long would Mickey be staying with Julie?

Cole looked thoughtfully at Mickey, with her beautiful dark eyes and her quiet, ladylike gestures and movements. And he thought about seeing her for the first time with Julie...at the station house before Thanksgiving. What was the connection, Cole wondered, as he accepted another pancake from Julie.

Cole once again found himself with cleanup duty while Julie got the bedroom to rights, the children's teeth brushed and hands washed. All the while Cole zeroed in on her voice, at once gentle and caring but firm. It provided him with a view not only of Julie but of how other people with normal lives lived. It was one of the reasons he'd wanted to come back. For the warm coziness, a phenomenon he had no real experience with. And there was the other reason, the more subtle and private changes that develop between a man and a woman. A relationship which Cole would now readily admit he'd not come close to having since Sharon Marie.

The children were playing a game of tag around Julie's coffee table, and Cole turned from drying his hands at the sink to see impending disaster in their energy level. He raised a brow at Julie. "Now what?"

"I don't know. I honestly hadn't given it much thought," Julie said with a frown.

"Why don't we walk them up to the Museum of Natural History for a while. Afterward we'll walk through Central Park. Maybe later we'll have McDonald's for dinner."

Julie smiled. "They'll be totally worn out by this evening."

Cole arched a brow. "That's the idea," he said in a stage whisper, causing Julie to suddenly laugh.

When they were all set to leave, Cole waited until the three children had filed out of the apartment into the hallway before taking his gun from the cabinet. He could tell from Julie's expression that she would have liked him to leave it behind, but Cole merely shook his head.

"I have to, Julie."

She nodded quickly in understanding.

It was cold on the walk uptown to the American Museum of Natural History, but it was very sunny again, and the children didn't seem to mind. At the start Tanya had hold of Julie's hand. Cole was not only surprised but he also experienced an odd sense of gentleness and protectiveness when he felt Mickey put her very small hand into his. It reminded him of holding her Thanksgiving night when she awoke in tears, when he had her trust so quickly and so easily.

Cole looked at Julie to find her watching him with a glowing smile. After a while the three children regrouped and walked together a few feet ahead of the adults. Cole glanced at Julie once again, enjoying the cheerful picture she made in her soft gray beret of angora wool.

"Tell me about your friend Lois. How did you get to be Aunt Julie to Tanya and Darren?"

"I don't know. It just happened. They've always called me that," Julie responded, her voice reflecting a certain pride and a great deal of affection. She watched as the two black children stopped as instructed at the corner, with Mickey, waiting for her and Cole to accompany them across the street.

"But you like being an aunt to them," Cole observed.

Julie nodded. "I've known Lois since before we both started working for Helping Hands."

"How long is that?" Cole asked conversationally.

"Oh . . . maybe seven years ago. Lois's husband had been killed in an accident on his job. She had Darren who was still an infant, and Tanya was on the way . . ." Julie stopped suddenly, realizing that Cole was slowly and effortlessly coaxing information from her. She stopped talking.

They reached the children at the corner and Julie used the moment to change the subject. "All right. Everybody hold hands," she instructed, reaching for Mickey's hand. But then she felt her other hand being grasped and realized it was Cole. When they crossed the street to the other side the children again started off on their own, but Cole continued to hold Julie's hand. For a moment she thought of pulling free, but she didn't. Her hand felt small, secure and warm being held by him.

Cole then transferred their clasped hands to his jacket pocket, big enough to accommodate both. Julie smiled to herself. It felt good. And with that came also a sense of harmony, compatibility.

"How did you meet?" Cole suddenly asked. He felt a fluttering in her hand because of the question. He could feel the hesitation in her long silence.

Julie thought about it, and knew she could give Cole no simple answer. She could not say how she'd met Lois without telling the why. The less said about that, the better.

"I...I had a new job, but no place to live. Lois had a large apartment, but with her husband gone she had no way to pay the rent. She also had two kids to care for. We helped each other out. I started working at the center first and later on she was hired, too."

Cole was silent for a moment. He had a feeling that while Julie had not lied, she certainly hadn't said everything.

"Then you were pretty lucky to have found each other."

Julie didn't respond. She would not have used the term luck herself, given the losses both she and Lois had endured. And even the exact time of their first meeting had been a trauma. Julie had been at a simple restaurant having a meal one evening, when she'd felt incredible pain grabbing at her. She'd passed right out from the sheer intensity. It had been awful waking up in a public hospital ward to find herself almost destitute. Lois had been in the bed next to her. She had just given birth to her baby. Julie had just lost one....

Cole made no further attempts to ask personal questions. Already he could sense Julie slipping away from him. He didn't want to lose what they'd established between them so far, as tentative as it was.

The museum was crowded and busy on the Saturday after Thanksgiving and there were children everywhere. Tanya and Darren took the noise and surroundings in stride, but Mickey, as she had at the parade, seemed only bewildered by the activity. Again, she was not inclined to explore, but stayed close to Julie and Cole. Again, in the crowd, Julie began to feel uncomfortably warm. Cole, now fully conscious of all the quick changes in her, saw her breathing change, saw the too-bright glow in her eyes and watched them dilate. He quickly took her hand. Julie looked askance at him even as her fingers closed around his.

"I don't want you to get lost from me" was all he said. But it helped to divert Julie's attention.

When the children began to lose interest with the many exhibits, they went in search of the holiday tree that stretched nearly to the ceiling of a mammoth hall. It was decorated entirely with origami animals made from colorful foil paper. Cole spotted a table in a corner where the children could actually be shown how to fold birds and dinosaurs and fish. Julie managed a simple star, but Cole tried the more complex monkey. His results sent Julie and the children into delighted laughter because it looked nothing like a monkey.

Outside once again Julie found herself the custodian of the origami efforts while the kids ate oversize pretzels purchased for them by Cole from a street vendor. They crossed the street from the museum and released the three energetic kids into the open spaces of Central Park. Julie and Cole followed slowly behind them as the youngsters invented games and ran over rocks and dashed behind trees and rolled on the hard, cold ground of dry grass. Julie hugged herself as she watched them play. She looked at Cole with a warm glow.

"Thank you, Cole. They seem to be having a great time."

Cole grinned at her and pursed his mouth. "What about you?" he asked.

"I...I'm having a lovely time, too," she admitted softly.

Cole stepped close to her, to look down into her upturned face. Her nose was getting red. "Nice enough to do it again?"

Julie drew in her bottom lip between her teeth for a second. She nodded. "Yes."

Cole's gaze roamed over her face. "Just the two us?" he questioned further.

Julie smiled. "Yes..."

"After my exam. We'll celebrate," he said easily, and let it go at that. But Cole felt a sudden elation and hope. Julie was still watching him.

"What will you do with your degree?" she asked. "Go into private practice?"

Cole was shaking his head. "I don't think so. I'll probably counsel in the department. Maybe in a few years I'll switch to another agency." Cole lifted a brow as he watched Julie's smile broaden. "What's so funny?"

"Not funny," she corrected, watching the sunlight make his hair look a lot blonder than it actually was. "I was just thinking you're not going to be like other lawyers."

"Why?" he asked, truly curious.

Julie blushed, and looked away for a brief moment. "Because...you seem too nice, too patient."

"Wrong," Cole corrected in a firm but quiet voice. His eyes were suddenly intense. "But thank you, anyway..."

His comment only made Julie curious, and her smile wavered. She glanced at the children. "I don't understand how come they're not cold."

"Children don't get cold," Cole said wryly. "They don't know that they feel any different than when they're *not* cold." He grinned at Julie. "Don't you remember when you were a kid you'd stay out in the snow no matter how cold it got, and then come home soaking wet with your nose running? But you'd still want to go out again."

Julie looked blank. She shook her head. "No."

"No? Where are you from?" he asked lightly.

"Southern California," Julie responded readily. And then she froze. She'd never admitted that to anyone except Lois.

"Well, that explains it. You had to worry about sunburn, not frostbite," Cole teased, but he could see the somewhat stunned expression on Julie's face. "How could you leave sunny California for the wilds of New York?" he now asked with purpose, although he tried to keep his tone light.

When Julie looked at him her eyes seemed vacant. Cold. It was clear to Cole that somehow Southern California was tied to her other secret and to her past.

"It was easy . . ." Julie said tonelessly, her face suddenly pale. She shivered, turning up the collar on her sport jacket.

"I've never been to California," Cole admitted, casually moving closer to her as he detected the tightening around her mouth. *Don't give in to it,* Cole urged her mentally. *Let it go . . .* Cole reached out and took hold of Julie's arm. "Come here."

He pulled her slowly around until her back was to him. The movement brought Julie out of her deep reflection and she frowned.

"What are you doing?"

"The kids are good for another hour or so. We can't start getting cold before they do."

Cole stood with his legs braced slightly apart. Putting his arm around Julie he pulled her so that she leaned against his chest.

The bulkiness of his coat made Cole seem bigger, wider, sturdier. Yet Julie still felt a bit self-conscious. She stood awkwardly against him, afraid of letting herself relax, not even admitting that already she was beginning to feel warmer. Not even acknowledging that with him she felt safe, because he was still a man and he might still expect something from her she couldn't give.

But Julie also remembered the last time he held her like this. The surprise of it and the unexpected delight that quickly melted her resistance.

"Relax…" Cole whispered softly, his hands making slow stroking motions on her arms. He bent his head slightly and Julie felt his breath at her temple. She let out a long sigh and her spine flexed and the weight of her body settled completely against Cole. "That's it," he encouraged in a caressing tone. "Are you warmer now?"

Julie nodded, briefly closing her eyes. "You're … like a furnace."

Cole chuckled richly. "At least I'm good for something."

They were both silent for a moment, Julie getting used to Cole once again holding and touching her with such ease and her not minding. As a matter of fact, it occurred to Julie that while her panic on Thanksgiving had been swift and overwhelming, once it was over, it was over and done. It was with that realization that she felt suddenly light inside. Not exactly carefree, but closer to it than she'd been in a long time.

Off in the distance the children romped, truly mindless of the temperature. It was a beautiful day. A wonderful time. And Julie realized it had been so long since she'd stepped out of herself and her history enough to enjoy feeling like a woman. She was beginning to feel that feminine softness that responded to a man, which allowed her to rely on and trust his strength. It was a sensation she was not only recognizing but was in fact experiencing in part because of Cole Bennett.

Cole settled his arms more comfortably around Julie. His chest took her weight easily and he had a very satisfying sense of protecting her. She felt not only good against him, but right. With some surprise Cole knew this was the first time he'd known simple contentment and pleasure in a woman's company that had not started out in sex. With Julie, it seemed infinitely more important that he not treat her casually or as a passing fancy. And in truth, since Thanksgiving night when he'd first held her and suspected that she had suffered a lot of pain, he had not thought to.

Cole bent his head. The fuzzy wool of her knit hat tickled his chin and nose. There was a sweet, subtle fragrance, through the wool, of her hair... of her. For a moment Cole had a vision of himself lying against her, his head on her breasts, enveloped by Julie's gentle giving and her warmth. He felt a stirring in his body at his own fantasy, and it took him completely by surprise. He shifted his legs back slightly so that Julie couldn't detect the change, and he sighed deeply for control.

Over the top of her head Cole could see and hear the children. He had another fantasy. What if they were his. What if when he went home at night there was someone there and the house was bright with lights and activity and he no longer had to listen to silence. What if there was always someone to hold just like this. Just like Julie.

Tanya suddenly tripped and fell and lay for a stunned second before starting to whine and whimper. Julie at once moved to go to her, but Cole's arms held her in place.

"She's all right," he whispered, watching the child pull herself up on her knees and examine her bare hands for scrapes or cuts. Discovering that she was really okay, Tanya got up and continued her play with the other two children. Julie relaxed again. "You love children, don't you?" Cole observed.

Julie smiled slightly. "Am I so obvious? Perhaps I get too involved."

Cole grew pensive for a moment, thinking about his own barren childhood, the parental input that he missed out on because of a father who didn't care and a mother who couldn't.

"I don't see how it's possible to love children too much," he replied.

"When they're not yours, I suppose it is."

"Well then, there's only one answer to that." Cole released her and turned her to face him. In the bright sunlight and cold, her cheeks had color and her eyes were almost a taupe gray.

"Give up being a surrogate aunt to other people's children," Julie supplied flippantly.

Cole smiled at her wistful tone of voice. Her brows lifted to give her a defenseless, hopeful look. Cole brushed a lock of hair from her forehead. "Wrong again," he said, and felt a sudden emotional and physical tension in himself as he said it. "You just need to have children of your own."

Julie blinked at him. All of the softness slowly went out of her face. It was replaced by a look of sadness. She glanced toward the children for a long time and then back to Cole. "You seem to be very good with kids yourself. Why don't you have any?"

Cole pushed his hands into his jacket pockets and shrugged. "It just didn't work out that way for me."

Julie's smile was almost grim. "Exactly," she said softly.

Cole frowned. "Then I'll give you the advice you gave me when I told you about Sharon Marie. It's not too late."

Julie looked as though she wanted to believe him, but then she closed her eyes and abruptly turned away. Cole put his hand on her shoulder and squeezed gently.

"I'm sorry. I didn't mean to sound thoughtless. I just meant that we can't do very much about the past, Julie. It's already been lived. It's dead and buried. It's already taught us whatever lessons were intended. Now comes round two."

She shook her head. "I don't understand."

Cole thought carefully for a moment. "We all get a second chance. I'm saying there's still time to have a dream or two come true. Think of all the women who come through your center looking for second chances. Isn't that what you give them? Hope and a second chance? How about one for yourself. You don't have to ask, Julie... you just do it."

Julie looked over her shoulder into Cole's serious countenance. "What about you?"

"Me?" Cole let his eyes roam over her face, and he who had been witness to more horror and sadness than he cared to remember, who went home alone at night because he'd come to believe that's how the cards were dealt, began to believe his own words. "I've had two chances," Cole said in sudden revelation. "Number one, I didn't die when I was shot as a rookie. And two... I met you."

Julie slowly began to blush with uncertainty. Cole stepped closer and took hold of her arms to slowly pull her closer.

"I'm glad you left California, because it's true what they say about West Coast women."

"Cole, I...I can't give you what you want from me. You know that..." she whispered, her voice shaky.

It made Cole's heart constrict and turn over at her attempt to deny that she held any attraction for him at all or that she wasn't capable of a deeper relationship. "I think I'm getting exactly what I want from you, Julie. So far I have no complaints."

They looked into each other's face at the instant recognition and discovery. Cole began to bend toward her, yet stopped with his firm mouth a fraction of an inch from her own. His blue eyes looked deeply into Julie's as his lips brushed erotically over her mouth, feeling its gentle pucker.

"You just let me know if you have any trouble breathing," Cole instructed hoarsely.

Julie nodded absently, completely mesmerized by the movement of his lips, the growling, seductive sound of his voice. And then Cole kissed her again.

While his mouth was every bit as gentle as he'd been the first time they'd kissed, there was more of a display of male mastery and expertise that held Julie fascinated. She could feel the slow movements of his mouth on hers, the pressure that manipulated the softness of her lips and stroked to send a spiraling warmth throughout her. It reached to the ends of her nerves and loosened her resolve.

Cole's large hand reached to Julie's face to cup around her jaw with his callused thumb under her chin, his fingers touching her cheek. He held Julie only by the positioning of his hand and her own fascination at his intent. The moment his mouth opened over her own, Julie could feel her will stiffen protectively, and then it burst abruptly like a bubble into air. She no longer felt cold. She felt his tongue, abrasive and warm and decisive as it explored and danced around hers.

Julie's hands came up to brace on Cole's chest, but not to push him away. It was to balance herself, to hold on to something firm, as Cole's provocative possession kindled a pleasant wave of desire. It felt strange to have her body respond to the gently rising heat caused by his kiss alone.

While Cole was still alert to her every reaction, he was finding it very stimulating to slowly build up his desire for her. There was an enormous sense of slow seduction, heady and ephemeral, which was emotionally as well as physically impressive. But it was the physical that he held in check while he tried to connect to Julie beyond any thought of sexual satisfaction. It came to Cole that he wanted Julie to *want* him, to need him . . . to trust him.

His tongue stroked and rubbed for a tantalizingly long moment before he ended their kiss and their warm breaths vaporized into the cold winter air around them. They opened their eyes to stare at one another. It was clear that the kiss had not been merely a kiss. It was like a key that had opened up and exposed a glimpse of the need in both of them.

Cole's hand still cupped her face, and his thumb now brushed curiously over the moist surface of Julie's bottom lip. She let out a deep sigh, releasing her breath. Cole's arms pulled her a little closer and Julie watched the wisdom and caring that made his eyes now so intense and dark. His fingers tilted her head up a little farther toward his own.

"Did I scare you?" he asked, his voice gravelly and low.

"Only a little," she confessed.

Cole grinned at her. The laugh lines around his eyes deepened and fanned out attractively. He kissed her nose. "Good girl . . ."

He would have kissed her again, except for the giggles and amused sounds from the children.

"Ohh. You kissed Aunt Julie." Tanya pointed at Cole, not so much shocked as finding it funny.

Cole only grinned at them, not making any attempt to pretend he and Julie were doing anything else. He felt Julie wanting to pull away, but Cole discouraged that easily by putting both arms around her and stroking her back.

Mickey only smiled shyly and silently, twisting back and forth as she held the doll. Darren's look was clear to interpret. It held both embarrassment and childish disgust.

"Ugh. How could you kiss him?" he asked Julie.

Cole and Julie exchanged glances, although Julie's was more concerned than Cole's. Cole looked at Darren. "Grown-ups kiss each other when they really like each other."

Darren frowned, pushing up his glasses on his nose. "You mean, like boyfriend and girlfriend?"

Cole winked at Julie. "That's right. Like boyfriend and girlfriend."

Darren grimaced. "I'm never going to do that."

Cole laughed gently, looking at Julie. "I'd like to be around when you change your mind," he said.

Chapter Six

Cole swept his hand through his hair and leaned back in his spring-action chair until the coils squeaked. He looked at his watch. Almost lunchtime.

He also looked at the text on his desk and shook his head in disgust. The exam was going to be a nightmare, and he couldn't seem to concentrate on the material that was going to be covered.

He had a meeting in half an hour to plan a stakeout to apprehend one Rodrigo Santiago, a nineteen-year-old suspect in a murder case. He had to get to court sometime this afternoon on the indictments in another case. He hadn't slept all that well last night...worse than usual. Worse than the heavy restlessness of being alone night after night, which he'd more or less gotten used to in his life. Worse because he'd been thinking intensely about Julie Conway.

He'd spent the night wishing her in bed with him.

Cole's body had responded via his fantasies and stayed painfully hard and unfulfilled the whole night because his brain had taken an unexpected erotic turn. He didn't fully understand why it was suddenly happening. He'd been prepared to wait until Julie was ready for more than friendship, and he was reasonably confident that more would happen.

Cole scrubbed the palms of his hands over his face, hoping to shake himself into alertness. Right now, more than anything, he was missing the sleep he hadn't gotten the night before.

"Four days off and you look like hell. Don't tell me you partied all weekend," Ben boomed from Cole's open doorway and followed it by a deep amused chuckle.

Cole opened his eyes to find a full cup of hot black coffee set in front of him. He swept the textbooks aside. Nodding briefly at Ben in appreciation for the needed caffeine, Cole took a deep gulp.

"Not hardly," Cole finally answered.

"You didn't have to spend it alone, either. Mama was prepared for hungry folks. Leftovers again tonight. Umph!" Ben moaned with a shudder.

Cole sipped at the coffee and thought for a moment. He hadn't exactly spent the weekend alone. "I was invited to dinner at the last moment and went."

Ben sat on the edge of the desk facing Cole. "Really? Anybody I know?"

"Almost," Cole said with a sly grin.

Ben raised his brows. "Excuse me?"

"A pretty lady with dark honey hair and very warm gray eyes..."

"The last pretty woman you've mentioned in a month was the mystery lady of last week."

Cole merely smiled.

"You're kidding. Her?"

"I'm a better detective than you gave me credit for."

"No. Just a fast worker." Ben chuckled again. "So what happened?"

Cole shrugged, remembering the close, cautious look on Julie Conway's face when he'd first met her, as compared to the warmth that radiated from her Saturday. The transformation had been gratifying. And promising.

"I met her, escorted her home, went to a parade with her..."

"Parade?" Ben sounded astonished.

"... had a great dinner and saw her again over the weekend."

"I take back all disparaging remarks I made about you. Is she a hot ticket?" Ben intimated slyly.

Cole winced. He shook his head. "I told you. She's not that kind of woman."

"Then you must be getting old. Or she's something really special. Tell me about her, anyway," Ben said, getting more comfortable on the edge of the desk, carelessly mutilating papers and files under his hip.

"I've only gotten a fraction of her life story," Cole said quietly, "and we haven't had a real date yet. She's been baby-sitting someone's kid, so there's been a third party."

"But the bottom line is, you like her. At least, I think that's what I'm hearing."

Cole nodded over the rim of the coffee cup. "I like her."

Ben sighed and got up. "A good woman is hard to find. She got a friend?" he asked jokingly.

"Are you looking for companionship or a hot ticket?" Cole asked with a silent chuckle.

"Yes!" Ben nodded emphatically, causing Cole to laugh.

"As a matter of fact she does have a friend."

Ben shook his head and smoothed his thick mustache thoughtfully. "Now understand me, Cole, I have nothing against blondes..."

"To be honest I haven't met her yet, but judging from her two kids, whom I did meet, I can guarantee she doesn't have blond hair."

"Kids?" Ben repeated blankly.

Cole gave him a lopsided grin, recalling the energetic and friendly youngsters. "You have something against kids?"

Ben grimaced. "I don't know. Tell me more about their mother."

Cole drained his coffee cup. "Her name is Lois. Judging by the kids I'd say she was attractive and probably a cross between Patti LaBelle and Gladys Knight."

"Umm," Ben uttered in interest. "How come you met the kids through your honey-haired lady?"

"Her name is Julie Conway, and she's sort of an aunt to the kids." At Ben's perplexed expression, Cole closed his eyes briefly and shook his head. "Don't ask. It's a long story and I don't know it all. But Lois is a widow."

"Ahh. The plot thickens."

"No it doesn't," Cole countered. "Like I said, I haven't met the lady. And who said she'd want to have anything to do with you, anyway?"

Ben laughed and stood up. "You're right. Well, keep me posted. Want to have lunch?"

"He does, but he can't..." came another male voice through the door. Both Ben and Cole turned their heads as Officer Danny Noonan came in and handed Cole a sheaf of wrinkled yellow, pink and white pages. "It's all there. In triplicate."

Ben shook his head and moved toward the door. "I'm so glad I didn't want to be a detective..." He waved briefly and left the office.

Danny crossed his short, thick arms over his barrel chest and stroked his ginger-colored beard. "All we gotta do is organize it and get the team together. I got search warrants and court orders."

Cole looked blankly at the papers for a moment, feeling almost lethargic. There was obviously not going to be any time to go back to his contemplation of Julie. No time to play out a variety of scenarios that, as of late, he found his mind fertilely manufacturing.

He sat back in the chair again and again the springs groaned. "Then let's do it," Cole said flatly.

COLE TESTED THE PORTABLE walkie-talkie, lowered the volume when he got back static and some breakup and put it on the table where other equipment was spread out. Next he checked his gun to make sure it was fully loaded. He put it in his waistband, under his left arm and put a clip with extra bullets in his pocket.

The other men in the room were telling morbid jokes, using crude language as they also geared up. Tough talk to keep them focused.

They all looked like hoodlums with their unkempt attire for undercover work and their scruffy looks. Except for Cole who was dressed in neat slacks, a crisp white shirt and another crazy tie. Over that he had the same navy blue breaker as some of the other men, with NYPD in iridescent white on the back.

The half dozen or so men were in the ready room at the precinct preparing to go and hopefully apprehend a suspect in the homicide case Cole had been investigating before Thanksgiving. The suspect, a young male of about nineteen, had been spotted over the weekend in the vicinity of the crime. He was known in the neighborhood, and with a certain cockiness had hung around, coming back to show he wasn't concerned about being caught.

Cole knew, as did his men, that there was also the real possibility the kid would try to manipulate them into an immediate action if they tried to arrest him, that would bring him down. He'd never see the inside of a jail cell. It had happened before.

The suspect, it was also known, was a good friend of the victim. In his investigation Cole had come to theorize that the friend was now dead because a pretty, flirtatious young girl, known to both of them, had come between the friends, playing one off against the other.

It wasn't a new story. It was so standard that the police, who were the ones called in after the harm was done, had long ago given up hope that people ever learned by example. They dealt constantly with men and women who let their emotions and pride rule their lives, often leading them to hurt other people.

The men around Cole laughed raucously, and he recognized the male bantering for what it was. A way to deal with the unspoken level of fear. Things sometimes went wrong, but the idea was to bring everyone back in one piece. The presence of guns made things more edgy. No one wanted to have to use them, but sometimes you had to. That's what they were preparing for as bulletproof vests went on and a strategy was planned for where each man would be.

Cole would go in with the rest of the men to take the suspect into custody. He was the person in charge. He was the one the men would turn to if quick decisions were needed or if something went wrong.

The nervous energy kept at bay all thoughts of wives and girlfriends, kids and Christmas just four weeks away. It was only as they got to this point in a case when anything could go down, that Cole ever felt more fortunate than his colleagues.

He had nothing to lose.

Or, at least, he never used to.

When he'd been shot as a rookie, it had never occurred to Cole that Sharon Marie would react as strongly as she had. He could still remember her coming to the hospital not expressing happiness that he was alive but a morbid premonition that sooner or later he would be killed. Cole could give her no odds on that not happening.

He had been young and untried, but he'd never thought of himself as invincible. That would have been stupid. And he'd been careful. It was years before it also occurred to him how lucky he'd been, because sometimes being careful didn't matter.

It had become easier for Cole to deal with the potential dangers of his job precisely because there had been no one waiting in the wings for him each time he came home a little bloodied or bruised, torn or dirty. On the other hand, when he came home exhausted and disgusted and wired because a case had been a nightmare, it would have been nice to know there was someone there to talk to, to stroke him and let him know he'd done the best that he could.

Someone who was glad he'd made it back intact.

Which might or might not explain his thoughts now of Julie Conway. Cole kept seeing her as someone who might care, but even more telling, as someone he'd *want* to care.

Cole had a clear vision that kept reappearing in his mind's eye of how Julie had looked in the sunlight the other day, how she had smiled at him. How she laughed with the kids and how loving she was with them.

His mind went back to Julie standing in her apartment after he'd kissed her Thanksgiving night. Not the first time, but the second when she knew it was coming. When she had opened her eyes, Cole could tell she'd been surprised, not only by the kiss itself but by her own response. He hadn't felt any fright in her during that second kiss, but there had been this level of discovery for both of them.

Cole had known by then that he'd have to be careful, but he hadn't given it a great deal of thought until later, which was probably just as well. His spontaneous desire to kiss her as he was leaving had been because the first one had not been finished. The second kiss had allowed him to feel Julie's soft mouth again, to touch the baby-smooth skin of her face and to inhale the essence of some sweet body talc.

And then there was Saturday.

He had gained some of Julie's trust because they could spend the day together, although the children acted as unwitting chaperones. Also because she had let him touch her and not all of it had been innocent.

They'd gotten the children back to the apartment by six o'clock, drooping and quiet and totally worn out. Cole had stood outside the apartment door watching as Julie gently herded the children inside to remove their coats. She had then turned to face him. For the first time there was no doubt, no hesitation, no confusion in her gray eyes. Just a sort of quiet peace and contentment as she smiled at him.

He wanted to touch her, to kiss her again, but he didn't. Quite a lot had happened and the day had changed everything between them. What didn't happen now would happen next time.

"Do you want me to help get the kids to bed?" he asked.

Julie chuckled, shaking her head. "No, I can manage. They're too tired to complain." She continued to look at him, seeming to feel her heart open little by little to him, to warm to him completely. "Thank you for your help today," she murmured.

She began to blush suddenly and Cole let his eyes grow tender with regard and understanding. He leaned toward her.

"Is that all?" he asked gently.

Julie looked up, her eyes wide, to find the question in his eyes. Her heart began to race because what he wanted was so clear.

It was a moment of truth.

She took a deep breath. "I'm glad you came. It . . . it was nice."

Cole's eyes twinkled. "Nice," he repeated. But he certainly wasn't laughing at her. He just would have used a different term himself. He grinned and raised his brows. "We're getting better."

And then Cole changed his mind.

He lowered his head even farther and kissed her. He enjoyed the brief complete consummation of their mouths even more because Julie had anticipated it as she lifted her head slightly to meet him. But Cole possessed only the soft surface, not wanting to start anything that couldn't be finished.

He let their lips separate. Julie gave a furtive look over her shoulder to the open apartment door.

"Don't worry about the kids," Cole said, stepping back toward the stairwell. "They think kissing is yucky. But I like it." He grinned, looking suddenly boyish.

Julie looked at him a long moment. "Me, too," she'd said before disappearing inside and closing the door.

All the way home Cole remembered and repeated that to himself, grinning foolishly from ear to ear.

The memory of Julie's simple response lived in Cole. The image of her surrounded by her own aura of peace and calm created a sudden urgency in him he'd never known before. And like the other men, now, there was something more than the moment to consider.

"Are we ready?" he asked, his voice cold and firm, bringing himself back to the business at hand.

The response was that the men gathered the rest of the equipment on the table and began filing out of the room with Cole bringing up the rear. They passed through another room and out into a hallway, making a turn toward a metal door with heavily gated fronting. The door led out to the back of the precinct, where a number of dark cars awaited them.

It was six-thirty in the morning and overcast and cold. There had been a forecast of rain, possibly turning to snow in the afternoon, but the skies looked like it could happen a lot sooner. If it did, the weather could make their job even more difficult.

"Whatta ya got today, Bennett?" a voice said from Cole's shoulder as he exited the station. But he kept walking toward the cars, not breaking his stride.

"As if you didn't know," Cole said dryly to the rumpled-looking man with cameras strung around his thick neck.

The man cackled.

"I told ya I'd make a good detective. I know what you know sometimes even before *you* know it."

"Then you don't need any answers from me," Cole said, opening the trunk of the car to throw in a jacket, a rifle and a box of other stuff. "Watch it, Hal..." he said as he slammed the trunk shut.

"I just want to know if I can..."

"No you can't and don't try to follow us," Cole said, and then gave the man a sardonic glance. "Since when have you ever asked permission?"

The overweight Hal, looking more like a derelict than a free-lance crime photographer, shrugged.

"I'm tryin' to play you guys straight. I gotta make a living, too, you know. What about all those times I was there right when you needed a good, quick picture, huh?"

Cole headed for the driver's side of his unmarked car. "This is not after the fact. We have no one in custody yet, and I don't want you in the way. Maybe you'll hear something on the radio if you hang around out front. Otherwise you get your pictures right here, later."

"That's it?" Hal moaned in disappointment. "You mean you're really not going to let me come along? After all I've done for you guys?"

"Give me a break..." Cole murmured as the car started to move.

Yet even as the police caravan pulled out of the lot single-file, Cole could see Hal hurrying to his equally derelict car in hopeful pursuit.

It took more than an hour to set up so that there were men at the back of the building and on the stairwell one flight up and below the floor Cole wanted. The building was not supposed to be occupied, but it was not unusual for empty buildings to be squatted illegally by individuals, sometimes whole families, who had no place else to live. The infractions could go unnoticed by the city for long periods of time, which made the buildings ideal for someone trying to hide.

The structure was not safe, and there were cracked walls and shaky stairwells in the darkened building. Yet the information Cole had was specific and had led him and his team to this floor near the rear of the building. The silent signals were given and the adrenaline level in Cole's chest went shooting up. He was pressed flat against a wall from the stairwell that bordered the apartment they had staked out. He had his gun drawn.

With a nod from Cole one of the men pounded heavily on the door.

"Police. Open up, please."

No answer. They listened carefully for any movement or noise within. There was nothing. The pounding started again, louder.

"Open up!"

Another signal was given to force the door, and slowly the hallways came alive with shadowed people cautiously appearing to see what was going on.

The apartment door caved in with a resounding thud, and dust and debris clouded the entrance. The men rushed in, shouting commands.

From somewhere on an upper floor there was a sudden noise and commotion, followed by the running of feet and the jangling of metal objects and equipment.

"Up here, up here..." came down an urgent call.

Cole and the other men abandoned the futile search in the apartment and started up the stairwell. They didn't stop until they reached the roof, where they found the door swung open to the outside. When Cole reached it there were already five of his men searching cautiously around corners and in dark spaces.

"There he goes," someone shouted.

Everyone turned to see a slight, wiry figure maneuvering from one rooftop to the next and disappearing.

"Go after him . . ." Cole pointed to two men. He turned to two others. "You two stay here in case he doubles back."

Cole started back through the roof door and jabbed a finger at a fifth man. "You come with me."

Cole pulled his radio from his pocket and contacted his men on the street. The boy was playing with them, faking them out with his sure knowledge of the area and buildings. Cole didn't want any of his men hurt because the kid had the upper hand for the moment.

"Watch the streets," Cole ordered as he and the last officer bounded back down the stairs. A banister gave way under the pressure of their hands and went falling over to crash three stories below.

Cole kept going until he came out the front of the building. A few people had gathered, sensing police action, but they all stayed back. Cole signaled to his men positioned up and down the street.

"I want all those buildings checked, floor by floor," he said.

"Did you get 'im?"

Cole sighed in annoyance and frustration. It was just starting to drizzle.

"Get out of the way, Hal."

The dumpy little photographer trailed behind Cole like a puppy as Cole went about organizing the second course of action.

"I think he was tipped off," Hal offered.

"No. I think he was waiting for us. He knew we would come."

"So now whatta ya gonna do?"

"Now we go find him," Cole said, but the prospect was daunting.

He had the men thoroughly search out the building they'd started in, and the one the teen had disappeared into. The third building down was the one where they knew the kid lived with his mother and two sisters. But Cole already had that one covered, just in case the boy thought to sneak home.

He was somewhere on the streets, somewhere in the maze of alleys and spaces behind the buildings. Or in the cellars and old coal-chute spaces of the aging tenements.

The rain began coming down in earnest by ten o'clock, and a half hour later it was turning to fat snowflakes sticking to everything. The temperature dropped.

It was beginning to seem like a useless operation and Cole was about to call a halt when one of his men came running in search of him.

"I think we got something."

Cole looked up sharply and alertly.

"The guys over at 211 say there's a woman who knows the kid, knows where he might be."

"Who is she? How does she know?" Cole asked, already beginning to follow the man.

"She's the mother of the victim's girlfriend. Says she's afraid our boy is coming after her daughter because she jilted him."

Cole frowned. "Well, where's the daughter?"

"Says she doesn't know. She didn't come home last night."

Cole slowed and halted in his tracks, thinking hard. He looked around the dreary street, the gray freezing day. He scanned the buildings, his gaze returning to the ones they'd just searched, the one where they'd started. Good hiding places, but the kid already knew the police would look there.

So where would he go?

Not home. It was too obvious.

But someone had been back at the scene of the crime. Out of morbid curiosity? Or out of remorse? Was he playing hide-and-seek with them now because he was trying to be clever or because he wanted to be caught?

Then why not just come forward?

Pride again. And machismo.

Cole looked over his shoulder. The building where the crime took place was behind him, and they hadn't bothered with it.

"What's the woman's name?"

"Milagros Rojas."

"Go get her. And be quiet about it . . ." Cole said, as the officer left him.

Then Cole got on his radio and ordered two of the men to meet him at the crime building. The ever-present Hal was standing on the periphery, looking like a sodden and frozen bum.

"I want you across the street. And stay there!" Cole ordered in a tone that brooked absolutely no argument, before hurrying on to his new destination. His radio came to life.

"Yeah, go ahead . . ."

"This is Mike. I just got part of a call about some sort of disturbance on Eighty-seventh Street. That's just around the corner from here. You want us to check it out?"

Cole listened and at once Julie came to mind. It was unlikely that their suspect had found his way to the other side and to Helping Hands. But Cole still had an instant when unexpected apprehension grabbed at his gut.

He couldn't leave his team, and yet he felt an urgency that threw him into momentary confusion. Every instinct in him as a man wanted to race around the block to the center and make sure for himself that Julie was safe. He wanted to see her in the flesh, smiling calmly at him. He wanted to tell her he'd be back later when all the craziness was over.

Cole hesitated for only a second, because the cop in him took over. He gritted his teeth purposefully and shook his head to focus. He clicked the radio back on.

"No. Proceed as we planned. See if you can radio Lapone and Jacobs in their car. Tell them to see what's going on. If they can, get back to me when they have something to report."

THE DOOR to the conference room room opened and half a dozen women filed out and headed back to their various work areas. They continued to discuss the weekly staff meeting they'd just completed.

The first person out of the room had been Julie. Lois was right behind her.

The meeting had been an uncomfortable one for Julie. During the entire two-hour session she'd sat nervously shifting the papers in the report folder on the table in front of her. And she'd also sat avoiding eye contact with Lois who'd been silently prompting her to make an announcement. The announcement being that, for nearly a week Julie had been silently harboring an unidentified five-year-old left at the center.

Lois's arguments had made perfect sense, especially after coming to work the day before, Monday, and finding there was still no word at all concerning the little girl. Perhaps the director of the center, Marjorie Kennedy, would understand Julie's wanting to be responsible for this child in particular. On the other hand, perhaps Marjorie wouldn't. At this point, Julie wasn't willing to take the chance. She'd decided on a course of action and right or wrong she knew she had to see it through. She was responding to an instinct, to some internal mechanism that placed the little girl's needs first. Maybe in some unconscious way, Julie was fulfilling a need of her own.

Julie was shaking her head as she moved along the corridor with Lois now at her side.

"I know what you're going to say..." Julie said calmly.

"That you're a coward," Lois remarked, but it was done without sarcasm.

"One more day won't matter."

"It could mean your job. Have you considered that?" Lois asked.

Julie stopped to look at her friend, her blank stare indicating that she hadn't. She blinked as the possibility took hold and settled among the other decisions she had to make.

Letting out a frustrated sigh, Lois could see that that consideration carried no weight at all.

Julie continued walking. "Let's talk in my office," she whispered.

For a moment she hesitated outside the playroom, where only Mickey sat on the floor coloring in a coloring book. When Lois and Julie reached the office, Lois tried again.

"Julie, maybe you're being...well, overprotective. You may not be helping the child by what you're doing."

Julie looked at the deep concern on Lois's face and she smiled at her to let her know she had not gone off the deep end.

"I know she's not my child, Lois. I haven't begun to make that mistake. But am I supposed to care any less because of that?" She remembered Cole telling her that he didn't think it was possible to give a child too much love. Would he still think so if he was aware of what she'd gotten herself into?

"I don't know. I guess not." Lois sighed. "I've seen you with Tanya and Darren, and I know you love them. But this is different."

"Maybe it isn't."

"I know your heart is in the right place, but someone else who doesn't know you might not look at what's happened in the same way. I just don't want anything horrible to happen to you," Lois said sincerely.

What Lois had always liked about Julie was her honesty and her empathy for people and their problems. She had never been standoffish, had never presented herself as better than anyone else. Perhaps what had happened to Julie had tempered her—or at least made her realize how similar people were, rather than how different. Perhaps it made Julie see how very fragile and precious life was and that each life had to be handled carefully.

Lois knew that Julie had never gotten that assurance from the family she should have been able to count on, but from the helping hands of strangers. Julie had walked away from a privileged life, leaving everything behind in order to find and be the person she wanted to be. The kind of person someone might respect and love just for herself. She'd already had so much taken from her.

Julie gave a sad, ironic smile at Lois's worry. "Nothing horrible is going to happen that hasn't already happened."

Lois shivered dramatically. "Lord, don't say that. It can *always* get worse."

"Lois," Julie said softly. "You won't say anything, will you?"

"You know I won't. I'm not sure that what you're doing is right, but I'm on your side, Julie."

Julie's phone suddenly rang.

"I guess that's a signal that I have work to do and should get back to my own office," Lois said heading to the door. "I'll talk with you later."

Julie nodded as Lois left. "Hello?"

"Hi. This is Sylvia Novak from Immigration . . ."

"Oh, hello, Sylvia. We got your notices last week about illegal aliens. We haven't encountered any problems like that..."

A half hour later Julie was just getting off the phone when there was the gradual raising of several voices near the front reception area of the center. There was one distinct female voice, high and strident with anger and emotion.

Slowly Julie got up from her desk to walk to the office door to investigate. As she approached, Mickey suddenly slipped inside to stand next to Julie, her eyes also following the commotion down the hallway.

"Let go of me. You have my daughter," a woman's voice shouted.

Julie put her arm around the child's shoulder, her adrenaline starting to pump in a dread of excitement.

Then there was a thud, and a crash and the breaking and shattering of glass. The child huddled closer to her side as Julie tried to separate and identify the figures near the door. Her stomach somersaulted with the anxious notion that Mickey's mother had finally returned.

There were several people already lining the hallway to see what was going on.

"I want my baby," the woman screamed, starting down the hallway in Julie's direction. "You have no right to keep her from me."

Julie looked down at the child next to her, who was peering around Julie's thigh and down the hallway at the hysterical woman. Julie held her breath, half expecting the little girl to break into a run as she caught sight of her mother. But the child never moved.

Instead, she took hold of the folds of Julie's skirt, as if holding on to something sure and safe. The few staffers in the hall stood frozen, not knowing what to do until the woman got closer and recognition was clear.

"Oh, my God. It's Marion Hayes..." Lois said in a shocked voice to Julie's right.

Marion stopped in front of Julie, looked frantically left and right and then down to find the small child cowering behind Julie in wide-eyed fascination.

"My baby..." the distraught woman cried, reaching out toward the girl. Her hands were bloody, and shards of broken glass still clung to the sleeve and front of her winter coat.

Instinctively Julie put out her hands to ward off the woman.

"You've made a mistake. This is not your child."

The woman began to struggle as Julie grabbed her by the arms. Julie felt the sharp stabs and quick stinging pain as glass fragments bit into her hands. She let go and quickly pulled her hands back.

Marion's arms were flailing to push Julie out of her way.

Julie put up her arm to protect her head and felt the blunt glancing blow on her arm and shoulder. The little girl began to whimper in fright.

"Marion, stop it," Lois ordered sharply. Marion stopped and looked blankly at Lois's commanding presence.

Julie pulled herself together and quickly stepped into the hallway between Lois and Marion. Her hand hurt, and was now bleeding, too. Julie curled it into a soft fist and held it at her side.

"Lois, let me talk to her."

Lois shook her head. "Julie, she is out of control. She could hurt somebody."

"Please..." Julie pleaded. "She's just upset."

Lois hesitated.

"What is going on out here?" came the voice of the center's director. Marjorie marched forward, took one instantaneous look at the gathering, spotted Marion and turned around. "I'll call her parents..." she murmured, heading back to her office.

Julie turned back to Marion, not waiting for Lois to agree to her request. Marion had her attention focused on the little girl.

"It's Mommy, honey. I came to take you home..." Marion crooned to Mickey, who stood against the door to Julie's office clutching her doll.

"She's not your little girl," Julie said softly.

Marion turned a wild tearstained face to Julie. "My baby needs me."

"You're absolutely right," Julie said, agreeing with the woman. "Why don't we both sit down and we'll talk."

The woman stopped crying and looked at Julie. "You'll help me?"

Julie took the woman's arm, steering her inside the office and out of the public viewing of a startled staff. "I'll try..."

"Julie, are you okay?" Lois asked anxiously, noticing the blood on Julie's hand and arm.

Julie looked over her shoulder to find Lois in the doorway, watching Marion with a guarded look.

"She's bleeding all over the place. It's all over your clothes," Lois said quietly.

"I'll take care of it later. Will you keep an eye on her?" she said, beckoning the little girl forward and giving her a gentle push in Lois's direction.

"Are you sure you should be alone with her?" Lois asked concerned.

Julie only smiled. "I'm going to sit and talk to her until her parents come. Just keep everyone out of here until then."

Julie saw the bright confusion in the little girl's eyes and patted her and stroked her hair reassuringly. Then she stepped inside the office and closed the door.

Julie looked down briefly at her hand, opening the palm to see the two open cuts that were bloody but no longer bleeding. She closed her hand again, the torn skin protesting. Then she looked up at Marion Hayes who stared forlornly and with eyes glazed with pain and suffering.

"You have my little girl. You've kidnapped her. Where's Linda?"

Julie looked at her for a long moment and quietly moved toward the woman. "You came here last spring with Linda. It was soon after your divorce. Do you remember?"

The other woman nodded slowly. "Yes."

"You came to us for help. But there was another reason."

Marion nodded again. "I was running away. I didn't want my husband to take her away from me. Linda was all I had."

Slowly Marion was becoming lucid, and Julie tried to talk to her calmly to keep her that way. Julie reached for her shoulder bag resting on the floor by her desk. She opened it, looked inside and pulled out a handful of facial tissues.

"You told us he was trying to kidnap her. But you didn't say he had legal visitation rights granted by divorce court. We didn't take Linda from you. But we had to comply with court orders."

Julie gently took Marion's hand, so bloody she couldn't tell where the cuts began and ended. She dabbed carefully at the hand.

"No one hid your daughter from you. The courts gave her to her father. But it's only temporary, Marion. I'm sure you'll be allowed to see your child as soon as you're feeling better," Julie said with conviction, hoping that it was true.

Marion looked completely blank at what Julie was doing to her hand. She didn't seem to be in any pain except what was in her heart. But her chin quivered.

"I thought we'd be married forever. We had so many plans. We were going to have more children. We wanted to buy a house," Marion moaned.

"Sometimes it doesn't work out that way," Julie said, feeling a tightening in her chest, thinking of her own life in disarray, remembering her own losses.

Marion's face began to crumble and she pressed her free hand to her mouth, perhaps so that she wouldn't scream out in helpless anguish.

"I don't know if I'll ever be better."

"You will," Julie promised firmly. "You'll make new plans and start over again. You and Linda."

Marion sobbed quietly, shaking her head. "You don't know what it's like to lose everything."

Julie felt an awful rush of memory wash over her in a cold wave. She recalled the doctor telling her she'd miscarried. And she hadn't even known she was pregnant. There would have been a baby from the horror of what had happened. A baby might have wiped the slate clean, given her a chance, helped her to forgive.

"Yes I do," Julie answered in a whisper...

When the two uniformed officers arrived, they found an elderly maintenance man sweeping up the shattered glass, which had been knocked out of an inner door at the entrance.

There was still a chair turned over and magazines from a nearby table dumped on the floor. A poster was half torn from a wall where there was also a bloody handprint.

"We got a call about an altercation," Officer Jacobs said to the man.

"I don't know nothin' about it," he said, never looking up. "Talk to her..." He pointed absently toward Lois.

"We didn't call for police," Lois said, using her I'm-not-intimidated approach.

"Maybe. But we got one anyway. What's going on here?" Lapone asked, his eyes assessing the hallway.

"There was just a small accident."

"Whose blood?" asked Jacobs, the female officer no less forthright in her questioning than her partner.

Lois shrugged, thinking fast for any excuse. "One of our clients. She slammed the door too hard and the glass broke."

Jacobs raised her brows at Lois. "But where did the blood come from?"

"She cut herself," Lois said easily. "It wasn't serious."

"Is she still here?" Lapone asked, walking past Lois and heading slowly down the hallway, following the few drops of blood that spotted the floor.

Lois sighed. "Yeah, she's still here," she answered with real reluctance.

"We'd like to see her, please."

"She's all right. As a matter of fact someone is helping her."

Lapone nodded, ignoring Lois's excuses. "Yes, ma'am. We'd like to see her."

Lois moved toward Julie's office, the officers following, their equipment belts jangling with the dozen or so items hanging from them. A small radio being carried by Jacobs occasionally blurted out an unintelligible message and went silent.

Lois turned to Jacobs and Lapone. "You know, this is a waste of your time. The woman is fine."

"Why did she slam the door?" Lapone asked.

"She was upset."

"About what?"

Lois shrugged. "Look, we're a self-help center. We counsel women, but we don't ask them their life stories. Many of them are going through hard times..."

"Now what's going on?" Marjorie's voice could be heard again as she walked briskly from her office to where Lois stood with the two officers.

"We're responding to a call about a disturbance."

Marjorie was shaking her head patiently. "It's just a distraught woman."

"What was she distraught about?" Jacobs asked, pulling out her notebook to start a preliminary report.

"Her daughter. She thought we were hiding her daughter from her. It's a little complicated. You see..."

Jacobs knocked on Julie's door. "Ma'am? It's the police. Could you open the door? We just want to see if everything is okay."

The door opened and Julie stood there. Her eyes were a bit misty, but she seemed calm. The officers could hardly help but notice that she had dried blood in patches over her blouse and skirt, her hand, and her hair was slightly disheveled.

Julie stiffened when she saw the uniforms. "Everything is fine."

Marion came to stand next to her. She looked at the police. "Did you find my baby?"

Julie sighed and looked helplessly at Lois. The police weren't going to understand.

"Your baby?" Lapone asked blankly.

Marjorie stepped forward. "Officers, this woman recently suffered a breakdown. She just thinks that..."

Marion pushed past Julie to stand in front of the nonplussed officers. She wrung her hands. "She's been kidnapped." She looked around, seeing the child again, reaching out for her. "There she is."

The little girl ran to stand with Julie as Marion again slipped into delusion.

Marjorie pointed. "That's not her child. Her daughter was given to her father by the court."

Jacobs pointed to Marion's hand. "That's really bad. You need to see a doctor..."

Marjorie frowned at Julie. "Who is that little girl?"

Julie froze.

Lois froze.

Lapone looked at Marjorie. "You mean, you don't know who she is?"

"I remember her..."

All heads turned at the incredulous voice of Phyllis. "That's the child from last week."

Marjorie's head turned. "What do you mean, *last week?*"

Phyllis looked to Julie for guidance but only saw her standing stock-still, her face drained of color. The two officers exchanged looks.

Julie felt her heart begin to pound in her chest. She took hold of the little girl's hand and faced Marjorie, Lois and the police. "She was dropped off at the playroom. Last Wednesday," she added weakly.

"I told Pat about it when I was going home. And Pat said she'd tell Julie," Phyllis explained to Marjorie.

"The kid is not this woman's daughter?" Lapone asked, just to try and get one straight answer.

"No," Marjorie answered.

"But you don't know who she is?" Jacobs asked.

"No," Lois filled in the silence.

"She's been around for almost a week, and you didn't know about it?" Lapone pointed to Marjorie.

Marjorie shook her head.

"Then, who's been taking care of her?" Jacobs asked.

Julie bit her lip, looking at Lois who felt just as helpless as she did. "I have. She's been staying with me. I was sure that someone was going to come back for her, but..."

"Oh, boy..." Jacobs groaned, shaking her head.

"You didn't tell anyone?" Lapone asked.

"I knew about her," Lois spoke up.

"You lied to me," Marion accused Julie tearfully.

Lapone sighed and shook his head. He took the radio from his partner and turned it on. He ordered an ambulance to take Marion Hayes for medical attention. He tried to get information from Lois and Marjorie. The little girl wouldn't talk.

He turned to Julie. "Why didn't you bring her in to the police?"

"She was frightened. It was just before the weekend . . . I didn't want to leave her alone," Julie explained simply.

"Well, now you have no choice."

"You're not going to arrest her, are you?" Lois asked in disbelief, as the officer beckoned Julie and the child.

"No, ma'am. Not if she comes along voluntarily. But I think we'd better go down to the station to get this straightened out."

Everyone looked at Julie. She looked down at the trusting little face of the child who believed she would not let anything happen to her. Julie looked back to the waiting officers and to Marjorie Kennedy.

"I'll go," she nodded quietly.

Chapter Seven

The flashbulbs going off and the lights of the video cameras were irritating. Normally Cole didn't mind the half dozen or so scavenger reporters who hung out at the precinct and somehow managed to find out when an arrest was imminent in a criminal case. They were always the first ones at an arraignment. But at the moment Cole was tired, all out of patience . . . and he was hurt.

Cole flexed his right hand into a fist and relaxed it again, feeling the pulling of the nerves and broken skin around the cut on his arm. It hadn't been caused by a bullet or a knife or any other handheld weapon, but by something as innocent as a wooden beam studded with exposed nails.

A scuffle had taken place between the suspect and three of the stakeout officers, including Cole, when they'd closed in to arrest him. They found the young man and a badly frightened girl exactly where Cole thought they'd be. At the apartment where the murder had taken place. The girl had been taken from the apartment in hysterics. She'd been forced there by the Santiago youth to witness whatever was going to happen between him and the police. To show her he wasn't afraid. To show her it was all her fault.

Cole had warned his men what to expect. They knew the boy would have a gun, and he did. He never actually pointed it at the officers, but he'd refused to put it down, forcing the men to charge him. He was in no way a match for their size and strength.

A cluster of male bodies had tangled and twisted, crashing through a door, through a damaged wall that had brought the beams plummeting down on Cole with three-inch carpenter nails ripping through his coat, and into his arm.

The desk sergeant read the charges as Rodrigo Santiago stared blank-eyed and indifferent into space, and several weeping women could be heard from an outer room.

"Cole, you sure you don't want to go to the hospital? The Captain thinks you might need stitches or something," one of the officers from the stakeout said.

Cole shook his head. He knew that his arm was no longer bleeding. He could feel that the fabric of his shirt had stuck to the wound. "I'm all right. I don't have time to go to the hospital. There's something I have to take care of."

The officer shrugged and turned away.

The first thing Cole had thought of once Santiago had been taken into custody was Julie. He wanted to get to a phone and call the center. Although it was after five o'clock, she might still be there. But he hadn't expected it to be so difficult to get away from the booking of his suspect.

"Thanks, Cole. Those were some of the best shots I've gotten in a month," Hal exclaimed from Cole's left side as he rewound a finished roll of film. "There's a great one of you with that girl just as you're comin' outta that building. The one where you're tellin' her she's fine and everything's okay. Great image. Shows compassion and understanding. My editor's gonna love it. Wanna copy?"

"No…" Cole shook his head absently, listening to the end of the arraignment and watching the prisoner being led away. Santiago was accompanied by two men from the stakeout team.

Hal hurried after them, already reaching for his second camera.

"Hey, Cole..."

Cole turned around to see an officer from the Youth Squad raise a hand for him to wait. Cole took a look at his watch and was already turning in the direction of the hall-way that led to his office.

"I have a call to make. What is it?"

The officer looked him over seeing the dust, now caked, over Cole's jacket and pants. He glanced at the torn sleeve and Cole's drawn features. He shook his head.

"Looks like it was a tough arrest." He looked down at his pad and flipped through a few pages. "Lapone and Jacobs checked out that call at that women's center..."

Cole became instantly alert again. "They never got back to me."

"Yeah, I know. Things got weird. There was something about someone kidnapping someone else's kid."

"Kidnapping..." Hal suddenly said from behind the two men.

The officer frowned at the photographer and waved him away. "Beat it, Hal. This is not official. You understand?"

Hal shrugged and walked away.

"Who's the someone?" Cole asked.

"It's all in here," the man said. "But we had to bring in one woman, send another to the hospital, and then there's this kid. I don't think it's a real kidnapping, but it's real complicated."

Cole rubbed his hand across the back of his neck, fu-tilely trying to ease the tension. "Okay, cut to the chase. What's going on?"

"Well, it's just that when the woman was brought in she asked for you. By name. Do you know someone named Ju-lie Conway?"

Cole stood stone-still for a moment.

Maybe he didn't. Maybe he knew nothing about Julie, after all. Maybe all he thought he knew was simply what he wanted to believe.

He didn't answer his colleague directly, but instead asked one question of his own, one that made him feel tight and anxious inside.

"Is she being charged?"

The officer rubbed his chin. "I don't think so. There's probably a misdemeanor here, but I don't see any malicious intent. We had a caseworker from BCW come and get the kid and take her for a complete medical."

"Where did you put Julie Conway?" Cole asked, already beginning to walk in the direction of the precinct offices. The officer followed.

By the time they reached the third floor and the interrogation rooms, Cole had been given the details of the situation. At least from the police point of view. And all the while Cole kept getting a vision of Julie and the little girl as they appeared at the station on the night before Thanksgiving. He knew instinctively that the beginning and the end to what was going on happened on that night. He didn't know what had caused Julie not to tell him then that she might have a problem or that she might need his help. But Cole felt a strange emptiness and a sense of defeat that at no time since they'd met had Julie trusted him enough to confide her secret or that of the little girl . . . whatever it was.

Cole only knew a grim reality that he couldn't respond to her now as he would have over the past few days. He and the other officer encountered Ben Bradshaw after they'd gotten off the elevator.

Ben tilted his head back in surprise. "I heard you finally got back." He looked at Cole's appearance. "Glad to see you're mostly in one piece. You need to see about that arm?"

"No, I'm okay."

Ben let it go. "I thought you might want to know about the call this morning to Helping Hands." He fell into step beside Cole and the officer.

"I'm filling him in now," the man said.

Ben touched Cole's arm to gain his attention. "Anything I can do?" he asked quietly, just between the two of them, remembering Cole's recent account of his time spent with Julie Conway.

Cole kept walking. "Thanks" was all he said.

The other officer went back to the information he had gathered so far. He shrugged after he finished reading from his notes, unaware that Cole had only half listened because he was busy trying to figure out what story Julie Conway might make up to tell him now.

"That's it. She's in there." He pointed to a room to their right.

"How is she?" Cole asked flatly, afraid he'd betray some emotion or thought, some feeling.

"Quiet. Very cooperative. She keeps asking about the kid, but you know I can't tell her anything at this point."

Cole nodded.

"Look, I was going to make one or two more calls and finish this report. We'll probably just let her go." The officer walked away, leaving Cole to a private contemplation of the closed interrogation-room door.

Ben slapped Cole lightly on the shoulder. "Let me know how it works out, my man . . ."

Cole reached for the handle.

"Excuse me. I've been sitting here for hours and I can't get anyone to answer any questions or give me any information."

The female voice was filled with annoyance and impatience. Cole and Ben looked to their left to find a black woman seated on the edge of a bench against the wall. She stood, when she saw she had their attention, and approached the two men with brisk strides.

Cole only vaguely registered that there was something familiar about her, but the thought quickly faded. The woman was tall, a bit stout but shapely, with a very self-confident air. She had attractive dark features but with eyes that held suspicion. And although she seemed somewhat put-out at the moment, there was also no disguising the concern that brightened her eyes and made her nervously finger the fringe on her wool scarf.

"What's the question?" Cole asked quickly, his hand tightening on the doorknob to the interrogation room.

"I want to know what is happening to Julie Conway. We work together at the women's shelter on Eighty-seventh Street. There's been a terrible misunderstanding. Julie was..." she stopped suddenly.

Ben and Cole exchanged brief glances.

Cole turned back to her, looking the woman over carefully. He smiled slightly. "Are you Lois?"

Her brows raised, and she took another closer look at Cole. "Yes I am. How did you know?" Her brow cleared. "You're Julie's detective," she stated.

Then Lois's eyes passed carefully over Cole to see the dirty and wet clothing, the long rip in his jacket sleeve, the dried blood. This man had been about the business of police work. She looked at the silent black man next to him. He was staring too openly at her and made Lois feel as though he was looking right inside of her.

"This is Officer Ben Bradshaw. Ben, this is Julie's friend Lois..."

"Henry," she supplied. She gave Ben a look of quick, furtive interest, but addressed herself only to Cole. "They won't let me see Julie."

Cole nodded. "I understand. You're concerned. The officer will be finished in a while and then Julie can leave."

Cole hated sounding so official and cool, but he didn't have a choice.

Lois's annoyance returned. "Julie hasn't done anything. How can you let them . . ."

Cole raised a hand. "I haven't seen Julie yet. I just got in."

Ben smiled at Lois reassuringly, liking the way she was willing to stand up to them on behalf of her friend. "She's not being mistreated. Rubber hoses weren't used."

But Lois was in no mood for joking. She let out a deep breath and gave Ben Bradshaw a scathing look of disgust. "What have they done to her? She was only trying to help."

Cole couldn't answer. He didn't know yet what Julie was trying to do.

"Don't let them frighten her," Lois appealed to Cole softly. "She doesn't deserve to be treated like some criminal." Lois started to say more but abruptly stopped.

Ben shifted and scratched his jaw, sorry that he'd been so flippant. That was not the way to win and influence this woman.

Cole touched Lois's shoulder. "I promise, I won't let anything terrible happen to her."

Lois nodded. "I believe you."

"Maybe you know something more about all this. Can you talk with Ben?"

Lois frowned and looked at her watch. "I only have a few minutes. I have to go pick up my kids and get home. I wanted to see Julie."

"I'll tell her you were here most of the afternoon. Call her later at home."

"And I promise this will only take a few minutes," Ben added. He gently took Lois's elbow and he looked for a long moment into her face. "Why don't we go to my office. It's on the first floor . . ."

JULIE FELT NUMB.

At the moment she wasn't capable of much more than just staring at the dingy wall of the room where she'd been sitting for hours. She was trying not to let the throbbing pain from her headache make her sick to her stomach. She was trying not to let the awful humiliation of being accompanied to a police precinct, under suspicion of endangering the welfare of a minor, tear at her insides. Trying not to let the irony of the situation make her hysterical.

Julie was also trying to block the painful cries of the little girl from her mind as the child was forcibly led away by a female officer when they'd arrived at the station house. She could still feel the anguish twist at her as she helplessly watched Mickey leaving her. Julie closed her eyes against the image of the frightened little face as the child suddenly and unexpectedly screamed out "Mommy . . . Julie" in the same breath.

Julie glanced down at the doll in her lap. The Annie-Fannie doll the girl had attached herself to for comfort from the beginning, but which she'd let drop to the floor as she was led away from Julie.

Julie was also trying not to put any real significance to the fact that after she had finally built up the courage to ask to see Det. Cole Bennett, it was only to be told he was not available. She had then tortured herself all afternoon wondering what that meant.

Did it mean Cole couldn't see her, or that he wouldn't see her? Did it mean he was busy with work? Away from the precinct? Avoiding her?

Julie sighed. The officer who questioned her had been pleasant to her, but even after repeated explanations from her he obviously didn't understand why she had made the decision she had to keep the little girl instead of turning the unidentified child over to the authorities.

The question answered itself. But the officer had only shaken his head, bewildered. And Julie continued to feel, as a result, that she'd made the right move to begin with, even though she now faced a legal reprimand and could lose her job. Marjorie Kennedy had not been pleased with her story.

The only problem was they had taken Mickey away and would tell Julie nothing of what would happen to her.

Julie let her eyes close, again hearing that plaintive cry. Hearing her name burst forth from the previously silent little girl. Hearing the cry for her mother. She had confused the two for a moment, Julie realized, but it was nevertheless a heart-wrenching moment. It evoked in Julie the hollowness of having lost her own baby.

Her child had been conceived out of hurt and pain, and she had lost it the same way, never knowing of its existence. Completely unaware she was even pregnant as she struggled for peace of mind, desperately in need of a helping hand, understanding ... love.

What she couldn't have herself, she'd nonetheless learned to willingly give to others, to a five-year-old child. Someone's baby.

She didn't hear the door open, and for an instant Cole saw her seated at a long wooden table, the battered, scarred surface emphasizing Julie's frailty. Her face was pale and oddly calm. Her hair feathered around her face wildly, tendrils trailing against her cheek and jaw, against her neck. But when she opened her eyes suddenly, Cole only saw wariness and a dazed faraway look laced with sadness.

Julie, for her part, felt an immediate spark of joy at suddenly seeing Cole standing so large in the doorway. But her joy was short-lived. There was obviously much more than one table separating them, and Julie could see it in the cool distance of Cole's blue eyes.

They were cautious. And remote. She blinked, thinking it an apparition borne of her exhaustion and anxiety. But it was clear to her that she now faced Det. Cole Bennett, the cop. Not the Cole Bennett who had teased her gently and made fun of her in a familiar way. Not the Cole who made her feel both shy and responsive to his kisses and touch. Not the Cole who could comfort her and a lost little girl with just his presence.

Julie's eyes traveled over him, from the hard features of his face, with the closed expression and grimly set mouth, to his disheveled appearance. She saw the sleeve of his jacket and went still. Her gaze went back to his face.

"You've been hurt," she said quietly.

Cole tensed his jaw. The genuine concern in Julie's voice went straight to his chest. "It's not serious."

She opened her mouth to ask what had happened, but his quiet stare made her bite the words back and she made no more effort to bridge the gap between them. Instead she tried to pull herself together, to be more in control than she actually felt. It was clear that Cole had heard about what had happened that morning at the center. He'd been told the news about the child and Marion from the other officer. But Julie felt tremendous disappointment because Cole had not asked her.

Her voice was stronger. "How's Marion Hayes?"

Cole tilted his head, surprised that Julie's concern was still on someone else. "I understand she's being kept at the hospital overnight for observation. Her parents are with her."

Julie nodded. She unconsciously bit her lip and her eyes grew dark with emotion. "And . . . and Mickey?"

Cole stepped into the room and closed the door. But he just leaned back against it and put his hands into the torn pockets of the nylon windbreaker.

It reminded Julie of the walk they'd taken with the kids, from her apartment to the museum, with her hand intertwined with Cole's and stuffed into the pocket of his jacket for warmth.

"I understand her name isn't Mickey."

Julie raised her brows and shook her head, readily agreeing. "No, it's not."

"Why Mickey?"

There was, surprisingly, a small smile on Julie's mouth as she remembered that night. She raised her hands from under the table and ran them palm-flat down her torso. The right hand was wrapped in cotton and bandages. Cole reacted silently at the evidence that she, too, had been hurt.

"She had on this cotton shirt with Mickey Mouse characters," Julie responded softly. "It seemed like a good choice. It was cute."

Cole merely nodded, watching her face. "What happened to your hand?"

Julie looked down at her hand, having forgotten the bandages. She quickly put both hands in her lap again out of sight. "I cut it on glass," she said flatly.

Cole's expression didn't change.

Julie suddenly recalled a young officer who'd listened to her tearful story of a sexual assault without one iota of understanding or compassion. Who'd been more interested in the details than in the physical and emotional impact on her. She would have been better off to have kept silent. Perhaps she would have been better off not to have asked for Cole in the first place.

Except that she had had this overwhelming sense of needing him. Had that been a mistake, as well?

Julie had some insight as to why Cole was aloof with her. She also knew he had no right to be. She was the one, after all, who had taken all the risks. Her not telling Cole about Mickey from the beginning had not so much to do with him, as it had to do with the needs of the little girl. Julie had simply put the child's comfort first.

"Where did they take her?" Julie asked in a thin, small voice.

Cole didn't pretend not to understand. And even though he was confused about what had happened, Cole was in no doubt that Julie had cared for the mysterious little girl as if she had been her own. He also knew Julie wasn't going to like or be prepared for the answer to her question. He walked to the table, keeping it between them, bracing his hands on the back of an empty chair.

"She was taken to an area hospital for examination."

Julie's eyes grew round. "Why? There's nothing wrong with her."

"It's procedure..." Cole stopped. Even he didn't know how to say it. "They'll want to eliminate the possibility of..."

"No..." Julie suddenly whispered in understanding. Her face completely drained of color and her eyes filled with tears. "No..." she moaned, shaking her head, her chin quivering.

Cole wanted to go to her then. But he didn't. His hands tightened around the chair back and his jaw muscles flexed furiously. What a fool he'd been to *think* any differently about Julie from what he *knew*. He was wrong to have begun to suspect that she was anything more than what she'd always been to him. But the damage had been done and Cole cursed himself.

Julie closed her eyes in total despair. She shook her head. When she opened them again she was angry and her voice quavered with it.

"How can you believe that I..."

"I don't," Cole interrupted firmly. And then he repeated more softly, his blue eyes searching over her face. "I don't. But this is not my call, Julie. It has to be done. This is a child welfare matter now. It's out of your hands and mine," he added, as if suggesting that it might have all gone differently had he known everything from the start.

"They'll check to make sure she's okay. Then she'll be placed in foster care."

Julie's anger was quickly replaced with apprehension. "They can't, Cole. She's not lost. She's not abandoned."

"How do you know?" he asked quickly.

She gnawed on her bottom lip, rubbing her hand across her forehead to ease the pain. "I just know." She looked openly at Cole with her gray eyes appealing and bright. "Listen to me. When Mickey was brought to me last week she was clean and properly dressed. She was cautious, but she wasn't skittish or afraid of me. She was alert and attentive and very well behaved. Later, when I put her to bed in my room, I could see there were no sores or bruises on her.

"Cole, she wasn't left on the streets, or at Grand Central Station, or at a hospital, or with the *police*. Someone brought her to the center. *Not* because they were leaving her forever, but because it was intended that someone would come back for her."

Julie had to stop because her throat was threatening to close, making it hard to breathe as tears swelled up again, but she was determined not to cry. Crying never got her anywhere.

"They, whoever they are, knew their little girl would be safe at the shelter with women. They knew she'd be cared for. You've seen her. You've spent time with her, playing with her, hoping she would talk but happy to hear her laugh. Did Mickey strike you as a child that *anyone* would not want?" Julie's voice cracked on the last words.

Cole believed her. He realized that she was right. And Julie had had more insight than even he had. She might not have told him what was really happening or that she found herself in a circumstance where she might have made poor judgment calls, but there was no evidence that she had anything but the child's interest in mind.

Cole began to relax. His gaze softened and he saw how long and tiring and upsetting a time Julie had had. And not once since he'd met the interviewing officer or spoken to Julie had she asked for anything, even understanding, for herself.

"Why didn't you tell me?" Cole asked simply.

Julie looked openly at him, not hiding any emotion. "I didn't think I had to."

"I would have understood. I would have helped you."

She shook her head. "You would have taken her into the station. Just like they're doing now. You're a police officer. You wouldn't have had any other choice. I did."

"If I had asked about Mickey, would you have told me?"

"Is there any reason why you would have asked?" Julie frowned.

Cole grimaced. "No," he said, sighing. "You were taking very good care of her."

Julie looked down at her hands, at the doll in her lap. "I thought someone would be back for her by now."

"You still believe that someone will?"

"Yes."

"Julie, there's no evidence to support that feeling."

"This isn't about evidence, Cole. I just know. Can I see her?"

Cole shook his head, suddenly unable to look her in the eyes. "I'm afraid not. You won't be told anything more about her."

"Dear God..." Julie moaned, turning her head away.

Cole reached a hand halfway across the table toward Julie. "It's going to be all right."

But she wasn't listening. Julie was suddenly cold and empty inside. Lost. Perhaps Lois had been right, after all. Perhaps she should have gone to the authorities right away. But they still would have done what they were doing now. Being official and not remembering that above all else they had a young child who was separated from her family and who, for the moment, was alone in the world.

Sometimes you didn't even have to be a child for that to happen.

The door opened and the interviewing officer stepped halfway in. He spoke to Cole.

"We're all done. It's clear that there was no mischief intended."

"Can I go now?" Julie's voice cut between the two men, suddenly a flat intonation curiously without emotion.

Cole looked at her. She'd withdrawn. Closed down. Cut herself off. She'd reached her emotional limit and needed to get out of there.

"Sure," the officer said, handing a paper to Julie. "You might want a copy of the report. Sorry we kept you so long..."

He left the room, and all the while Cole kept his eyes on Julie. He wanted to hold her now, but he'd waited too long. He wondered if he'd ever get a chance to again. Had he blown his second chance because of male pride?

"Come on, Julie. Let me take you home," Cole said quietly, standing straight.

Julie stared blankly into space. "You don't have to."

"I have to. I'm not letting you go home alone."

She turned on him. "I don't need you to."

Cole narrowed his eyes at her defiant features, her raised chin but sad, tired eyes. "Oh, yes you do..."

After a moment Julie got up from the table. Cole saw that she held the calico doll the little girl had carried everywhere. She suddenly looked small standing opposite him as she listlessly pulled her coat on and walked around the table to meet him by the door. Cole made a half move to take her hand but stopped. Julie wasn't going to let him.

Cole steered her out of the room where they were met by a flashbulb going off, momentarily blinding them. It was quickly followed by another as the two of them looked with surprise at the rumpled photographer preparing his camera for yet another shot.

"Boy, you sure have been busy," Hal chuckled as he aimed his camera.

Cole impatiently pushed the man aside. "Knock it off, Hal..." he said irritably as he quickly led Julie to the elevator.

From the time Cole and Julie walked out of the precinct to his car, their footsteps padded by the three inches of snow on the ground, until he'd parked down the block from her building, Julie said not a word. In answer to his hesitant question as to whether she was hungry and wanted to stop for something to eat, Julie shook her head no. When Cole said he wanted to come up for a minute, she only looked at him with a frown. When he told her that Lois had waited at the precinct most of the day to see if she was all right and would probably call later that evening, she nodded her head.

But Cole was not put off by her silence. He understood. He himself was trying to buy time with her. More than wanting to know what had happened to her hand, more than wanting to find out more about the child, Cole wanted to be with her and to say he was sorry.

Better than anyone, he should have known what the experience would be like for someone like Julie, being questioned impersonally, indifferently. He should have remembered, as Lois had said, that Julie wasn't capable of hurting anyone.

For reasons that hadn't been immediately clear to Cole when he'd returned to the precinct, with another homicide solved and a suspect in hand, he'd felt overwhelmingly lonely. There had been less of a sense of satisfaction and no particular pride in the work done. He'd come back to the station with the usual adrenaline rush, but rather than wanting to celebrate a victory with his men, he'd only thought of getting to Julie because he suddenly needed from her now what he'd never gotten from another woman. Peace and a haven of sanity. Cole admitted wryly that he hadn't given much thought as to what he could give to her.

It seemed to him now, as they silently climbed the stairs to Julie's second-floor apartment, that she didn't want much of anything for herself. She had always been more concerned for those around her. Yes, he needed her. But did she need him, too?

When they were inside and the door closed on the outside world, the silence they stood in was charged with wariness and expectation.

Julie stood indecisive in her foyer looking down at the cloth doll. For a moment she didn't seem to fully know that Cole was there behind her, appraising her and trying to read into her silence. She slowly reached out and put the doll on the counter. Cole took a step closer to her.

"How did you cut your hand on glass?" he asked.

Julie looked down at her hand, running her fingers over the crude bandaging. "It's not important, no more than scratches." She turned to face Cole, finding him looming close and large. "How did you hurt your arm?"

Cole grimaced with a sigh. "You don't want to know."

Her eyes thoroughly searched his face. For the first time Julie could see exhaustion, tension and uncertainty in Cole's blue eyes. She'd never had a chance to know him as a cop, but now she realized that his daily work was hard and filled with pressures she'd never given thought to. What he did was very likely dangerous, and there was often not enough time for sensibilities when lives were at stake. Julie had come to know the other Cole, the one she was discovering deep feelings for, but they were one and the same man.

Her eyes grew relaxed and warm because the man who'd shown so much gentleness and energy with three small children was the same one who went out on the streets and risked himself to protect perfect strangers. Had she under-estimated Cole? Would he have understood?

Julie's gaze roamed carefully over his dirty clothing, the cuts and scrapes on his hands, the torn sleeve. She took hold of his tie, as bright and as colorful as the one he'd worn when they'd first met. A contradiction, and yet so fitting. *One and the same.*

Cole looked down as Julie silently appraised his tie. He lifted a corner of his mouth in a smile. "There's a perfectly reasonable explanation for my ties."

"I'm sure there is."

Cole cupped the hand holding the tie. "Someday I'll tell you all about it," he promised in a low voice. Julie raised her face to his, their eyes meeting and trying to communicate. He wanted to take her in his arms and hold her.

She wanted to throw herself against him for his strength and tenderness. Julie moved her hand to pluck at the sleeve. "Take this off. Let me have a look at your arm."

"That's not why I came here."

"I know why you came here," she responded as she slipped out of her coat and held out her hand for Cole's.

Keeping his eyes on Julie, Cole shrugged out of the coat and gave it to her, following her movements as she hung them up. Then she went silently about gathering a towel, a washcloth, gauze and tape, a pair of scissors.

For the first time ever, it was Cole who felt awkward with her. He wanted to get past Julie's cool efficiency and know what she was really thinking and feeling, to find out what it was she really wanted.

But Julie didn't have a choice in what she wanted for the moment. She, too, was tired and cold and hurt. It was not just her hand. It hurt that anyone could think she would deliberately jeopardize a child, that Cole could doubt her. And maybe it wouldn't hurt so much if it hadn't also occurred to Julie that she was falling in love with Cole Bennett. What he thought mattered to her.

She also didn't have a choice because she was so close to losing control. She had to concentrate on something other than herself or be completely consumed by bewilderment and pain.

Cole stood and waited until Julie set everything on the pine table. Then he moved, walking to the counter cabinets to put his gun in its familiar place out of sight. He turned to find Julie staring at him with a strange, flushed expression on her face.

"You'll have to take your shirt off," she said softly.

Cole hesitated only a moment, but keeping his gaze riveted to her face he unbuttoned the shirt with one hand, loosening the tie and pulling it off with the other. Julie's eyes also stayed focused on his face, but with a deliberateness that was obvious to Cole. When the shirt and tie were removed he stood for a second holding them before placing them over the back of a dining chair.

Julie blinked at Cole. Seeing his bare chest sent a pulsing of tension through her body. She stood rigid, swallowing hard. He was a big man, with large hands and a broad chest and thick neck, but it was still a wiry masculinity, not heavy and lumbering. She could see the power in his arms and shoulders. Cole had clearly defined muscles, without being overly muscular. And his chest hair was a thick curling fur that was much darker than the hair on his head, but also mixed with strands of gray.

The sight of him half dressed began a sudden heated quickening within her, unexplainable and distantly familiar. Julie quickly lowered her gaze from staring so openly. She felt disoriented and vulnerable.

Cole took a seat at the table and held out his arm to Julie, all the while watching her, aware of her sudden confusion.

Julie looked at the ragged tear in the upper arm, which was nearly two inches long. She took hold of Cole's arm, feeling strange to be touching him this way, feeling elementally female standing so close to his naked torso. Julie gingerly began to wipe at the open cut, loosening the dried blood and cleaning around the wound.

Neither of them said anything for a long time, neither inclined to talk because what they would talk about suddenly seemed so personal and suggestive. Julie knew that Cole watched her closely and when she took a quick, furtive glance at him it was to find his eyes intense and probing. She drew in a sharp breath at his clearly sensual regard of her and nervously chewed her lip.

She could see that the tear was not so deep. Julie applied an antiseptic to the cut and put a wad of gauze over it, securing it with tape. When she was done she had a sudden desire to stroke his arm, as if to comfort him, as if the stroking would make the wound better.

"You probably should have stitches, but I think it will heal without..." she whispered, now unable to meet his gaze. She then tried to busy herself with gathering the equipment, but Cole reached out and took her hands to still them.

He pulled Julie just enough so that she faced him, standing in between his spread knees. He wanted to pull her onto his lap, but instead he began unwinding the Ace bandage from her hand. When he lifted the cotton there were several small cuts in her palm. Cole ran his thumb over them and Julie drew in her breath again. The sensation was far from being painful.

She watched his bent head with the ash-color hair slightly disarrayed, saw the curious way Cole examined her hand. It looked so small held in his. He was being so careful with it.

"We're a fine pair," Cole said in an amused undertone. "We get battered and bruised trying to help others." He looked up into her gray eyes. "Who helps us when we need it?"

The question was laced with innuendo and hidden meaning, and Julie knew it. Cole asked and answered the question at the same time, his eyes waiting for her reaction.

Julie felt her resolve cracking and disintegrating. She didn't want to be strong. She didn't want to *not* care. She could see in Cole's face what she was feeling in her heart and right now it would be nice if there was someone who could understand, who wouldn't ask questions or pass judgment or even necessarily say anything. It would be nice to just be held for a little while until she didn't feel quite so helpless and exposed.

A wave of sadness washed over Julie and she closed her eyes. Her hand shook in Cole's and the tremor went up her arm.

Cole could see the struggle, but he knew Julie was going to lose. And he was both glad and relieved. He stood up slowly and in one fluid movement had Julie in his arms. Her effort to maintain self-control was a mere token. She had been through too much and it was all catching up to her. They had been through too much *not* to need to hold on to one another now.

It seemed so perfectly natural. Once she was pressed against his furry chest, Julie let out the breath she'd been holding. The awkward moment passed very quickly and she wondered why she'd waited for so long, an eternity, for someone to give her what she needed. As a matter of fact, Julie suddenly felt so comfortable, so glad, so relieved to be in Cole's arms that everything in her relaxed. Her tension dissolved. She began to cry.

Cole hadn't expected that, but he also wasn't surprised. In fact he felt rather complacent, and smiled to himself as he cradled her head under his chin, stroking the slight shaking of her shoulders. Cole was going to enjoy comforting Julie Conway, because it showed so clearly that she was giving him her full trust. And it was too soon for him to put into words exactly what he was feeling, except that it was pretty good. For the first time in almost eighteen hours Cole was exactly where he wanted to be.

Julie wasn't absolutely sure why she was crying, except that she felt weak and raw and unable to stop. She felt that she'd been self-contained and invincible against the opposite sex. It had always felt unnatural, but for a time it had been an instinct of survival.

But Cole was warm, his chest cushioning her nose and mouth while she cried, his chest hair tickling her. The strength of his arms was gentle and secure. The tall, hard width of him was so right, so perfect, after so long. There was a heady exhilaration about wanting the touch of a man again. This man.

Cole didn't know how long they stood that way, except his concern for Julie began to give way to other needs and desires, ones that had been building gradually since Thanksgiving. The muscles in his arms and legs tensed as he tried not to give in to the physical excitement gathering within him.

Slowly Julie's crying subsided and she merely rested against Cole with her eyes closed. His chest was damp with her tears. Julie's arms had rested loosely around his waist, but now her left hand began to tentatively explore the smooth surface of his back. Her right hand drew up to his chest, her fingers gliding into the hairy surface until she could feel his heartbeat and breathing. Julie's fingertips inadvertently passed over the rigid, nubby point of his male breast and a jolting shock of desire made her head come up abruptly so she could look into Cole's face with wonder.

It was suffused with a quiet but intense regard for her. His eyes seemed very dark and completely unfathomable. She raised her hand, the one with the cuts, to touch his face, but

Cole caught it in midair and pressed her open palm to his mouth. His lips seemed hot. He felt hot.

He could see in her teary eyes what Julie couldn't say. Her mouth was slightly parted and her face was suddenly flushed. Julie watched him as if she had suddenly discovered something new and wonderful, and it was with profound relief and promise that Cole slowly bent to cover her mouth with his.

Her response was instantaneous.

Cole's lips seemed to grab at hers, to fuse with the soft surface. His entire being grew taut and urgent with desire for her, but he didn't feel the need to rush. He waited until Julie shifted her mouth to a comfortable position under his and her eyes drifted closed. Then he rubbed across her lips erotically, forcing them apart.

Julie's mind went blank. She was responding with pure instinct and feeling she thought never to know again. When she opened her lips Cole's tongue slowly eased inside with such delicious intent that a soft whimper escaped and her stomach curled into a jittery mass.

His arms drew her closer until he, too, could detect her heartbeat. It fluttered rapidly in her chest. Cole's hands came up to her hair, blindly searching until he found the clip that held her French braid in place at the base of her neck. He pulled the clip free and let it drop to the floor. Then his fingers forayed through the golden-highlighted locks, spreading them full.

Cole broke off the kiss. He wanted to see her face, see her hair around it. It made Julie look sophisticated. It was both sexy and alluring, with her face color heightened and her lips moist. Cole shaped her hair with his hands, fascinated with its heavy, silky texture. He bent to find her mouth again.

This kiss was a tantalizingly slow, deliberate kiss that was more than the exploratory ones they'd shared earlier. This kiss was familiar, and allowed each of them to taste and absorb the essence of the other. This kiss was filled with expectation and hope. It was warm and electrifying. This kiss had healing powers.

Julie unconsciously clung to Cole while he encouraged her. He stroked her back, forcing her chest against his. He kept her mouth a willing captive while his tongue danced teasingly with hers. Julie's fingers curled into his chest hair, gently massaging Cole's skin.

He gasped at the subtle pleasure.

Julie felt Cole's body change against her. His legs were braced apart but his hips were pressed forward and there was no mistaking how aroused he was. His mouth released hers again and she was left feeling oddly abandoned. His kisses were stimulating and comforting at the same time. But Cole's mouth only searched for her jaw, working his lips to her neck and throat. Julie caught her breath, and the tantalizing swirls inside her grew until she couldn't let the breath out. But it was for an entirely different reason and sensation than seven years ago.

Julie needed to be held. She needed to become familiar again with the feel of a man's arms and caresses. She'd come to rely on the sheer solidity of Cole, his gentleness. But it was one thing to reason that he was in control and that she could trust him to understand her unspoken concerns. It was quite another to feel that he, too, had limitations to that control and perhaps she'd unfairly tested him.

Cole had never tried to hide his interest in her as a woman. He'd been careful in holding and kissing her, restoring her faith in herself as someone worth desiring. But she was reminded now that he would want more from her.

It would be the full, complete expression of love. It would be the physical culmination of what had been growing between them. Unconsciously her body stiffened and she finally expelled a soft swish of air against his chest.

Cole felt the difference and stopped the slow marauding of her mouth.

"Cole..."

"It's all right," Cole interrupted, his voice hoarse and low. "Just don't move yet."

They stood quietly, their breathing rushed and quiet. But Julie's body shifted and her hips curved into his. It only made Cole harder. He groaned.

"Cole..." Julie tried again, tilting her head back.

"I'll stop. I won't do anything you don't want me to do."

"I'm not afraid."

"What?"

She sought his eyes, seeing that they were slumberous with desire. "I'm not afraid."

Cole swallowed and arched a brow. "Well, I am."

Julie smiled, finding the comment endearing, and telling. "Don't be. I won't break," Julie whispered ruefully, thinking of the irony of this man's honesty and the lack of such from a man she would have married. Had the fates been cruel... or had they ultimately saved her?

Cole shook his head. "Maybe the timing is all wrong."

"When will there be a better time?"

"When your feelings aren't clouded by what happened today. When we come to each other because we both want to be together. When you're sure you're ready."

Julie closed her eyes and laid her cheek on his chest. He was so warm.

"Then it's time."

"Julie," he started, and then stopped. She didn't move.

Cole would have been kidding himself if he'd said he didn't want to make love with her. He was about to burn up with need. But he didn't want it to be for himself alone. If Julie meant it, if she wanted him, too, *if* she was ready... if it was time...then he wanted her to realize it was to be a start upon which they would build. He didn't want a one-night stand for either of them.

He touched her hair, running his hand under the mass to gently rub her neck. He moved the hand to her throat and upward to raise her chin. Her eyes were bright and damp, but peaceful.

"Julie..." he whispered simply, touching her lips briefly with his.

Cole released her, took hold of her hand and headed for the bedroom. He hit a wall switch and the ceiling light went out. They were two ghostlike figures disappearing into the room.

Standing next to the bed facing each other, Cole began to undress her. First her sweater and blouse, then the long skirt and her boots, until Julie was left in only bra and panties. Cole stopped and began to undress himself, watching her face for reaction but only finding a shy curiosity. She was openly curious when he removed his jockey shorts, finally lifting her gaze to his face.

When Julie didn't move and didn't say anything, Cole put his arms around her drawing her close to him. He kissed her cheek as his hands found the bra clasp and released it. The bra was tossed aside, but he left the panties in place.

When Julie was in his arms again Cole felt his throat grow dry at the feel of her silky, smooth skin against his, her breasts, rounded and pert, with the nipples rubbing on his chest. He kissed her, his mouth eager and hungry without being demanding. Julie felt the air of the room on her skin, but Cole's wandering hands quickly warmed her. Their breathing deepened and the physical urgency in him pressed hard against her through her underwear. But she wasn't afraid.

Cole lifted her onto the bed, but lay next to her rather than on top. For long, delirious moments his hands and mouth sought out all the sensitive spots, which drew deep sighs and soft mews. Her body began to undulate with each touch and sensation.

Julie thought it would be more difficult than it was; that Cole's intimate touches, the very feel of his body might trigger some memory, not only of her past helplessness but of hands that had been rough and had hurt her. But Cole's every movement was slow, seductive and careful. Her nipples grew turgid and instead of shrinking from Cole's questing mouth, the provocative pursuit of his tongue around the sensitive buds, Julie found herself arcing into the source of dizzying pleasure.

Her hands were restless on his chest, loving the feel of the hair-covered surface, the ridges and flatness of his stomach. Where his mouth first claimed and scorched, his large hands then soothed with gentle massaging strokes until she was so sensitized she twisted languidly against his hands and sought to come closer to the feel of his body.

Cole knew when Julie was ready, but he did not move to take his natural place between her legs. Instead he curved his body down so he could kiss her stomach, kiss her through the panties before slowly pulling them down her legs and kissing the triangle of soft, curling hair. Julie gasped out his name, her hand combing through his hair.

Cole's lips moved back up her body. His hand stroked a breast, rubbed over an already stimulated nipple. He glided over the rib cage and the barest curve of her tummy to the thatch below. Instinctively she pressed her knees together and Cole stopped.

Julie's eyes flew open and she looked at Cole. In the dark his face was just planes and shadows.

"Am I rushing you? Do I want you so badly that I'm risking everything on this moment?"

Julie sighed. She slowly pulled his head down so she could kiss him. It was her turn to give reassurance.

"If we don't risk this moment we might never know."

She relaxed her knees apart.

Slowly Cole's fingers trailed a path to the delicate open center of her, touching and slowly seeking until a roiling of sensation began to tumble inside of Julie. Like thunder. Like an impending explosion.

Her heart pounded as Cole's touch encouraged the gathering storm and she braced her hands on his chest. Her head went back and she tried to utter his name. But Cole had found the rhythm of her body, coordinated with the writhing of her hips, and she could only concentrate on a mindless need for release.

Cole leaned to kiss her, to take the remaining breath and surprise from her. The erotic rubbing of his mouth and his exploring hand drew a final labored breath of air and then there was a crash, a bursting that rocketed almost painfully through her body. The sheer bliss of it melting every nerve in her, squeezing through her pores until her skin was damp and hot.

Cole felt Julie's body responding freely, completely, and was so relieved that it was enough for him just then to pull her limp body into his arms and hold her. His right arm around the area of the wound was throbbing a little. So was his heart and other parts of him, but it had been quite a while since Cole had been happy merely to hold someone this way.

Julie's head was on his shoulder and when she could catch her breath, when she could even open her eyes, she realized that Cole had made no move to join his body to hers. No move to seek a physical satisfaction she knew he must have wanted, too. Instead he had taken the time and care to reintroduce her to the aspects of intimacy that made loving so exciting. Julie thought of all the people who had actually cared about her enough to show it.

Lois. And now Cole.

Her family wouldn't approve of either of them, but they were beyond any doubt in Julie's mind the most important people to her. And whatever lingering hesitation she might have felt about Cole, or his feelings and intentions, had vanished along with her fears in the past hour.

"Thank you."

Julie's voice was so low Cole wasn't sure he'd heard her. Then he smiled and threaded his legs with hers.

Thanks were hardly necessary. But it was the kind of thing Julie would say. It was one of the things he loved about her. And actually he should be thanking her for openly accepting him as he was, with no questions and no need for justifications. For trusting him enough to let him try and show her what love was really all about. Not taking but giving.

Cole could feel her body grow heavy and limp against him. Julie was falling asleep.

Later he would thank her, too.

Chapter Eight

Neither of them responded to the phone until it rang for the second time. Julie moved first, her arm extending from under the quilt to reach for the receiver. But a second arm, longer, stronger and faster, also extended from the covers to grab her wrist, stopping Julie.

The phone rang a third time and Cole half twisted over Julie's body to answer.

"Detective Bennett," Cole answered in an authoritative tone meant to discourage any more nonsense calls, such as the two that had come the night before. Both had been clumsy attempts to get information from Julie about her appearance at the precinct earlier in the evening. Cole made her hang up on both callers.

A third call had been from Julie's center director. But she hadn't discussed that with him.

There was a long pause before anyone responded on the line to Cole's announcement.

"I was calling to make sure Julie was all right. I guess the answer is yes?"

A slow grin lifted Cole's mouth and he looked down at Julie who lay almost under him. She was spooned into his body, her bottom snug against his stomach. Her hair was fanned out over his arm where her head rested, and her cheeks were suddenly a very attractive shade of pink.

"Yes..." Cole answered and passed the phone to Julie. Her expression showed she was reluctant to take the call. "It's Lois," Cole whispered as he gave Julie a warm, brief kiss. "Good morning," he said against her mouth as he settled down into the covers.

"Hello," Julie said into the phone, while trying to hoist herself up out of Cole's arms and keep herself covered. But he would have none of that. He pulled her back to rest against his chest with an arm round her waist.

"It's a good thing I didn't go through with my plan to come over this morning. You sound like you would have been *very* indisposed," Lois commented dryly.

"Not really, but..."

"But it would have been real bad timing. Are you okay? Am I going to have to give that man a piece of my mind? Or should I just shut up for once and mind my own business?"

"Not really, but..."

Lois laughed. "I can see you don't have much to say. Men can sometimes do that to you. I don't suppose you'll be in today?"

"No," Julie said, trying to concentrate as Cole's large warm hand made lazy stroking motions over her midriff.

"Or tomorrow?"

"Probably not."

"You got a call from Marjorie," Lois correctly guessed.

"Yes," Julie sighed. Cole rubbed his chin against her hair.

"Well, I was worried about you being alone, but I guess I don't need to be."

Julie closed her eyes as Cole's hand rose slowly to find her breast and a stiff, quivering nipple. "N...no," she said breathlessly.

Lois chuckled.

"Just promise you'll call me later."

"I will . . ."

Julie hung up the phone, and for a moment Cole stopped his sensual stroking of her and they were both still.

"She's very protective of you," Cole said, but Julie didn't look at him. She merely nodded.

"I hope she realizes that I have no intention of hurting you."

"I'm sure she does."

Cole came up on his elbow to look into Julie's flushed face. "And how about you? Do you believe it, Julie?" Cole wanted to know, aware of the slight stiffness in the way she lay. So unlike the middle of the night when she willingly cuddled against him, unafraid of letting him wrap his body around hers.

"Yes," Julie finally answered in a small, thin voice. She sat up suddenly, away from Cole, and he made no attempt to stop her, although he did frown.

Julie's hair hid her face, falling forward and preventing Cole from seeing her eyes. He wanted to pull her back into his arms because he sensed her awkwardness at waking up with him in bed next to her. Cole wanted in this moment only for Julie to be soft and satisfied, warm and still willing. He didn't want her to feel embarrassed or shy with him. Not now.

Julie made a helpless gesture with her hand. "I . . . I owe you an apology," she whispered painfully.

Cole stared at her. Was he losing her already? "What are you apologizing for?"

"For losing control last night."

Cole grinned and reached out a hand to trail it down her spine. "When? The first time or the second?" he asked caressingly.

"That's not what I mean. I think I was . . . hysterical."

Cole relaxed and lifted a brow, remembering.

For a quick moment after they'd awakened in each other's arms around midnight, Julie had panicked and struggled in his arms. For a devastating instant she was recalling the weight of another man holding her down, using a superior strength to get his way. Julie had cried in relief when she realized she was with Cole and completely safe. As for the second time...

Julie lifted her head when she heard Cole's quiet chuckle. His hand circled her and pulled her gently back down to the mattress. He kissed her throat, her jaw and chin, and laughed into her eyes as he caressed her face.

"I understand it's been a long time. But you weren't *that* hysterical," Cole countered. "As a matter of fact, I remember that last night was pretty fantastic."

He kissed her, not allowing any more protest. It was meant to silence Julie, to wipe her mind free of any doubts and second guesses. He succeeded.

It also helped in quickly restoring the memory of their middle of the night lovemaking. Cole had been slow and very careful in letting the full naked touch of his body rest against Julie. They'd finally joined together, as nature had devised, and under Cole's tutelage Julie had experienced the physical delight possible when two people care for and trust one another.

She couldn't breathe again, couldn't catch her breath. But the experience was meant to be breathtaking. Although she was bound by the arms and large body of a man, there was no show of will or force. Instead there had been murmured endearments and soothing kisses, as large, knowledgeable hands stroked her back and a strong, muscled thigh lifted to free her legs.

For a long moment she had lain in his arms, her face buried in his neck. Their chests and stomachs pressed together, the growing hardness of Cole insinuating between them, urgent and needy.

Julie's breath quickened, her hand stroking Cole's chest and then slowly, boldly, beginning to travel down. A small muscle or nerve rippled in his groin under Julie's feather touch of curiosity. Her fingers had closed around him, making Cole surge against her hand.

And then everything happened as it was supposed to. Choreographed by instinct and desire, care and meaning. Her hand caressed, and Cole's hips gyrated toward her.

As he held her, Cole had rotated the two of them slowly until Julie was on her back. He used his knee to push apart her unresisting thighs. His intent forced Julie to release him and put her hands elsewhere. Cole's hips rocked against her, drawing a surprised sensual growl from him, a deep sigh from her.

He was unerring in finding her waiting open essence. He'd slowly sheathed himself within Julie, and then half sat up drawing his knees in so that he wasn't laying his full weight on top of her. But his position left Cole's hands free to touch her, to massage a breast or her stomach, to cup her hips and lift her to him.

Cole watched her. Felt her. Listened to her sounds as the rhythmic driving of his body sought to find in Julie the aching resolution to his hunger. But he wanted her to come with him on the enchanted ride and was gratified when Julie's body movements matched his own.

With her legs resting over his, Cole began stroking the insides of her thighs with his callused palms. Julie gasped, stiffening her back, reaching for him suddenly as Cole aided her release. Her sweet clutching reaction drew on him, buried deep inside, and Cole, too, skyrocketed to the end of the journey, bending forward to cradle Julie's face and kiss her with tenderness...

The phone rang yet again, breaking their early morning kiss. Cole lifted the receiver, disconnected the call and laid the receiver next to the phone. He looked into Julie's puzzled eyes.

"They've got your number."

"Who's got my number?"

"The press," Cole said, combing his hand through his disordered hair and slouching back against the pillows.

"The press?" Julie repeated blankly, resting in the crook of Cole's arm. "How would they get my number? Why would they even want it?"

"Remember getting our picture taken last night as we left the precinct? That was a reporter. He sometimes uses slightly unethical ways of getting information, but that's what news is all about. It's how he makes a living," Cole said wryly.

"But why me?"

"Because of the hint of a kidnapping. It was enough to set him off."

"But it's not true," Julie said bewildered.

Cole rubbed her shoulder and neck. "I know it's not true. You know it's not true. Hal probably knows it's not, but doubt and scandal is what sells newspapers, Julie."

She thought silently for a moment. "Sooner or later I'm going to have to answer the phone. I don't know what else to do."

"Well, I do," Cole said, brushing a kiss against her temple. "I want you out of here. At least for a few days."

"I can't."

"Why can't you?"

"I won't be harassed out of my own home."

"Can you handle the phone ringing every five minutes? Will you be able to deal with the clever ones who manage to get into the building and find your apartment? Especially the ones who will lie to get you to say something about the case?"

Julie sat up abruptly, worried and angry. "It's not fair. They don't have the right to do that. I haven't done anything wrong."

"It doesn't matter. This isn't about fairness, Julie. They'll start asking questions at the center. They'll talk to employees. Probably find Lois..."

Julie looked at Cole, her eyes filled with indecision. "They can't do that, Cole. She'll come to my defense and get angry. I can't risk her losing her job over me. Over *this*. She has children to worry about."

Cole watched her carefully. He took hold of her hand. "Then come home with me."

"What?" She raised her brows.

"Just for a few days until some of this blows over."

Julie shook her head. "I can't."

"Are you afraid to be with me?" he asked quietly, watching her begin to blush.

"No, that's not it," she answered quietly. She could no longer imagine being afraid of Cole.

"Then what is it?"

She looked poignantly at Cole. Julie let her hand explore along his jaw, which was slightly bristled with hair growth. "I don't think I'm worth getting into trouble over, Cole. You're a policeman with a very long career. I understand if..."

"You're worth more to me than you realize. Don't worry about my reputation. It can take care of itself. And if I can't use what I am to protect the people I care about, what's the point?"

"But I can't hide forever."

"Sometimes it's okay to hide. Sometimes it's the only way to protect ourselves. Do you have anywhere else to go?"

There was home, of course, except she'd fled there for the same reasons she might have to flee now—lack of sympathy and understanding. "No." Julie shook her head.

Cole sat forward, the bed linens falling to his hips. He lifted Julie's chin so that he could see right into her eyes. "You're very good about caring for other people. Let me help you. Believe me, I'm very good at it, too."

Julie loved the protective feel of his hand against her cheek. "But what can you do?"

Cole smiled at her naïveté. "The first thing I do is get you out of here so no one bothers you or gets you upset. The second thing I do is to find Mickey's family."

Her eyes grew round in her face. "How can you? We have no information to go on. And she hasn't said a word except..."

"*Mommy* and *Julie*," Cole interrupted gently. "The report was pretty thorough. Just leave everything to me."

Julie blinked, but she found herself nodding and agreeing to Cole's command. She felt a sudden relief flow through her. She'd forgotten what it was like to depend on someone... to *have* someone to depend on. To *need* someone.

Cole smiled at Julie's expression and kissed her with lingering tenderness. It wasn't a passionate kiss, but it was one of caring and strength. His lips tugged at hers sensuously and then let go.

"It would be really nice to make love to you again. But you and I have things to do. I have some calls to make. In the meantime I want you to pack a bag of things you need to bring with you." He gave her another quick kiss and got out of the bed, striding naked to the door.

"Where are you going?" Julie frowned.

"To take a shower. Coming?" Cole asked with a grin.

Julie bit her lip and shook her head. "After you. I'll make the coffee."

"I like my idea better." He disappeared out the door.

"Cole!" Julie called out. His head and shoulder leaned back. "What... what will I do at your house?"

Just be there was the thought that went instantly through his mind, already looking forward to the experience. "Anything you want." Cole shrugged. Then he slowly returned to the bed. Reaching for Julie he easily lifted her from the tangled sheets and stood her on the floor next to him. Cole wrapped his arms loosely around her as Julie looked into his face. "There is one other thing I want to do with you."

"What is it?" Julie asked in a whisper.

Cole grinned. "Watch the sunset."

WHAT JULIE DID at Cole's house was to make herself at home. Almost as much as Cole had succeeded at her apartment. What she also did was help him prepare for an important exam in his law class. But that came much later.

First had come the shower and coffee, during which Julie changed the dressing on Cole's upper arm as he outlined his plans for the day. It included calling in a marker or two, which would give him free time to pursue the mystery of Mickey and set to rest Julie's persistent concern about the girl's situation. It would also include making sure that Julie was kept clear of nosy reporters looking for a story, even one that they might have to embellish.

After dressing once again in the clothing of the previous day, Cole had made a series of calls to people he knew in the city. Julie didn't try to decipher the cryptic jargon and subtle cutting of deals and return favors that Cole went through to get the information he wanted. She didn't understand the bargaining, or the hard no-nonsense, sometimes scathing persistence of Cole's efforts. Julie only recognized that he obviously had tremendous clout in the bureaucratic maze that operated New York's social service agencies, and he was going to use it to help her and, hopefully, the little girl. The Cole Bennett who was the cop, and the man who had loved her in the night, keeping at bay the last vestiges of a past horror, had come together in one person again.

Julie was having just as much trouble trying to decide what to pack to take with her. If she'd been going to Lois's, it wouldn't matter. Whatever she forgot she was always able to borrow from her friend. Everything from a nightgown to dental floss. But with Cole it was different. Going with him would be infinitely more personal.

She, nonetheless, absently packed a canvas tote, feeling an excitement that was hard to explain. Some of it had to do, no doubt, with the fact that for the first time in her adult independence Julie was letting a man take charge and make decisions for her. The excitement was also in knowing and trusting that Cole only had her best interests at heart. And the excitement had to do with it just being Cole. Hearing his masculine voice, which was full of assurance and strength, gently lulled Julie into a feeling of safety and care.

Cole only needed to place three calls to get enough information for what he wanted to do. The first had been to the precinct. Since he'd made one of his stakeout men the arresting officer on the homicide case, he wouldn't have to appear in court this morning for an arraignment. He wanted today and the rest of the week free.

He got it.

Next Cole found out what process the little girl was put through by the Bureau of Child Welfare when she was taken from Julie. Where was she being sheltered? The agency had no obligation to give Cole the information, but here again his intuitive understanding of not only how the system worked, but people, played in his favor.

The third call had been to a friend at one of the daily newspapers. She was someone he'd had a fling with more than ten years earlier, but they'd always remained friends. Julie had a sense that the party on the other end of the line was female, simply by the tone of Cole's voice. And she could tell by the inflections and softer manner in which Cole addressed her that their relationship might have at one time been intimate.

For a moment a wave of intense insecurity attacked Julie as she began mentally to compare herself to the unknown woman, wondering if she was more attractive, more interesting…a better lover. But the call between the woman and Cole was not really personal, and he succinctly kept to his purpose. Cole wanted his acquaintance to document any strange stories in the past week of missing or abducted kids.

After his last call, the phone in Julie's apartment began to ring. Incessantly. And it was barely nine o'clock in the morning.

Cole wouldn't let her answer it, and Julie finally realized that Cole was right. Someone, reporters or whoever, had gotten hold of her phone number and were trying to reach her. And Cole had also been right that she would not have been able to handle the sudden barrage of attention, or the sense of being pursued and trapped. Each time the phone rang it made her jump. Julie herself had only one call to make. She wanted to let Lois know she was leaving the apartment for a few days with Cole.

The second thing they'd done was to get out of the apartment and the building without being detected. The day was dull and overcast and snowing again lightly. The snow of the previous day was now slushy and impeded the flow of traffic. All of this worked in Julie and Cole's favor as people worried about their footing on the slippery ground, or bent under umbrellas held against the wind. No one paid much attention as first Cole and then Julie, her hair completely tucked under a knit winter hat, left the apartment and walked slowly to his parked car.

They drove to the precinct where Cole wanted to use the computer networking of departments to check additional information. He in essence wanted to check the same information he'd requested from his reporter contact, but through the precinct records of the past week.

Cole and Julie stepped inside the precinct and instinctively Cole felt Julie's hesitation. He didn't blame her. He took hold of her hand, and with his other, pulled off the cap so that her hair fell loose. Cole looked into her wary eyes.

"This won't take long, I promise. Will you mind being left alone for a while or would you rather wait in the car?"

"Let her wait with me. I can be trusted. And my office is warm."

Julie and Cole turned simultaneously to see Ben Bradshaw coming out of an office down the corridor. He held a cup of coffee in his hand and had a Cheshire-cat grin from ear to ear. He came to a stop in front of Julie and looked her over carefully, his grin still in place. Cole lifted a tolerant brow, while Julie only looked a little nonplussed by the big man's comment.

Ben took hold of Julie's free hand, bowing over it and kissing the back of it gallantly.

"You must be Julie Conway."

Julie glanced briefly at Cole and then back to Ben. "Yes, I am."

Ben's grin turned to a pleased friendly smile. "It's nice to meet you, Julie. I've heard some wonderful things about you."

Julie began to blush. "From . . . from Cole?" she asked surprised.

Ben raised his brows. "No. From Lois."

Cole squeezed her hand and entered the conversation. "Julie, this is Ben Bradshaw. He's from Community Affairs . . ."

Ben frowned. "Well, don't stop there. Tell her I'm also an all-around great guy!"

"Don't push it." Cole grinned dryly.

Julie smiled at the other man. "How do you know about Lois?"

Ben released her hand. "She was here yesterday waiting for you. We met and spent a little time in my office talking." Ben turned to Cole. "The sergeant said you weren't in today."

"I'm not. I just wanted to run some information through the computer." He looked down at Julie.

Ben easily read Cole's expression and stepped casually between him and Julie to take her arm. "If you don't get to the computer now you'll miss your chance until late this afternoon. Julie here can keep me company till you're through."

"Thanks, Ben." Cole nodded. And with a final quick wink of reassurance to Julie went off down the corridor with brisk strides.

"Come on in here..." Ben said graciously, leading Julie to his crowded little office and seating her in a chair opposite his desk. "It ain't much but we call it home," he teased, and Julie chuckled.

Ben then added more coffee to his cup and held up the pot to Julie. "Would you care for some? It's industrial-strength caffeine, but that's what keeps us going."

"No, thank you. I've already had two cups this morning. And I'm nervous enough as it is," she added with a self-deprecating smile.

Ben took his seat and watched Julie over the rim of his cup as he drank. "Rough night?"

Julie's eyes flew open and locked onto Ben's dark features, but his expression was bland and interested, and blushing deeply she realized he wasn't referring to the night with Cole. She shrugged.

"My phone's been ringing all morning. Cole said it was reporters."

Ben nodded. "Don't let it throw you. They'll lose interest by tomorrow, when they don't get anything."

Julie nodded and began to look around the office with curiosity. It was not attractive. Like the rest of the building it was obviously not meant to be comfortable or pleasing. But Julie wondered how Ben and Cole could work in a place that was so unwelcoming.

"Cole's office is upstairs," Ben offered. He glanced around his own space indifferently. "I'm afraid it's not much different than this. Except Cole has more books. He's a reader."

Julie was interested.

"What does a detective do?" she asked Ben suddenly.

Ben gulped the bitter coffee and grimaced. "Cole never talked to you about his work?"

Julie blinked. No, he hadn't. Other than his condition the night before with the terrible cut on his arm and, of course, the ever-present gun, she had no real idea what he did day-to-day. Yes, she knew he was a cop. But Julie also realized he was a special kind of cop...in many more ways than one.

Seeing her expression Ben pursed his mouth and fiddled with his mustache. "Probably just as well. He's a homicide detective. That means he investigates murders, deaths, killings. It means he sometimes has to deal with some pretty nasty findings, and the people who do them.

"He's good. No, he's better than good. Cole worries about people and what happens to them. That alone makes him a cut above most of us."

Ben saw the strange stillness in Julie, as the details and truth of Cole's work took hold of her.

"It's all right, now. Cole is street-smart. He knows how to take care of himself. He got a good collar last night. We owe him another tie."

Julie slowly relaxed in her chair. "Tell me about his ties."

Ben chuckled deep in his chest. "You noticed, eh?"

"I kind of like them. But it seems strange for a detective to dress so..."

"*Cool* is the word you're searching for." Ben shook his head and rolled his eyes toward the ceiling as he thought. "Let's see... He got the first one from his partners when he made detective. That was eleven years ago. We wanted to give him something that would really make him stand out, set him apart from the pack."

"You succeeded." Julie smiled.

"Then each time Cole had an arrest that went to conviction, he got another tie. The arrest he made last night will probably rate another one. Our big problem is what to get him when he finishes law school. Any suggestions?" Ben asked unexpectedly.

Julie just shook her head. "I'm afraid not." Then she looked down at her hands, seeing the dark lines of the cuts on her palms, which no longer stung but which made her hand movements stiff. She didn't want to consider that in Cole's line of work he could be seriously hurt. Or worse. He'd already been shot once. Her stomach rolled in distress.

Ben cleared his throat.

"I want you to know that Lois was really there in your corner yesterday. As a matter of fact she was fully prepared to rip my heart out, if anything had happened to you."

Julie smiled, her eyes twinkling. "That sounds like Lois. But she's a good person. A good friend."

"Everyone should have a friend like her."

"I'm afraid Lois thinks I need constant watching over against the big bad world."

Ben nodded. "I wouldn't mind having her on my side." He drank from his coffee, and cleared his throat again. "She's a very strong woman. No-nonsense."

Julie looked closely at Ben for a moment and was suddenly alert to the open question in his tone and comment. Her brows raised slightly in surprise.

"I never knew Lois's husband. She was a recent widow when we first met. She's raising her two children alone. She's also very supportive, assertive and fun to be with."

"I'll keep that in mind."

Julie tilted her head. "Are you interested?"

Ben looked off across the room and played with his mustache again. "Let's just say that she made me sit up and take notice. I like her spirit."

Julie thought silently for a moment, and then looked speculatively at Ben. "Not that you asked, but my advice is to be straightforward and honest. Lois will see right through you, otherwise."

Ben grunted. "I've already got one strike against me."

"How?"

He looked uncomfortable. "I made a bad joke at your expense. I don't think she liked it."

Julie laughed. "But she didn't rip your heart out, as you say. For whatever reason, Lois forgave you. Pass Go. Proceed with caution. Collect two hundred dollars..."

They were laughing when Cole came back to the office nearly an hour later.

"Can I get in on the joke?" he asked, giving Julie a warm, caressing look from the office doorway.

"No," Ben said bluntly. "This is between me and the pretty lady."

"Are you done?" Julie asked Cole as she stood up.

"Here, yes." He held out his hand to her. "Come on. It's going to be a long day."

"What's going on?" Ben asked as Julie joined Cole at the door.

"We're trying to find out what happened to the parents of the little girl who was brought in with Julie yesterday. Julie thinks someone will be back for her."

"Umm . . ." Ben said with a thoughtful frown.

"Do you have any ideas?" Cole asked.

Ben shrugged and pulled his bulk from the chair and stood with his hands in his pockets. "Not that come to mind. But then I haven't had lunch yet. I'll think on it."

"Nice meeting you," Julie said.

"Oh, we'll see each other again," Ben said confidently as the two left his office.

Cole and Julie did not bother with lunch. Instead they spent the better part of the afternoon checking in on Cole's contacts but without any positive results.

First was the news that Julie would not be allowed to apply through the courts for temporary custody of Mickey until the child's parents or family were located. She had to fight against tears upon hearing this news. Julie reasoned to Cole, and he had to agree with her, that if someone was to return to the center looking for the child, she would not be there and the process of reuniting her with her family would be that much more complicated. Cole tried to reassure Julie that it wouldn't come to that, but he wasn't so sure himself.

Cole had managed to learn that the little girl had been placed with a reliable and caring family. While that was somewhat comforting, Julie continued to be upset that she was not going to be allowed any contact with the little girl.

Cole's contact at the newspaper also came up with little. The few stories and rumors Cole's ex-girlfriend had been able to put together didn't work for Julie's situation. It also did not help that Hal's hastily shot picture of Cole and Julie as they were leaving the precinct the night before had made the inside pages of the metropolitan section of a rival daily. The image showed a wide-eyed, bewildered Julie walking next to a stern and weary Cole. The caption only mentioned "...Julie Conway, cleared of a kidnapping charge, as she left a police precinct accompanied by Lt. Det. Cole Bennett."

"Oh, no..." Julie groaned when the caption also clearly identified her as being an employee of Helping Hands Center.

"It's all right, Julie," Cole said to her. "It's just a filler. A throwaway item that no one will remember."

"Except perhaps the board of trustees, our sponsors and a lot of women who might become nervous about seeking our help."

Cole had no response to that, because he suspected that Julie was right.

It was cold, dark and after five when Cole put a halt to their fruitless efforts. The light snow of the morning had gotten serious and turned icy and slippery on the streets. Julie suggested that maybe she should just stay home, but rather than argue with her, Cole had driven slowly through her block allowing Julie to see, to her astonishment, that there were half a dozen men and women waiting in the wintery weather, along with a mini-cam crew, presumably for her to appear.

After that Julie had silently nodded in agreement when Cole suggested dinner before driving out to his house in Huntington. However, she remained pensive as they waited for their meal at a restaurant near Julie's apartment. Cole had hoped to distract her with suggestions as to what they would do the following day, but it hadn't worked.

For one thing, it finally occurred to Cole that this was probably the first time that Julie was spending intimate time with a man since whatever had happened to her in the past. She was reluctantly willing to go with him to his house, but she was nervous. He had been greatly encouraged spending the night with her in the apartment. Julie had been wonderfully loving and responsive to him, easing many of his own doubts. But there was much between them that had not been settled because of Julie's past. Cole had never asked her what had happened, not sure how to approach so delicate a subject. It wasn't anything he knew how to deal with, particularly now that his heart and feelings were engaged. But he wanted Julie to know and believe that it didn't matter to him.

Finally Cole had reached for her hands across the table and looked with understanding into the soft gray eyes.

"Don't try to figure it out all by yourself," he advised gently. And Cole was talking about much more than decisions about Mickey, but Julie chose to think he was talking about the child.

She smiled at Cole's concern. "I've dealt with some of the agencies in the city, Cole. They mean well, but they don't always work. Foster care still leaves a lot to be desired."

"It did okay by me," he responded smoothly, studying her face, and watching her eyes grow round with regret.

"I'm sorry. I never considered that you'd lost your family so young."

"My dad, yes. My mom was never able to take care of me, so I was placed in foster care. She died when I joined the force."

Julie looked at their clasped hands. "She cries in the night," she said, her voice low.

Cole squeezed her hand. "I know. Let's just hope that the new people she's with will understand as well as you did."

It was after eight when they got on the road to Long Island. Almost ten when they finally reached Cole's house. It was a small but attractive ranch set back from the road and surrounded by trees. At first, Julie didn't say much, feeling a sense of disorientation as she shyly followed Cole on a quick tour of his home.

One of the things that Julie could voice right away was how much she liked the house. It was a surprise. It was furnished with comfortable traditional pieces and laid out for function and convenience. But it was also cozy and surprisingly quaint. It contradicted what Julie knew so far about Cole, but it also added a dimension that she liked: that of a man who belonged somewhere.

"This is my room..." Cole said easily, pushing open a door and turning on a light. Julie looked cautiously into the room as he watched her for reaction.

The room had all the normal outfittings, including a wonderful lived-in quality with items of Cole's clothing and personal possessions laid about. A stack of books on top of a portable TV, a half-eaten pack of chocolate-chip cookies, which made Julie's mouth curve into a slight smile. The queen-size bed was neatly made, and the thought that came unbidden into Julie's mind was that it was bigger than hers, and probably a lot more comfortable.

Cole stepped out of the room and walked several feet down the hall. He opened another door and waited. Julie slowly approached.

"This is the guest room."

Julie looked into a very nice but much smaller room, which had a clear look and feel of underuse. The first thing that Julie felt was relief. There was no evidence that Cole was in the easy habit of having female companions in his home. But he had also not taken for granted that she would share a bed with him again. Last night had had a certain spontaneity and surprise to it, but he clearly understood that she would have to take one step at a time.

Whatever hesitation Julie was feeling on the ride to Cole's house now vanished as she turned to face him.

"Do I have a choice?" she asked softly.

Cole flexed his jaw muscles. "Of course."

"I want to stay with you." Then she grew nervous and seemed to regret her hasty words. "I mean…if you want me to. Otherwise I don't mind…"

"Julie…" Cole interrupted, his voice hoarse and low. He put his hand on her waist. "Yes. I want you to."

THEY WERE BOTH very still. Very quiet.

They'd sunk into a soft layer of peace and contentment and were afraid to move for fear that the mood would be broken. It was sometime after the loving, but before the sleep of having been sated. Soon enough the world would intrude into the magic, but for now there was only this extraordinary feeling that everything was perfect.

Julie let her hand glide over Cole's hair-covered chest. There was something so utterly virile and masculine about the wiry softness there, and the hair of his armpits, that Julie felt a feminine weakness and stirring within. She was aware that with Cole she had a very definite sense of her own uniqueness and frailties as a woman, a sense that Cole played on to make her feel precious and tenderly cared for.

Julie's fingers found a lump of hard flesh under his rib cage and played over it gently. She'd felt it for the first time the night before as they'd explored one another's bodies. Then, as now, Cole found her light touch erotic.

"Is this where you got shot?" Julie asked, her voice holding both awe and horror.

"Umm," Cole murmured drowsily as he stroked her hip and thigh.

Julie tilted her head against his shoulder and looked at him, but she couldn't see his features distinctly.

"What went through your mind when it happened?"

Cole thought a moment and then sighed deeply. He put a hand behind his head and his biceps tightened. He'd thought a lot of things at the time. One had been a youthful, almost macho sense of satisfaction that he had gone through a rite of passage, that he had completed some unspoken initiation. But it had also burst his bubble of ideals that, in some way, he was special because he was a cop. The truth was he didn't want to be hurt because in the long run it made no difference and few people would remember. He was not heroic, invincible or automatically right. He was as vulnerable as any other man.

Cole had not given up his work because he'd been shot. He'd not stopped being a cop even for Sharon Marie Sutton. Yet somehow he knew beyond a shadow of a doubt that he would if Julie asked him to. Perhaps it was her question and wanting to know how he'd felt. But Cole also knew beyond a doubt that Julie would never ask him to.

"Lonely," Cole answered at last. "And scared. A little bit higher or lower and my life might be different. Or I might not be here at all."

Julie's fingers deserted the scar tissue, and her hand settled on his chest again, playing idly with his male nipple. For just a moment Julie wanted to tell him about her attack. She wanted to tell Cole how she'd felt helpless and hurt, deeply humiliated and insignificant. But suddenly Julie knew it didn't matter anymore. Cole had countered all of that with the overwhelming strength of his own gentleness and understanding. And because she knew she didn't have to tell him, she loved Cole with an intensity that shook her from head to toe and made her struggle to hold back tears of relief and gratitude.

Julie considered the twists and turns and tragedies of their lives that had brought her and Cole together. She was glad that it had been Cole over the Thanksgiving holiday, along with the child, to make her life seem normal once again. Julie was especially glad that it had been Cole to gently coax her back to her own sexuality. It was awful to think that it might not have happened or would have taken longer without him.

"What happens to the force when you become a lawyer?" Julie asked quietly.

Cole hugged her to him. He brushed a kiss into her hair. "It'll still be there. I guess it will always be a part of my life. I won't have to carry a gun. My life will be more normal. Maybe people won't treat me differently..." He stroked her hip again. "Maybe I'll even find someone who'll love me just as I am."

Cole shifted his big body, leaning over Julie to kiss her with great care and lazy passion. There was a shy quality to it that was so unlike him. "Do you think that's possible?" he asked, unaware and unable to keep the hope from his question.

Julie felt warm tenderness for Cole. And a love that had, in that instant, taken a giant leap forward. Her hand stroked his hard, firm jaw, bristled and scratchy with hair. Her fingers found his well-shaped mouth and lightly explored the shape. Cole's mouth puckered into a lazy, affectionate kiss against her index finger. Julie lifted her head to kiss him back. His question made her smile in the dark.

"I think it's very possible," she whispered.

Chapter Nine

Julie stood on tiptoe and peered out the window over the kitchen sink. The yard was heavily laden with snow and the covered surfaces seemed dazzlingly white as the sun reflected off the still untouched layers.

Julie squinted against the light as she strained and contorted to try and see Cole. His car sat in the driveway, partially dug out of the snow, but still silent as Cole continued his efforts to get it going. With the car door open, he half sat in the driver's seat with one leg outside and his head bent to the wheel. He listened, in the way that men seem to do, to the internal workings and mechanics of his car.

There was a long, sputtering hesitation. The car engine strained, but finally it turned over and came to life.

"Yes!..."

Julie could hear Cole utter in triumphant relief. He'd been trying for the better part of an hour to get the car started, in temperatures that had fallen into the high teens twenty-four hours ago. And he'd been trying to do so dressed only in jeans, heavy work boots, a fleece-lined sweat top, and without coat, hat or gloves for protection against the cold.

Julie allowed herself a smile at Cole's vitality and the comfortable ease with which he went about everything. Including making her feel very much at home in his house, giving her the run of it, and not treating her any differently than when they were in her apartment. She was afraid to admit that she loved being with Cole here. Loved the total sense of home, companionship and domesticity that they were able to create together with so little effort.

Julie turned from the window and with a sigh began to industriously clean the countertops and the stove, wiping around the still plugged-in coffee maker that kept coffee warm for his return. She felt a giddy lilt of excitement flutter through her as she waited for Cole. It was the anticipation of the trust and safety she felt with him that enveloped her like a blanket made entirely of love. Julie felt unbelievable happiness.

One week.

That's all it had taken to crack the safe shell of her solitary existence.

That's all it had taken to realize what was missing in her life that would bring personal happiness for the future, forgiveness and understanding of the past.

That's all it had taken for Julie to begin to dream again. One week during which she had fallen in love.

It was with a sense of irony that Julie now recalled the caution with which she'd approached her first crush at sixteen, taking months to mull over the new emotions she'd developed for the older brother of a school friend. It had taken her nearly two years to finally agree to her engagement. And of course that experience was to teach her that caution did not always matter.

It bothered Julie only a little that it had only been one week since she'd met Cole Bennett, because on the other hand there were people she'd known all her life she couldn't trust as well.

Julie and Cole had fallen into a comfortable pattern together over the past day and a half since arriving at his home in Huntington, Long Island. Yet neither of them had to adapt. There was simply a surprising meshing, an easy blending of their individual ways. There had only been an initial shyness on Julie's part upon waking up the morning after in a strange bed.

The snow was still coming down, and the world seemed closed in and very quiet. It was the quiet that had awakened her to find Cole already gone from the bed. Julie had lain quietly in the bed, still feeling the warmth of his body, recalling how his presence in the night had made her feel protected and secure.

Finally with a lazy sensual stretch, Julie had climbed out of the bed. Then she'd heard his footsteps and his low whistle from the hall before there was time to run back for cover. Instead she'd reached frantically for a discarded T-shirt hanging on a doorknob and quickly pulled it on. Julie was still pulling it down to cover her bottom when Cole breezed into the room, big and cheerful and very nearly naked.

His hair was damp and spiked from his shower, a barely adequate towel tucked loosely around his hips.

Cole grinned when he saw the flushed color in her face. Her hair was all loose and sleep-tangled. Her mouth had a full, soft sensuality to it, slightly parted then. That had come from their lovemaking, their passionate kissing all during the night. Julie's total responsiveness was still a surprise, but he was grateful that her past experience had not stopped Julie from being so eloquently loving and willing with him.

"I think you look a lot better in my T-shirt than I do. Better than Mickey looked in yours," he teased.

"I hope you don't mind. I don't want to seem..." She stopped in confusion.

Cole arched a brow and slowly approached her. "Seem what?"

Julie shrugged, smoothing the navy blue shirt over her thighs. Her eyes searched Cole's face only to find a gentle amusement and tenderness.

"You know. Seem too...familiar. Or take anything for granted."

Cole cupped her chin and raised her face, examining her smooth features. His thumb rubbed over the rounded curve of her chin. "But I want you to be familiar. I want you to think of here as home. My house is your house. Even my T-shirts."

Julie grimaced prettily at him. "You're making fun of me again."

Cole nodded. "Yes, I am," but he tempered that with a peck of a kiss.

He looked around the room then. Their clothing was piled on a chair, some of it on the floor. Out of the mess hung a strap from Julie's bra. On the table next to the bed was her hair clip, near the dresser her shoes. It hit Cole in that instant that having Julie here made an enormous difference. He suddenly felt that his house was filled and being used the way a house should be. One person alone is not a family. With two people, with Julie, it was a start.

Cole felt an odd quake of emotion stiffen his shoulders, making him take a deep breath. He might never have met her, and never come to know this feeling of need...this sense of completeness. He smiled at her. "You belong here," he'd said simply.

Everything fell into place after that. Over a late breakfast they'd talked more about the strange circumstances of Mickey being left at the center. Julie speculated on the possibilities that would drive a mother to leave a child behind. And she spoke with a kind of innate observation that made Cole wonder if she wasn't speaking from experience.

For a moment it bothered him. He had no idea if Julie had family. If she'd ever been married...if she'd ever had children. Cole thought for a moment how he could broach the questions with her, but the timing seemed wrong and he reluctantly let it go. Everything between them was still new, still fragile. He didn't want to risk what they were enjoying now, for questions that could be answered later.

Expecting to get calls at some point during the day from his various sources, Cole suggested they not leave the house, which was fine with Julie. Instead the day was spent doing mundane household chores, which took on a surprising sense of fun because they were shared activities.

In the afternoon Cole had turned to his law books and Julie had helped him prepare for an important end-of-the-semester exam. She devised a method of prioritizing the cases and the points of law Cole needed to know. The questions she asked him made Cole sit up and take notice, because Julie seemed to have an astute understanding of the text material. Yet, when he tried to question her on her knowledge, Julie would only admit that she once worked part-time for a lawyer before rushing on to question Cole on his exam material.

The afternoon had been idyllic, the evening even better. They'd made dinner together and Julie had been impressed to find that Cole really did have culinary skills. At one point, as he carefully concocted a cream sauce for their sautéed chicken dinner, Julie could only wonder how his fiancée could ever have let him go.

But the wonderful day together, even the feelings she recognized she had for Cole, hadn't made anything easier for Julie. Cole was strong and kind. He was street-smart and energetic. He was gentle and passionate, but was Cole only feeling sorry for her? Was he just a cop, albeit a more concerned one than most? And when this unexpected adventure was all over, where would that leave them? What was she to do with her love?

Cole was having more or less the same thoughts, but with fewer of the anxieties that surrounded Julie's concerns. It had only taken twenty-four hours with Julie at his house to cement the emotions that Cole had. He had been surprised by them, and they'd had an unexpected intensity, but he wanted the feelings and he wanted Julie. He wanted her to be part of his life...

When the engine was turned off and Cole didn't immediately return to the house, curiosity forced Julie to the door. She stepped through, out to the bright morning, the cold air feeling sharp but invigorating against her. Her breath formed vaporish clouds.

Julie crossed her arms over her chest and picked her way along the snowy path until she could see the car. Cole was brushing snow from the side and rear windows. She watched him for a moment undetected, and felt a constriction in her chest. She wondered if it was at all possible that what was between them now could grow into a solid relationship. Dare she try again? It was a fantasy that she'd not had at all, not a single thought since that episode years before, until she'd met Cole Bennett.

Julie frowned slightly and tried to think what it was exactly about Cole that allowed for the changes in herself, the willingness to take a chance. She wasn't sure, but perhaps it was nothing more complicated than that he'd respected her uncertainties, her frailties. More than that, Cole had also shown Julie that she was desirable and worthy of love. That's what she wanted.

Cole suddenly looked over his shoulder and saw Julie standing against the background of the house. He blinked at the picture she made. Julie began to smile at him and his heart turned over. Just seeing her there, waiting for him, made Cole feel hopeful. Forgetting about the car, Cole turned and began walking slowly toward her. On the third step Cole's right foot flew out from under him. He lost his balance and landed backward on the ground, his fall cushioned by the thick layer of snow beneath him.

Cole was surprised and annoyed at his ignoble downfall. And then he heard the giggles from Julie. Her reaction was spontaneous and natural and he suddenly decided to play on it. Cole rolled onto his side and, grabbing the arm he'd injured, he winced and moaned.

Julie's amusement stopped and her eyes rounded with instant concern. "Cole..." His name came out on a ragged note and Julie hurried to him, slipping and nearly falling herself. She dropped to her knees beside him on the wet gravel, a hand on his back as he struggled to sit up.

"Cole, are you all right? Is it your arm?" she asked. Cole grimaced and moaned again. "Oh, Cole..." Julie's voice quivered.

The empathy that made her voice shake made Cole feel suddenly guilty. He sat still for a moment and then squinted open one eyelid to look sheepishly at Julie.

She instantly understood what was going on. She froze. But even in the frosty winter air Julie's cheeks turned to pink as she began to feel foolish. She released Cole abruptly and sat back on her heels. "You were making fun of me. I...I thought you were really hurt," she said in an accusing tone.

Cole sat looking at her expression. "It's one of the oldest tricks on record."

"I'm not used to people playing tricks on me," Julie said, and began to scramble to get to her feet.

"Julie..." Cole called as she stood. "Julie..."

When she didn't stop, Cole quickly came to his feet and started after her. She was already several yards ahead of him, headed toward the kitchen door. Julie stopped unexpectedly to gather a handful of snow. She hastily packed it tight in the cupping of her hands and, turning, hurled it straight at Cole. It caught him at the throat and neck.

Julie had almost made it to the door when Cole grabbed her arm. She tried to pull away so hard, as Cole kept his hold on her, that she pulled them both off balance and they tumbled down into the snow. She landed on her back with Cole on top. The wind was knocked out of her.

Cole grabbed her wrists and forced Julie's arms over her head. They were both breathing hard. She glared at him.

"Okay. I wasn't really hurt. But admit it. You thought it was pretty funny when I went down," he said smoothly, ignoring the twisting of her slender body under him, which was having a stimulating effect on a certain part of his anatomy.

"It...*wasn't* funny."

"It made you laugh," Cole countered. Julie bit her lip and turned her head away.

"It didn't."

"Admit it."

Julie's chest heaved. "Cole...Cole, I can't breathe."

Cole went absolutely still. All of the humor and teasing and the excitement of the moment went out of him and the grin faded when he realized exactly what he was doing. He was holding her down by force. She couldn't move. Julie was helpless.

"Oh, my God," Cole groaned.

"Let...let go of my...my arms," Julie said in a weak voice.

Cole complied at once. "Julie, I'm sorry..."

Julie's arms closed slowly around Cole's neck, preventing him from getting up. Her breathing was still labored, and her face was rosy. But when she looked into his face, her eyes were bright...and mischievous. There was also an awareness and surprise and a great deal of amusement.

Cole frowned at the instant change in her. His blue eyes scanned her face, and relief flooded through him when he didn't see any panic or hysteria. There was merely a kind of open, curious regard of him. His brow quirked up at her superior expression.

He'd been had.

"It *was* funny," Julie said softly, running her hand through the hair at his nape.

The weight of Cole's body on top of Julie relaxed and he made no more attempts to move. It didn't matter that they were lying in the snow getting very cold and very wet.

"I thought..." Cole began emotionally.

"Serves you right," Julie said.

They simply stared at one another for a moment. Cole began to smile and to shake his head in amazement. "You are deadly with a snowball for someone from Southern California."

"Beginner's luck," she whispered.

Cole's expression became tender and caressing. He put his arms under Julie's back, and pulling her tightly to him, began kissing her with an urgency that shook them both.

Everything on him was ice-cold. But his tongue plunging with passionate force into her mouth was hot with sudden desire and it quickly ignited Julie's own.

"I'm sorry..." Cole breathed against her lips, his mouth frosty but his breath warm. He hugged her close and nibbled under her jaw. "I would never hurt you, Julie. I tease you because..."

"Because I'm easy to tease. And I suppose...if you didn't care about me, you wouldn't bother," Julie supplied, her face again growing flushed with a realization that suddenly made her bold.

Slowly Cole bent his head to brush his mouth sensuously over her. His lips gently grabbed and pulled, his tongue played and was both provocative and teasing. Cole brushed back the loosened wild tendrils of blond-gold hair from her cheek and forehead. He shook his head slowly.

"I more than just care about you," he whispered simply.

Julie smiled in a peaceful and contented way. "I know," she said as Cole again began to kiss her.

Bells began to peal in the distance.

It was a long moment before either realized it was the telephone ringing. The awareness broke their kiss abruptly.

"The phone . . ." Julie said dazedly.

Cole struggled to his feet grabbing Julie's hand to pull her to her feet, then hurried back into the house. They were both still out of breath when Cole answered the phone.

"Hello."

"Hey. I was just going to hang up."

"Ben . . ." Cole said, identifying the caller for Julie. He watched her eyes widen and she clutched at his arm. Cole pulled her to his side. "What's up?"

"A whole bunch of stuff. You know I don't believe in coincidence, but I have some information that could tie together and mean something."

Cole heard the hesitation. "Go on."

"I don't want to get your hopes up *too* high, but I have a feeling I know where Mickey's mother is."

"You do?" Cole asked astonished. "How? Where?"

"Whoa. Like I said this isn't one hundred percent. But it's close. A lot of things make sense.

"Remember my report a little over a week ago? The one where some woman collapsed on the street and went into a coma?"

Cole frowned. "Sorry. It doesn't sound familiar."

"Never mind. The thing is, we found her just a few blocks from the center."

"So?" Cole prompted.

"She started to come out of the coma yesterday. She's pretty incoherent yet, but the doctors think she's asking about her child. A little girl."

Cole inadvertently squeezed Julie's shoulder. The concern on her face changed to one of fear. "Cole . . ." she began, anxious for information.

"It's okay, sweetheart," Cole crooned, stroking her back.

"*Sweetheart!*" Ben uttered in confusion.

"Not you. Julie," Cole said on a chuckle.

"Listen, why don't you and Julie come in and meet me. I'm at St. Luke's Hospital. The IC unit on the ninth floor."

"We're on our way..."

Cole hung up and turned to Julie, but he was careful in what he said to her. He didn't want Julie to expect too much yet. He caught her hands.

"Ben wants us to come into the city. St. Luke's Hospital."

"St. Luke's? Has something happened to Mickey?" Her voice was strained.

"No, no..." Cole assured her, trying to smile. "But it may have something to do with Mickey."

Julie frowned. "How?"

"I'm not really sure, but we're going to find out." Cole glanced at her clothing and then his own. He turned toward the hallway and the bedroom, pulling Julie after him. "But first we change into dry clothes..."

ON THE DRIVE in to the city Cole told Julie the scant information he'd gotten from Ben. Granted it wasn't a lot to go on and it was very circumstantial, but Cole could tell by Julie's pensiveness that she was already putting considerable store in the possibility that the unidentified woman in the hospital could be Mickey's mother. It had never occurred to Julie that one reason no one had returned for the child might be illness.

Julie found herself growing tense as they got closer to Manhattan and absolutely silent as they arrived at the hospital. Cole could only guess at what she was feeling, but he wisely didn't try to convince her of *anything* regarding the only lead they'd gotten in two days.

Cole identifying himself as a police officer was enough to get them onto the ward floor where they were met by several doctors, a nurse standing to the side awaiting instructions, and Ben Bradshaw. Ben greeted Julie with a smiling nod and shook hands with Cole.

"Thanks for calling, Ben. What do you think?" Cole asked, glancing at the two doctors.

Ben shrugged. "It's still anybody's guess." He gestured to the doctors. "They say the woman started coming out of the coma yesterday around six in the evening. She was only alert for a few moments, but she was responsive before falling asleep again."

"Has she said anything?" Julie asked.

"Not much. And it wasn't very clear. *And* they think she spoke in Spanish."

"Spanish," both Julie and Cole softly exclaimed. They exchanged surprised glances.

Ben nodded with a rueful look at Julie. "Is your little girl Spanish?"

Julie looked dumbfounded. She shook her head, her brows drawn together. "I don't know."

"The thing is, Ben, the child hasn't said anything since Julie got her."

"Well maybe that's part of the answer. If she doesn't speak English, then she wouldn't understand a thing you said to her."

"Oh, Cole..." Julie said on a thin note of acknowledgement, "I never even considered that."

Cole put his arm around her shoulder. "It still doesn't mean anything for sure."

"But it does make sense," Ben insisted.

"Ben?"

Ben turned to Julie.

"What caused the coma?"

"Diabetes. The young woman wasn't getting her insulin. Without it a person can lapse into a coma and die. Sometimes. She was pretty lucky."

Julie looked beyond Ben, beyond the doctors to the ward with only six patient beds, four of them occupied. She looked at Ben again.

"Which bed is she in?"

"The middle bed on the right wall."

Julie slowly walked to the ward door and stood silently looking in at the woman in the bed. She wasn't at all what Julie was expecting to see, but then she hadn't given much thought as to what Mickey's mother might look like.

The woman in the bed was very young, hardly more than a girl. Her hair was thick and dark. It had been tied to the side, probably by an attentive aide, in a ponytail so that it was out of the way. But with her hair so combed, Julie could clearly examine the woman's face. Julie stepped closer to the bed. The face was softly rounded with a firm little chin. Although the skin color was somewhat pale, it was smooth. She was very small in the bed. Petite, and overwhelmed by machines and tubes and monitors. As Julie watched the sleeping young woman with her rather sweet but frowning expression, Julie had the sense that she had been through a lot recently. Unbidden, Julie felt empathy and a certain affinity for the young woman.

And in her heart of hearts Julie knew she was looking into a more grown-up version of the little girl she'd cared for for more than a week ...

Cole and Ben silently watched as Julie left them and stood in the ward door watching the sleeping woman. Cole made a move to join her, but Ben put a restraining hand on his arm.

"Let her alone for a while."

Cole didn't question Ben's advice. And in truth Cole felt Julie was going through something at the moment, something to do with the woman and possibly Mickey, that he didn't quite understand. He turned back to Ben.

"What happens now? Do we just wait until she comes around again and try to question her?" Cole asked. His gaze returned to Julie.

"We could. But I think I can get the doctors to agree to something with a little more guarantee, and it would take less time." As he spoke, Ben signaled for the two doctors and introduced them to Cole.

"Do you know anything else about her?" Cole asked the older of the two doctors, a graying woman in her fifties.

"Well, she's probably not from New York. As a matter of fact her clothing leads me to believe she may not have been here very long. She had nothing really suited for this season."

"Officer Bradshaw says you think she's Hispanic."

The doctor nodded. "Maybe. We could only make out a word or two of what she's been trying to say. Spanish may be her primary language. She may be bilingual. We just don't know yet. She had no ID when she was brought in."

"When was that?"

"The Wednesday before Thanksgiving," the second doctor answered, referring to a metallic clipboard of charts and data. "We were more concerned with stabilizing her than with finding out her identity. It was only a few days ago that we notified authorities we had an unidentified coma patient here. There was a small item about it on the eleven o'clock news last night."

Cole pushed his hands into his jacket pockets and again glanced toward Julie, his eyes sparkling with a pleasant memory. They had been otherwise engaged at that hour.

"Officer Bradshaw has explained your problem and investigation. We don't think there's any harm in bringing the child in."

Cole looked sharply at Ben.

Ben shrugged again. "It seemed the quickest thing to do. If that woman is the child's mother, she'll let us know one way or another."

One of the doctors nodded in the direction of the silently waiting nurse. "Nurse Morales will act as translator if needed."

Julie slipped quietly back to Cole's side. He looked at her to try and see her response, if any, to the unconscious woman. But Cole could tell nothing. Julie's smile of reassurance was tight, and her face seemed pale and drawn. In front of the doctors and Ben, Cole was more circumspect with her than he really wanted to be. He could certainly at least sense that there were a lot of emotions at play within her at the moment.

"I've arranged for Mickey to be brought here," Ben informed Julie. She only nodded silently. Ben looked at his watch. "She should be arriving with her foster parents any minute now."

"I have other patients to see. The nurse will let me know if you need me," the doctor said as she and the resident walked away.

The three remaining adults stood in awkward silence. Ben cleared his throat.

"Well, with any luck if this works, Julie, your little mystery guest will be reunited with her mother."

Julie winced. "I know. I'm sure she'll be very happy when this is all over."

"I guess you will be, too," Ben added.

Cole put his hand on Julie's shoulder and squeezed gently. He suddenly had no adequate words to say to her. Suddenly he couldn't read into her body language or her quiet, withdrawn state. Cole didn't think this should have been so hard for her.

"I think I'll wait by the elevator," Ben said striding away and leaving Cole and Julie alone.

"Julie . . . are you okay?" Cole asked gently.

"I'm fine." She laughed nervously.

But Cole was not convinced. He cupped his large hand around the back of her neck and looked into her eyes. "I guess you were right. It looks like Mickey wasn't abandoned. Your maternal instincts were right on target."

Julie raised bright eyes to Cole, and he was surprised to see the glimmer of tears. But before he could question it, they heard Ben's deep voice from behind them.

Julie jumped and inadvertently grabbed hold of the sleeve of Cole's jacket. Ben was approaching with a couple . . . and Mickey. When the little girl saw Julie and Cole she hesitated. But suddenly her eyes brightened and she started running forward.

"Julie . . ." her childish voice lilted out happily and clearly.

Julie caught the little girl against her. She bit down on her lip and bowed her head over the child, which effectively hid the deeper emotions she was feeling. Again her laugh was nervous as she petted the little girl.

"So, you can talk after all . . ."

Cole squatted down on his haunches. "Hello, Mickey." The child peeked under Julie's arm at him and slowly separated herself from Julie to hug Cole.

Cole had not expected such open affection and was surprised when the child placed her small thin arms around his neck. Cole stood up, holding the little girl in his arms. He looked at Julie and he suddenly knew a little of what she might have been feeling. He knew a fleeting sense of longing and regret at not having had children of his own.

The nurse quickly summoned the doctor. Ben huddled with the doctor and the foster parents for just a moment before beckoning Cole to bring Mickey closer to the ward. The little girl had no idea what was going on, although a look of shyness and uncertainty made her cling to Cole as she was carried forward. The child looked over Cole's shoulder to Julie.

Julie smiled. "It's okay. Go on," she urged softly, knowing the child would understand, even if the words held no meaning.

The small entourage went into the ward quietly. Except for Julie who stood alone in the hallway.

The child looked at the woman in the bed. There was curiosity in her face, but she was otherwise so still that Cole and Ben exchanged looks that said they'd guessed wrong.

"Mommy..." suddenly came the small voice.

There was no mistaking the word or the meaning. Cole put the child on the floor and stood back as she hurried to the bed, calling the name again.

It was Ben who looked behind at Julie, saw the almost painful anticipation in her wide-eyed stare. He gave her a thumbs up sign.

COLE WANDERED RESTLESSLY around the living room. Julie's living room. It was almost seven o'clock and already dark outside. An odd quiet, reminding Cole of the kind of anticipation that comes with bad news, seemed to hang in the air.

He'd tried to persuade Julie that tomorrow, or even the day after that, was soon enough to do what she'd insisted on doing now—gathering Mickey's meager things together for transfer to her temporary foster home. The child would be with the couple until her mother was fully recovered and a permanent home and other assistance could be found for them both.

It was Julie who'd suggested Helping Hands as the place to go. Right back to where the mystery of Lucia and Dominica Valez first began.

Dominica. Not Mickey.

Domy...

Tanya and Darren had been right. They had somehow
found out the child's real name. They had somehow managed to communicate on a simple level beyond the understanding of adults. But it would be the adults who would
figure out that Dominica and her mother were illegal aliens
in the country, refugees from the horror of their embattled
Central American home. They were running to safety and
freedom. Julie understood that.

The search was over. The mystery was solved. Cole would
have preferred taking Julie back to Huntington. But he
sensed for some reason finding the little girl's mother and
reuniting them had not ended Julie's emotional involvement. Something else sat on the edge of Julie's feelings,
something that hadn't been spoken or expressed yet.

Cole stopped his pacing. It was so quiet. And it bothered
him. He suddenly felt that he had to get Julie out of there.
He went to the bedroom.

She was still folding small items of clothing, smoothing a
sleeve or a skirt with loving touches. Too loving. A muscle
tightened in Cole's jaw. She hadn't said much of anything
most of the day. Not since the call had come in from Ben
and they'd left for Manhattan and the hospital. Not since
Mickey . . . Domy . . . had recognized her mother.

Julie folded the Mickey Mouse T-shirt the child had been
wearing that first night, and placed it into a shopping bag,
already half-filled with clothing. She sensed Cole standing
in the bedroom doorway, but she didn't turn around.

"I'll take these over tomorrow. She might need them. You
never can tell. And children grow so fast . . ."

She was mumbling. She was talking for the sake of talking and there was this enormous knot in her chest slowly
making its way to her throat and threatening to squeeze it
closed.

"Julie . . ." Cole began, quietly stepping into the room.

"I should put in some of the toys. Maybe a book. She'll learn English very quickly." She hesitated as she lifted the Annie-Fannie doll, staring at one end before flipping it to the other. "Wasn't it wonderful that there was nothing wrong with her? I'll have to learn Spanish..."

"Julie..." Cole tried again. He simultaneously took the doll from her hands and turned Julie to face him. "Leave that stuff for now. I'll help you pack up later. Tomorrow. Or maybe the weekend. There's no rush. Right now I just want you to look at me and listen."

Julie looked up obediently, mechanically, but her eyes settled on Cole's chin.

"Remember that you always believed Mickey's mother would be found? Even when I wasn't sure, you never doubted."

"Her name is Dominica," Julie said tonelessly.

Cole pulled her a little closer. "She's always going to be Mickey to you. And remember that she was lucky to have you. You cared about her and...you loved her. You were the next best thing to her own mother."

Julie's eyes closed and a look of anguish began to twist her features. "Oh, Cole..." she said on a croaking note.

He pulled her into his arms, pressing Julie's face against his chest. "I know it's hard to see her go. Look. Don't give up everything. Keep some of it. Keep the doll," Cole suggested.

"What for?" Julie whispered, her voice quivering.

Cole smiled and kissed the top of her head. He rubbed the back of her neck. "You might need it later. For your own children."

Julie was very still for a moment. And then Cole heard the deep sob, the shudder in her body as she began to cry with an emotional depth that shocked him.

"Julie. Sweetheart..." he tried, but knew he didn't begin to penetrate her despair. It was unbelievably painful to listen to, and Cole began to feel as if he was absorbing it within himself. He hurt for her.

"I . . . I lost my . . . baby," Julie got out.

Cole stroked her back. "But she wasn't your baby. Mickey belongs to someone else."

Julie pulled her head back and shook it vigorously. Her face was streaked with tears. "*My* baby. I lost my baby, Cole."

Cole blinked in confusion. He stared at her. Then he understood. He swallowed hard and pulled Julie back to him, letting her weep from the heart. "Sweetheart . . ." he moaned.

He didn't try to say any more. The words that would have been right in a moment like this wouldn't have been right. Because when you put loss into words it doesn't mean as much. Cole couldn't deny what Julie was feeling or going through.

They both just shared it.

Chapter Ten

"All right. The food is ready. Who wants hot dogs and cream soda?" Ben asked from the doorway of the office.

"Me!" Darren said, looking up from a model of the space shuttle he was putting together. The pieces were all over the office floor.

"I do, I do," Tanya piped in, dropping her fistful of crayons and abandoning the colorful picture she was filling in. She wiggled and Cole lifted her from his lap and set the girl on her feet.

Ben looked at the children's mother to see her reaction. Lois was sitting in a chair opposite his desk, behind which was seated Cole. Her children had, in the meantime, run and each taken hold of Ben's hands, waiting to be escorted to the promised feast.

Standing between the two eager youngsters, Ben seemed to Lois tall and stalwart, dependable... and gentle. Nonetheless she sighed dramatically in mild exasperation and shook her head in defeat.

"Hot dogs and cream soda. Junk food."

Ben shrugged and smiled agreeably. "It's not supposed to be healthy, just fun. It's a party for kids."

"Please, Mommy," Darren coaxed.

"Please, Mommy," Tanya repeated with equal charm.

"Okay, okay. But only one hot dog each..."

The warning was lost in the ensuing squeals of delight. Ben grinned at Lois.

"Don't worry. We'll bring something back for you," he said wickedly and departed the Community Affairs office with the two excited children in tow.

In the hall and throughout much of the building were the sounds of children's voices, the sound of helium being pressed into colorful balloons, the exaggerated cheerfulness of a clown entertaining in another room, and the "Ho, Ho, Ho..." of a red-garbed Santa Claus, all clearly signaling the annual children's holiday party at the precinct.

Lois shook her head again and smiled at Cole. "I want to thank you. It was real nice of you to invite the kids to the party."

Cole returned the smile, but shook his head. "I didn't invite them. Ben did. It was only my idea."

Lois looked taken aback. "Oh..." she said surprised.

Cole continued to smile at Lois's expression. "It was the only way he could think of to see you again," Cole added openly.

Lois didn't look impressed. "He managed just fine two weeks ago, before he'd even met my kids."

Cole waited.

"He called and then came over to my house with a very lame excuse about wanting information on where Julie and I work. He said it was just to finish up the report about Julie's involvement with that little girl."

For a moment Lois saw a flicker of sadness flash across Cole's face. He idly picked up one of Tanya's crayons from the desk and examined it as if it was a vital piece of evidence. Then he gave her a brief grin.

"You're right. It was a lame excuse. Besides, writing the report wasn't his responsibility. So what do you suppose it all means?"

Lois grimaced and shifted in her chair. "I know what it means," she said dryly.

Cole tilted his head. "But you're not interested."

Lois hesitated, her features expressing uncertainty and doubt. "The kids seem to like him a lot. They took to him right away." Lois looked at Cole. "The way they took to you. I know you think I'm giving him a hard time, but . . . maybe I'm not ready for . . ." Lois let the sentence hang.

Cole looked down at the crayon he held and twisted it back and forth between his fingers. "Why not?"

Lois was silent for a moment and then she sighed, more deeply this time. "My first husband, Raymond, was a good man. He was kind and reliable and honest. And he worked hard. When he was killed, I just knew that was it. I was going to spend my life alone. Raise my kids alone. I didn't mind so much. I didn't believe there was going to be another man like Ray in my lifetime."

Cole looked at her carefully. "There won't be," he confirmed gently.

Lois understood. "I know. But Ben comes close," she admitted quietly. "I lost Ray. Then I lost Tanya's twin sister when they were born."

Cole looked sad again. "I know."

"Julie told you?" Lois asked. Cole merely nodded. "Then you know about . . ."

Cole looked up and caught her gaze. "Yes." He hesitated. "Lois, have you heard from her?"

Lois knew from the question that Cole had not. She knew it bothered him that he had not. She was not concerned. She wanted to smile and sigh in relief and utter *thank goodness* because it was so clear that Cole Bennett was in love with her friend Julie Conway. It was certainly what Julie needed.

Lois would guess that Cole now knew quite a bit about Julie's background. But oddly Lois also suspected it wasn't the physical and emotional trauma that Julie had suffered that caused him any doubt. It was probably the knowledge that she came from wealthy circumstances, that she was the stepdaughter of an influential state senator, that Julie was well traveled and educated at superior schools, even holding an MBA from Stanford University.

The Julie they both knew was much more down-to-earth and vulnerable than the facts indicated. But the facts had shaken Cole's confidence in their relationship. Julie was out of his league in more ways than he could count.

"No, I haven't heard from Julie. She'll call me the minute she gets back," Lois answered.

"Will she come back?" Cole asked. There was no bitterness or sorrow, just a kind of fatalism adopted probably from his training and line of work, and probably also due to his own unstable upbringing, which told Cole he could never really be sure of anything.

Lois nodded. "She'll be back."

"She has family there. Her mother. There's not much reason to return to New York. Why would she? What can New York offer her?" Cole asked bluntly.

"Maybe New York holds Julie's happiness. She's never wanted to go back to California."

Cole tossed the crayon back onto the desk and ran his hand through his blond and gray hair. Julie *had* gone back, nonetheless.

Lois thought for a long moment as she watched Cole. She didn't want to interfere in anyone's business. But she cared what happened to Julie because despite their backgrounds they weren't so very different. It was true that Julie had grown up with many things many people would kill for, but none of it had given her happiness or peace of mind. Julie still struggled to make her own happiness, just like everyone else. But Lois was not above stacking the cards in her friend's favor. She settled back in her chair and smiled at Cole.

"Look, let me tell you something. Since I've known Julie she's had exactly three dates, if you want to call them that. She went to a fund-raiser for the center once with a lawyer who represents us. He's close to sixty and his wife was baby-sitting grandchildren at the time and couldn't attend."

Cole raised his brows, but he was listening.

"The brother of one of our staff counselors invited Julie to see an off-Broadway play he'd produced. But he's gay. And then once Julie went to the circus as a specially planned outing for elementary-school kids. Darren asked her to take him."

Cole arched a brow and grinned sheepishly. He reluctantly admitted to himself that Lois's information helped. A little.

"So there's a guy who's way too old, one way too young, and one with a different agenda altogether. Julie hasn't exactly made herself available to the opposite sex, Cole, but you've managed to get next to her in just one week. I know Julie, and I know that counts for a lot," Lois finished sagely.

Cole wanted to believe that. Julie had been gone three weeks. That was two weeks longer than he'd known her, and he couldn't remember the last time he'd felt so lonely, so displaced. Cole rubbed absently at the arm that he'd injured during the arrest of Rodrigo Santiago. The one he'd reinjured just last week. He could feel Julie's cool, capable hands as she'd first seen to the bad cut. He needed her cool touch now.

Finding Mickey's mother had only solved the mystery surrounding the child. Cole was to find out there were unexpected ones involving Julie. For instance, learning that Julie had lost a child of her own had left him stricken with silence. How do you say you're sorry? It had been a kick to the gut to learn the baby had been the result of her rape. It had left Cole livid with rage to know the attacker had been her fiancé.

Cole remembered how Julie had sobbed out the story, and helplessly all he could do was hold her and whisper her name and his love over and over. Even now the memories made Cole's insides twist, made him ache just to hold her again. He'd told her that it was okay because she would have more babies. But it was another instant before the implications fully occurred to Cole himself. Who would be the father of her babies? No answer had come forward for the unasked question.

There had never been a real moment to talk about their relationship and what they were to each other. Their mutual feelings had not yet defined their future, and Julie's sudden departure from New York had put everything on hold.

When the call had come in from California, Cole learned that Julie had not been home or had contact with her mother or stepfather in more than seven years. And Julie herself hadn't known that her stepfather had died two years earlier, leaving her mother alone again.

"Why did she leave California in the first place?" Cole asked Lois smoothly, and saw Lois carefully consider her response.

"After what happened to her, there wasn't anyone who would help her. No one who understood. Julie had to deal with all that stuff by herself."

Cole nodded. "Everyone blamed the victim," he said tersely. "Then why did she go back?"

"Because her mother needed her to. And because I think Julie needed to, also."

"And what if our picture hadn't made the West Coast papers?"

"It would have just taken a little longer for this to happen. The past hasn't finished with her yet. When it does, Cole, she'll come back," Lois said simply.

Cole flexed his jaw but didn't respond. He couldn't admit to Lois that he hoped she was right. It had been so long since he'd really hoped for anything for himself. Julie still wasn't his. Maybe she couldn't be until she'd closed the chapter in her life labeled The Past.

"Have you gotten over the past, too?" Cole asked Lois.

She seemed surprised by the question and then chuckled. "Oh, yeah. My husband isn't coming back, so it's just me and the kids."

Cole looked at her. "What about Ben?"

Again Lois was nonplussed.

Then there was the sound of two childish voices in the hall and quickly two small bodies burst into the room and Ben appeared quietly in the background. He carried a hot dog wrapped in a napkin and a paper cup of cream soda.

"Look what I got!" Darren exclaimed, rushing to his mother to show her the shiny police badge pinned to his shirt.

"Me, too," Tanya said, going to Cole and lifting her arms out to him. Cole picked her up and sat her once again on his lap.

"How nice," Lois said quietly, casting a sly glance at the watchful man in the doorway.

"Ben said we could have a ride in one of the squad cars one day. Can we?" Darren asked as his mother rubbed dried mustard from his cheek.

Lois looked at her son's eager face. She looked at Cole, who merely tilted his head and bounced Tanya playfully, making her giggle. Lois looked once again at Ben and slowly she smiled, reaching to take the hot dog and soda from him.

"That's very nice of Ben," she said and smiled.

JULIE STEPPED OUT OF the courtroom and walked to a bench halfway down the marbled corridor. Her face was a little pale; three weeks in Southern California hadn't changed that. There were faint smudges under her eyes because she hadn't been sleeping well. But Julie knew that that would end now. In fact, everything was finished. She sat on the bench and with a tired sigh realized that she could now return to New York, and back to Cole.

Julie looked at the closed courtroom door. It had taken more than seven years, but justice was about to be served at last. Julie had not even considered that when she'd been asked to fly to California she'd also be asked to give testimony in a rape case against the man she once would have married.

Right now, however, her immediate thoughts were that she wanted to go home. The last of the tension drained out of her and she sat quietly and alone reflecting on the past few weeks. Julie was sorry she hadn't known of her stepfather's death. Not so much for herself as for her mother, who needed someone to depend on, someone to take care of her. That single revelation had answered a hundred questions for Julie about her childhood and her relationship to her mother.

It was seeing her mother again, after seven years, that the doubts had been cleared up as to whether her mother really loved her as a daughter. Cynthia Conway Gardner *did* love her daughter, but she was like a child herself in many ways, needing a lot of care and tolerance. Her husband had been willing to cater to her helplessness, but Julie had been left to fend for herself emotionally.

Martin Gardner might be gone but when Julie arrived in California she found that there was already someone waiting to take his place in her mother's life. Brian Whitaker was fifty-five, handsome and wealthy. He was a private developer who owned real estate in five states, and he wanted to make Julie's mother Cynthia Conway Gardner Whitaker.

As if that wasn't enough of a surprise for Julie, there was the news that her former fiancé was going on trial for charges of sexual assault. The prosecutor was sure of at least one infallible testimony. Her own. It had taken three days for Julie's mother to admit to an ulterior motive for calling her daughter home. But, then, Julie had her own reasons for consenting.

Julie and her mother had strolled out to the patio, beyond the solarium and outdoor pool, to a garden tastefully organized and cared for. In the golden glow of a late afternoon Julie could observe that her mother had changed little in seven years. She was still a strikingly pretty woman at fifty, still slender and well-dressed. She had a sweet vulnerability that two men had already found irresistible and to which a third was about to succumb. Julie noticed that the girlishness was gone, the desperate need which had made her mother seem so nervous and flighty when she was growing up.

The two women sat in cushioned lawn chairs, Julie sitting openly in the fading heat and glow of the sun, her mother protected beneath an awning. Cynthia Gardner leaned over to study her daughter with an open, appraising stare and smile.

"You are very pretty. Thank goodness you inherited your father's best features." She chuckled softly. "It feels very strange to have a grown daughter. I've often felt like I was too young to be a mother."

Julie shrugged easily. She could forgive her mother many things since she'd lived on her own and taken control of her own life. "Mother, you're very beautiful. There certainly have been enough people who were happy to tell you so."

Her mother raised her brows and shook her head wistfully, her still blond hair short and permed into an attractive hairdo. "It's a good thing. I had nothing else to offer. I wasn't smart or strong like you are." Her voice trailed off onto a sad note. "I . . . I couldn't have survived what you went through."

The comment surprised Julie and she stared at the woman sitting opposite her, whose love she'd never been sure of, only to see now it was because her mother had been so unsure of herself. Julie stared off across the yard, not sure how to respond.

"Julie? I am sorry. I just didn't know what to do for you or what to say. And Martin thought it best at the time not to do anything or create a fuss."

Julie shook her head, dumbfounded that her mother would believe doing nothing was acceptable. "I would have liked you to have at least listened to me. I needed you to believe I'd been hurt. Martin did what he thought was best for Senator Martin Gardner, not for a stepdaughter whose presence he'd always resented. About the best thing that can be said about him was that he truly loved you."

"He tried, Julie. I know he made mistakes, but he was really a good man," Cynthia defended him.

Julie could only stare at her mother's obvious loyalty, and she felt helpless. But she no longer felt any anger or rancor. There was no longer any point in holding on to it. She could see by her mother's confused expression that she had only done what she was capable of doing. For better or worse, that's all it had been.

Julie reached to take her mother's hand, surprised at how fragile and cool it was, how it trembled. Julie looked into her mother's eyes. "It's all right, Mother. It's over."

Her mother squeezed her hand. "Maybe it's not too late to . . . to make things right."

Julie smiled at her mother's innocence. "There's nothing to make better. I've gone on with my life."

Cynthia Gardner gave her daughter a hesitant stare. "Why did you leave like that? Why haven't you wanted to talk to me in all these years? I wouldn't even have known you were alive except for those letters once or twice a year."

Julie blushed. The answer had seemed so obvious seven years ago when she was a younger woman. Now it seemed less clear. Had time healed the raw wounds? "I didn't feel I had a place here in your life with Martin Gardner. I felt too much that I wasn't his daughter, and you were too much his wife. There was nothing here for me. Especially after what happened."

Her mother looked uncomfortable. "It was my fault..."

Julie smiled softly. "No, Mother. It wasn't anyone's fault. It just was. And I'm not angry with you."

Julie could see the relief in her mother's face. Cynthia smiled with a wistful sigh, as she regarded her daughter.

"Even as a small girl you never called me Mommy," she said quietly.

It was too late for such terms of endearment.

"Tell me about the child. The little girl that the papers said you found."

Julie took a deep breath, grateful for the subject change. She told about her adventure. Her mention of Cole was only incidental to the story, and Julie kept all personal details of their relationship to herself. Her description of Mickey... Dominica...was laced with gentle amusement, affection and a heartbreaking sense of loss. Her experience with the little girl was a dear one. One which had softened Julie but left both an aching memory and a yearning.

The two women were quiet for a moment until Cynthia suddenly blurted out, "He's done it again. Twice, this time. He's been arrested, Julie, and there's to be a trial."

Julie's stomach churned. She knew who "he" was. But the news gave her no satisfaction. She felt as if time had stopped, and when it started again Julie realized that her life was no longer tied to the past or what had happened.

"I thought you might agree to testify."

Julie shook her head. "They don't need me."

Cynthia Gardner shook her head, too. "But this isn't about him. This is for you," she said with insight, persuading her daughter to tidy up all the loose ends before she returned to New York....

Julie heard the court door open and she jumped. She saw her mother signaling to her and she got up to retrace her steps to the courtroom.

"They're back," her mother whispered, "the jury has reached a decision."

"No."

Cynthia stared at Julie blankly. "No?"

"I'm not going in," Julie said.

"But, don't you want to know?"

"Why?"

"Well, don't you think it's important?"

Julie shook her head. "Not to me. It was only important that I face what had happened squarely and be done with it." She smiled at her mother. "I owe you thanks for that, Mother. And for helping me make another decision."

"You're going back to New York, aren't you?"

Julie nodded. "There's someone there. A man I'm in love with. I have to go back to let him know."

JULIE WAS SO ANXIOUS to get back to New York she took the red-eye flight, leaving California at nearly midnight rather than wait for another day. She gave up reasonable comfort in exchange for time and speed, and still the flight seemed to last forever. Sleep was impossible because nervous tension pumped her adrenaline and her imagination shifted into high gear. She wanted Cole. She needed him.

Julie recalled in vivid detail the last time they'd made love. It had begun the night before she was to leave for California and had continued until an hour before she'd caught her taxi to the airport. There had been no frenzy in the way they'd loved each other. Instead, their passion had been poignantly tender, with a languid spirit and heat that had kept them helpless with desire. They had communicated in the most basic, elemental way... as intimately as possible. Cole had known just how to stoke the heat of desire until Julie was sure they would melt and meld together as one.

In the droning hum of the plane engines Julie could imagine she detected the repetitive moans and the deep sighs of delight that Cole had elicited from her. He had taken a tantalizing pleasure in the way she'd responded to his gentle hands and fingers, to his lazy, erotic kisses. A churning, nearly painful throb reverberated through Julie at the almost physical recall of the way Cole suckled at her breasts, his tongue bathing the pale peaks until they were sensitive and turgid.

She had gotten used to the weight of Cole on her, loved the way he nestled between her thighs with his hairy chest cushioned against her as the hair tickled her skin. She loved the way his muscular legs controlled his in-and-out movements, directing her own and maintaining the rhythmic rocking that ended in explosions of sheer mindless bliss.

Julie felt a swirl of abdominal tightening and desire ripple along her nerve ends. She'd especially come to love the throbbing manliness of Cole sheathed within her body, and he'd taught her to fully appreciate all the many sides of love. But Julie also recognized all that night and the next morning, Cole had loved her with a deliberate slow purposefulness, as if it was going to be the last time.

It wasn't. It *couldn't* be.

That's why she had to get home as fast as she could.

The wait for her luggage was interminable, and it was already seven-thirty in the morning when Julie climbed into a cab for the ride to Manhattan. All of the night-long anticipation, the lack of sleep began to play on Julie's nerves. Her heart began to palpitate with a rush, knowing that she was getting closer to seeing Cole again. She wondered where he would be. Huntington? The precinct? Away elsewhere...

The cab was on the approach to the Queens Midtown Tunnel when Julie noticed the inordinate number of police cars, vans and dark unmarked vehicles in some sort of irregular caravan. Julie sat up, suddenly alert, her heartbeat picking up speed. There were police everywhere, all around her. And they all seemed to be dressed in ceremonial blue. The way they dressed for official events, presentations and parades, visiting dignitaries...funerals for one of their own.

Julie clutched at the seat in front. Her throat went dry and she felt a wave of heat and panic grab at her insides. *No, no, no...* she kept saying over and over to herself.

"What's going on?" she asked the driver. "Why are there so many policemen?"

"There's services today for a dead cop," he said bluntly.

"Do you remember the name?" she asked.

"Sorry." The driver shook his head with indifference.

Julie sat back after that. She didn't have the strength to ask any more questions. She wasn't sure she wanted the answers. Instead of having the cab take her home, however, she gave him the location for Cole's precinct. If something had happened to him Julie wanted to know at once.

Again there were police vans and uniformed officers gathered around the precinct. No one paid much attention as her cab pulled up in front of the building, and Julie instructed the driver to wait.

"Look, lady. I got a livin' to make..."

"Please! This is an emergency. It will only take a few minutes..." That was all the time she would need to find out if Cole was all right.

"The meter is still on..." the driver warned as Julie got out of the cab. She couldn't have cared less what the fare was going to cost. It was going to cost her much much more if anything had happened to Cole.

Julie made her way into the building, her heart beating painfully in her chest. She looked at every man wearing a uniform who had blond and gray hair, who was tall and broad-shouldered, because she was afraid to ask where Det. Cole Bennett was.

Julie headed toward the Community Affairs office, whose doors stood open. It was the only office she clearly remembered from previous visits. Maybe Ben was there. Maybe Ben...

"Julie?"

Julie stopped in her tracks at the voice. It was deep and clear and familiar and alive. She turned around and there stood Cole. Julie just stared and blinked and tried to breathe again. He was okay.

Cole was in full uniform, complete with white gloves, and holding his blue hat. He was extremely handsome in uniform and Julie was suddenly overwhelmed with love for him. She tried to smile. She felt more like crying.

Cole stepped forward and taking hold of Julie's arm led her through the open office door and closed it behind them. Then he released her and stood looking at Julie. He couldn't believe it. She was suddenly there, just like that. Just when he was beginning to believe he'd never see her again. Cole's eyes drank in the sight of her, yet noticing that there were some differences. There was a new serenity about Julie, and it showed in the way she looked at him. Her eyes were bright and completely focused on him.

Julie was afraid to say anything. She was so glad to see him in one piece it was all she could do not to fall apart.

"You're back," Cole said somewhat flatly.

"I... I just got here. My bags are still in the cab outside."

It was not lost on Cole that Julie had apparently come to the precinct first, before even going home. Had she been looking for him?

"Where are you going?" he asked.

He seemed careful, almost remote, and Julie felt her spirits crash. Perhaps it had not been a good idea to maintain total silence with him while she'd been in California. Maybe this meeting wouldn't be so painful if he'd been assured all along that she loved him with all her heart. But why didn't Cole just take her into his arms and hold her? Why didn't she just rush to him and say, "I love you?"

"To the apartment. But, I thought...I heard that..." Her voice cracked. All the fear that she'd felt on the way into the city began to catch up to Julie, but Cole was not making it any easier for her.

That was only because Cole had decided he was in love with Julie Conway and she'd been thousands of miles away, and he didn't know if he was going to have a chance again to tell her he loved her. If he had to live with that, he could only do it by not giving in to his need and desires now.

"Are you going to stay?" Cole asked simply.

"Yes." Julie nodded, watching him.

"What about Southern California?"

Julie shrugged. "You can't go home again. Someone famous once said so. But I never had any plans to stay there anyway."

Cole began to relax. He looked down at his hat and seemed uncertain all at once. "Do I still have a chance, Julie?" he asked with startling openness.

"Do I?" she asked softly.

Cole looked at her again. She could see her name forming on his lips and didn't wait any longer. Julie walked to him, and let Cole's strong arms crush her to his chest. Their words and endearments and emotions all tumbled together.

"Cole, I was so afraid. I saw all the uniforms and I thought..."

He was whispering reassurances, trying to get Julie to stop shaking, denying the run of her thoughts. "No, no. I'm fine. A state trooper was killed in New Jersey. A show of the New York force is going over this morning for services. I'm fine, Julie. God, I feel even better now that you're here," he admitted in a low growl, kissing her face, touching her.

"Are you sure?" she questioned.

He nodded, his gaze roaming over her face. "I missed you. I love you. I think I hurt my arm again."

Julie's eyes shimmered in tears, but she laughed lightly. "In that order?"

Cole shook his head. "Not necessarily. But the first order of business is..." He bent his head to kiss Julie with great hunger and need.

His uniform jacket was stiff and rough and smelled faintly of mothballs. But it was so satisfying to be in his arms again. Cole reluctantly released Julie's mouth, only to capture it again briefly before gently pushing her away.

"I have to go. I love you..."

Julie smiled. "Are you just teasing me again?" she asked softly.

Cole's jaw flexed and his eyes were intense with longing. "Not about this. Go to the apartment. I'll be back in a few hours."

"Yes..." she readily agreed.

"We're going to love each other."

"Yes," she repeated as he backed out of the door. He suddenly stopped.

"Then we're going to plan our future together."

"Yes." She waved as a tear rolled down her cheek. She watched Cole put his hat on and turn to join the other men.

Yes, yes, yes...

Silhouette Sensation

COMING NEXT MONTH

SUTTER'S WIFE
Lee Magner

Alex Sutter had a secret past – he'd told no one about the career he'd had in covert intelligence. But, suddenly, he was being asked to go on one last mission...

Sarah Dunning was horrified that her sister was in the clutches of a killer. To save her, Sarah would do anything, even pose as Sutter's wife. But Sutter wasn't the domestic type; would anyone believe he was just a honeymooner?

BOUNDARY LINES
Nora Roberts

The feud between the Barons and the Murdocks spanned generations...

Jillian Baron wanted to build on the work of her ancestors. She wanted to make the ranch successful and no one, not even Aaron Murdock, was going to stop her!

Aaron wasn't a man who asked – what he wanted he usually took. Jillian Baron was something he wanted...very much. Was she worth wooing?

Silhouette Sensation

COMING NEXT MONTH

SAFE HARBOUR
Judith Arnold

When Kip Stroud came to Block Island, it seemed like a wonderful omen that he immediately met Shelley Ballard. They'd shared so many happy summers on the island as children.

From the emotional darkness of grief and betrayal, they created a new life. Kip and Shelley were friends long before they were lovers, but what would they be once they were parents?

BETTER THAN EVER
Marion Smith Collins

Twelve years ago after the death of her policeman father, Bree Fleming had broken her engagement to Ryan O'Hara because he, too, wanted to be a cop. She didn't want to live in fear so she'd married another, safer man.

Now, a widow, Bree couldn't avoid meeting Ryan again. He was coming home as the new commissioner of police. But she hadn't expected the passion to be stronger than ever. They were older, wiser; this time could they make it work?

TAKE 4 NEW SILHOUETTE SENSATIONS FREE!

Silhouette Sensation is a thrilling series for the woman of today. They are a specially selected range of narrative fiction with a mix of suspense, glamour and drama. Featuring modern realistic stories, they are daring and sensual.

NOW YOU CAN ENJOY
4 SILHOUETTE SENSATIONS, A CUDDLY
TEDDY AND A MYSTERY GIFT FREE

♥ ♥ ♥ ♥ ♥ ♥ ♥ ♥ ♥ ♥ ♥ ♥ ♥ ♥ ♥ ♥

Now you can enjoy 4 Silhouette Sensations, a
cuddly teddy and a mystery gift absolutely FREE
and without obligation. Then if you choose,
you can look forward to receiving your new
Sensations delivered to your door each month
at just £1.75 each (post & packing free) plus a
FREE newsletter packed with author news,
competitions offering great prizes, special offers
and lots more. Send no money now. Simply fill
in the coupon below at once and post it to:-
Silhouette Reader Service, FREEPOST,
PO Box 236, Croydon, Surrey CR9 9EL.

NO STAMP REQUIRED ✄

Please send me, free and without obligation, four specially selected Silhouette
Sensations, together with my FREE cuddly teddy and mystery gift - and reserve
a Reader Service Subscription for me. If I decide to subscribe I shall receive 4
new Silhouette Sensation titles every month for £7.00 post and packing free. If
I decide not to subscribe, I shall write to you within 10 days. The free books
and gifts are mine to keep in any case. I understand that I may cancel or
suspend my subscription at any time simply by writing to you. I am over 18
years of age.

Mrs/Miss/Ms/Mr _____ EP22SS

Address _____

_____

_____ Postcode _____
(Please don't forget to include your postcode).

Signature _____

mps MAILING PREFERENCE SERVICE